FAITH OF THE FALLEN

THE CHAIN BREAKER BOOK 9

D.K. HOLMBERG

ASH
PUBLISHING

CHAPTER ONE

The ground rumbled.

Gavin glanced back at the city of Yoran to make sure none of the enchantments had managed to make it past him, but so far he hadn't seen anything to suggest that he had missed one. He had come to find the city itself quite lovely. It was a mixture of different construction types that had changed over the years. Much of the city's foundation had been made by the El'aras, and the simple stone structures were some of the stoutest throughout Yoran. Other buildings were newer with more decorative stylings, and they were made of either white stone or wood painted in bright colors. The bells trees grew throughout the city, giving everything a distinct smell and offering a specific danger from the sharp edges of the leaves.

Gray clouds obscured the sun, and the dark sky cooled the air.

"Can you see it?"

Gaspar's voice came through the small enchantment in Gavin's ear, but he ignored it for a moment as he stepped forward and focused on his core reserves. He called on the power of the El'aras buried within him, a connection he had somehow forged when he had been exiled to the prison realm.

"Boy, you had better answer before—"

"I don't see anything," Gavin said. "I feel it, though. I know there is something out here. It's just that I can't tell exactly where it is."

He focused on the connection again.

These days, Gavin was spending more and more time trying to connect to the El'aras part of him, wanting to understand that power. He didn't fully understand it yet, though he no longer needed to draw on the El'aras ring in order to touch the power available to him. Through the ancient bralinath trees, he had connected to that power more directly, a connection that had bonded him to a part of the El'aras he had never known existed. It filled him with power he could not have otherwise.

Nearby, he could detect another enchantment, though this one was with him. The massive stone creature rumbled along with him, though it was far enough away that Gavin couldn't even see it.

"We just have to keep hunting," Gavin said to Gaspar through the enchantment.

Gaspar grunted. "We've been looking for quite a while now and have not found anything. If you remain convinced there is something here, I will keep looking, but eventually, if we don't find something, I think it's safe for us to turn back."

Before Gavin could respond, the ground rippled. It sounded like a deep rumble of thunder that echoed from below, as if a giant stone golem would rise out of the earth itself to force them to act, but that wasn't what this was. Vines swirled out of the dirt, though they weren't made of wood or leaves. It was more like they were constructed of metal.

After pushing off the ground, he immediately called upon his core reserves. He unsheathed his sword and brought the blade down, hacking through the vine as it attempted to get close to him.

The metal of his sword clanged against the vine, and it shrieked. It was a strange, painful sound, but Gavin twisted and then darted forward to reach the enchantment.

It looked something like a man, though only waist high and made all of what seemed to be twisted metallic vines with thorns facing outward. Gavin had come to believe that most enchantments, at least ones that were animated like this, had real manifestations in the world, but what could this be?

Just an enchantment.

That was what he told himself.

He raced forward and brought his blade around, spinning through a series of quick, precise movements. He hacked at the enchantment and cleaved metal off. Gavin had to push power out from him and into the blade, which glowed with a gray light—a combination of his El'aras abilities and the nihilar that still flowed in him.

He spun and then jumped again. When he came down, he brought the blade through the creature, slicing it in half.

It started coming back together.

Gavin slashed at the enchantment, driving his blade through it over and over, while able to feel the strange energy that coursed within it. The fact that he could feel anything suggested that whatever power was within this creature had to be considerable.

He did the only thing he could think of: focused on his core reserves. He funneled energy out of him in a blast of power that slammed into the enchantment, shredding it to the point where it couldn't re-form again.

"What was that?" Gaspar asked through the communication enchantment.

Gavin turned around. "You're only about ten feet behind me, so why don't you get up here and take a look yourself?"

Gaspar's weathered face had a deep frown, his eyes more sunken and hollowed than they had been before. He swept his gaze around, looking at everything before turning back to Gavin. "Well?" he said.

"I've never seen anything like this before. Have you?"

Gaspar shook his head. "Never like this."

Gavin looked around too. They had been struggling, trying to make sense of the various attacks that had persisted despite having defeated the Sul'toral, and continued to find more of these types of enchantments to deal with. Both he and Gaspar had done all that they could to handle these creatures, but they continued to come across more.

His presence seemed to trigger them. The creatures made by Mekel and the other enchanters in Yoran simply didn't set off these attacking enchantments the same way. Gavin suspected that they only detected those with more power, such as him or the El'aras.

"I didn't realize the Sul'toral had left so many enchantments behind," Gavin said.

"Either that, or there is another sorcerer still lingering."

Gavin let out a low groan. "Don't say that."

Gaspar shrugged. "Well, we have to consider all the possibilities. Can't say I like the idea of a sorcerer hanging around outside the city, but if there is, I'd rather know about it so we can deal with it. Wouldn't you?" He scratched his chin, where a hint of scruff lined with streaks of gray had started to grow.

"I don't know any sorcerers capable of placing enchantments like this. That means it has to be the Sul'toral."

"And if the Sul'toral are making their presence known, then we hunt them down. You can take them on, boy. Especially with that new connection you have."

Gavin supposed that was probably true. If anyone could deal with the Sul'toral, it would be him. There were others who had taken on Sul'toral and succeeded, but they were sorcerers of considerable power, and he doubted that many people would be willing to confront that kind of magic. They wouldn't want to risk it or themselves.

"Let's keep hunting."

Gavin focused on his core reserves. More and more often, he found it difficult to determine where his core reserves ended and where the power of the El'aras that he'd connected to by bridging to the bralinath trees began. There was a blur between them, as if the two had been joined together. It was a peculiar connection for him to have, and one where he couldn't help but wonder if it put him in a uniquely powerful position. But it was one that also left him in a strangely sensitive situation as well. Having access to that kind of power meant he had an obligation to the source of the power—which, in this case, was ancient El'aras.

"We can make another pass through here," Gaspar said. "We thought we'd gotten them all the last few days, only to come to find that there *is* something out here."

Every day had been the same. The enchanters had sent their creations to sweep around the area, patrolling so they could try to uncover any other enchantments that might be active, but they had not come across anything.

Gavin supposed he should be thankful, but it also meant there were probably other things that remained unseen. Maybe it was time they placed their own protections around this part of the city so they could deflect any potential dangers.

"I'm getting tired of being the only one out here searching," Gavin muttered, shaking his head. "Since the

El'aras have decided to take up residence in the city, shouldn't they be a part of it?"

"You would think so," Gaspar said. "But I gave up on trying to understand those people."

A warm breeze started picking up, and Gavin couldn't help but be reminded of the Ashara. Knowing now that the El'aras—supposedly *his* people—had some ancient grudge with the Ashara, he worried about them returning. After they had freed Jayna and the Ashara from the prison realm, Gavin had not seen them. He had no idea what had happened to them, but at this point, he didn't think it was important. The only thing that really mattered was that he had gotten free.

The problem for him was that the El'aras didn't view the Ashara in the same way as Gavin did. They still viewed them as a threat. It was even more reason for the Ashara to have disappeared, though it did nothing to keep Anna from searching, despite Gavin's reassurances that the Ashara would not harm the El'aras.

Gaspar frowned. "I don't care much for the way the wind is shifting. Or the change in the weather. You think this is them?"

"I don't think the Ashara would come through here."

"Maybe they want to get revenge on the El'aras."

"I hope not," Gavin said softly. "We don't need to bring war to Yoran. We have enough difficulty with other things targeting the city."

They needed more defenses. Not only did they need more from the El'aras, if they were going to stay, but they were going to need the kind of protections that Gavin wasn't sure he could provide.

"She's still coming," Gaspar said, his voice going distant as he looked out to the east. "I haven't heard from her in a few days, but she's still coming."

Neither of them needed to say who Gaspar was talking about.

Imogen had been gone for nearly a year now, and Gavin sensed the sadness within Gaspar every time he mentioned her. Now there was something else. There was a sense of hope. He knew Gaspar missed her, though if Gavin was honest with himself, he missed having Imogen around as well.

"I didn't expect her to return so soon," Gavin said. They'd had the same conversation repeatedly ever since the old thief had first detected the activity in his enchantment.

"Me neither. But partly because she went to find herself, though I don't know that she ever lost herself," Gaspar said. Though his voice was quiet, it seemed almost as if he was trying to convince himself more than anything else. "Maybe it has more to do with finding her brother."

"I didn't spend much time with him."

Gaspar snorted. "You're lucky. You left before he truly showed himself."

Gavin arched a brow at the comment. "What do you mean by that?"

"Imogen liked to talk about how her people didn't care about sorcery." Gaspar shrugged. "When the two of us first met, she made it clear that sorcerers were the bane of her existence and that she had trained to deal with them from the moment she picked up her sword. Over time, I think she started to see things differently." He stared off to the east, his eyes narrowed and his brow furrowed. He fidgeted with something in his pocket. Gavin suspected it was the enchantment that allowed them to communicate with Imogen, though he had never taken it out of his pocket to prove either way. "Some of it had to do with that Toral we worked with, but some of it had to do with just facing enchanters, saying that they might use magic but that not all magic was bad."

"Well, we have all begun to see magic a little differently lately, haven't we?"

"We all have, boy. To be honest, as much as I want to say that I don't want to have anything to do with magic, at least I have these," he said, grabbing the enchantments wrapped around his wrists. "Without them, I'd feel like I was little more than an insect swatting at a monster. Now… I'm more like a large insect swatting a monster." He chuckled. "Don't mean I'm not going to try to annoy it, but it just means that I'm not likely to have much success against it."

"Well, you annoy me, so I suppose that's good?"

Gaspar grunted. "At least I know it works."

Gavin continued to focus on his core reserves, and he wished he had a better understanding of how he could sweep that power out from him and search for the different magic that might be around.

"There could be—"

There was a burst of pressure.

It was the only way he could describe what he felt. It came across him as a tightness along his skin, as if he had suddenly stood in front of an oven that was baking at an impossibly hot temperature.

Sorcery. And powerful, at that.

He squeezed his blade, sweeping his gaze around him. "Be ready," he said carefully.

"Ready for what?"

The air shimmered right in front of Gavin, and he immediately darted forward. He didn't know who was here, but the fact that they were hiding themselves suggested that they weren't here for any altruistic purpose. There had been enough enchantments around this place that made Gavin wonder if there might not be a sorcerer—possibly even one of the Toral—left behind who was concealing themselves.

He carved forward with his blade and flowed in the Leier techniques, using the pattern that he knew would disrupt magic, even if he wasn't entirely sure how it worked. As he neared the shimmering form, his sword cut into something.

The air crackled again.

An olive-skinned woman stood before him, with dark hair and eyes that were pools of black. The rings on her fingers blurred as she traced her hands quickly in a pattern, which solidified the enchantment she placed in front of her, blocking him from seeing anything again.

"Toral," Gavin called.

Gaspar bounded forward and joined him, but he took a position several paces away.

Gavin flowed toward the woman using the Leier techniques in an attempt to disrupt the Toral's magic. As he neared her, shards of metal shot at him.

They hurt, but not nearly as much as they could have. Gavin still had on the stone skin enchantment, so he doubted that they truly pierced his flesh. Instead, they only bit at him. He was forced to spin, deflecting the metal shooting at him. In one attack after another, each shard streaked toward him in a way that suggested the metal was alive.

Each time he carved through it, the enchantment came back together.

Gavin muttered to himself.

"Thought you said this was done," Gaspar said, grunting through the enchantment.

"I thought it *was* defeated," Gavin said.

He had never faced an enchantment quite like this that would continually reassemble itself.

Not that it was impossible to believe, though. Enchantments were simply power. They weren't alive, so it wasn't a matter of bringing something back to life, it was a matter of disrupting the enchantment. If she was able to somehow reassemble the enchantment, it suggested that she had a different level of control than others Gavin had faced.

He swept his blade around, carving through one of the pieces of metal flying at him, and then he stabbed, jabbed, and twisted. Each movement was designed to bring him closer and closer to the Toral. He had to disrupt her magic.

A band of power began to work around his legs, sweep its way up, and start to constrict.

Gavin clenched his fists around his sword and growled. He had dealt with that kind of magic many times before, and he hated it every time. It was almost as if sorcerers thought it was the easiest way to hold somebody. He wished he didn't have to use his Chain Breaker technique on it and that maybe there was some other way for him to do it.

And maybe there was.

He'd already reached for the power of the bralinath trees that connected him to the ancient El'aras elders. Though he knew he needed to do so now, he also had to do something different.

He pushed power out through him, into his sword. That power flowed out, creating a burst of incredible magic that allowed Gavin to explode through the band holding him.

He stormed forward and brought his blade up and around, hurriedly carving through the barriers protecting the Toral. He focused on his stone skin, using that enchantment to keep him powered, and soon he stood in front of her.

"Who do you serve?" Gavin asked, his voice low with fury.

The Toral moved her hands.

Gavin lunged at her and used grappling techniques rather than his blade. He chopped at her arm and heard a solid crunch, but it wasn't what he expected. Not the sound of bones breaking, despite how much power he pushed through his maneuver. It was like the sound of metal shearing.

The Toral continued to manipulate her hands, her black eyes glowering at him. She was a dark sorcerer, the kind Jayna chased. Where was Jayna now?

When Jayna had warned him about dark sorcery, he had never expected to really see anything quite like this. He had seen darkness in the world, and he had seen people with power, but this...

Gavin punched the woman in the shoulder, drawing on his core reserves to augment his strength and speed so he could add more force to the blow. When it struck, she didn't move back at all. She looked at him with a flash of irritation in her eyes.

Balls. That's new.

Maybe he had underestimated her. Maybe she was more than just a Toral.

Could she be a Sul'toral?

Gavin didn't even know how many Sul'toral remained, but the kind of power he'd seen from this woman and the control over the metal were different than what he had encountered from other sorcerers. It seemed as if it should be beyond a Toral, at least from what he knew of them. Maybe she really was one of the Sul'toral.

He sprinted forward, flowing quickly in a series of strikes—first on her arm, then to her neck, and finally a knee to her side. Each blow seemed to take something out of her, but she absorbed them all and continued to move her hands.

"Dammit, boy!" Gaspar shouted through the enchantment.

Gavin grabbed her and spun her around, then flowed through a series of movements, ending with him grabbing his El'aras dagger and driving it into her shoulder.

It sunk down only about an inch, but it did elicit more of a reaction from her than he had seen from her so far. He jabbed his fist in her chest and belly, and he brought his knee up to try to catch her in the kidney. Blows like that should incapacitate almost anybody, but she merely absorbed them.

Unless she was made of metal, as Gavin started to wonder.

It was time to focus differently and use his core reserves.

He had already blasted his way out of her power once. He thought he could do it again, but it was going to take a different kind of approach.

Though he didn't have the time to place protections with the patterns Anna had tried to teach him, he could still use his core reserves and release a blast of power. Rather than releasing it away from him, he released it *through* him.

He shot forward like an arrow loosed from a bow, striking her in the chest. She staggered back. Gavin followed up, driving the sword toward her.

Something hit him in the back, and he went staggering to the side. The metal enchantment had reacted again, and the barbed vines started to lash around his legs. He enforced his stone skin enchantment, drawing power through him. There would be a limit to how much power that enchantment could hold.

He carved through the barbed vine, and then he rushed toward the woman once more.

Something struck him again. Another enchantment?

He looked up. Two more barbed vine enchantments were making their way toward him.

"Keep using your stone skin!" he shouted to Gaspar through the communication enchantment.

Gaspar grunted. "Trying."

Gavin had to finish this fight with the metal enchantments, but he also couldn't leave the Toral alone.

There might be something he could do. He focused on the connection he shared with the stone golem and called on it until it came lumbering toward him, causing the ground to tremble.

Attack the Toral.

With that taken care of, Gavin could now focus on the other creatures. He knew he couldn't destroy them easily, but maybe he could overheat them somehow. If only he had enchantments that would do that, but he didn't.

Something Anna had told him once again came back to him, about how he could draw on the El'aras power and that he often drew too much. What if he did that now, letting it fill him, regardless of how unfocused it might be?

He drew on his connection to the El'aras as deeply as he could. As the two creatures came toward him, Gavin pushed it out, focusing that magic into a pattern Anna had taught him. The power solidified and took hold, and the metal vines started to glow. They became superheated, then drooped, before they withdrew underground.

He spun toward where the Toral had been. His stone monster was already battling with her.

With a strange explosion of dark energy, she disappeared.

Gavin rushed over to Gaspar. The metal enchantments were trying to wrap him up, forcing Gavin to rip them free to get Gaspar out of their grasp.

When he was done, Gaspar frowned at him. "Why didn't you do that from the beginning?"

Gavin ignored the question. "That's a different kind of Toral than we've ever seen before."

"These days, that's all we are seeing," Gaspar said. When Gavin looked over to him for clarification, the old thief shrugged. "Something new. It tells you that whatever is going to happen is coming. And it's probably coming soon."

CHAPTER TWO

Gavin traced his way around the outside of Yoran for a while longer, looking for additional enchantments, but he didn't find any. The stone golem, a creature nearly fifty feet tall with boulders for arms and legs, lumbered around him as a layer of defense, though Gavin wasn't expecting to need it.

Behind him, Gaspar muttered complaints about the attack, though Gavin knew it was just his irritation rather than anything specific. When he turned to him, Gaspar was looking off to the east once more.

"Has she contacted you again?" Gavin asked.

"I'm going to wait out here a while longer," Gaspar said. "I'm hoping she will get back to me soon."

"She already told you she's coming."

"She said she was, but I also want to make sure I'm here for her. If she needs help…"

Gavin glanced over and grinned at him. "If she needs help, she's going to let you know."

"Unless she doesn't," Gaspar said. "These days, I tend to work with people who think they don't need help from anyone."

Gavin chuckled. Gaspar wasn't wrong about that. Gavin probably needed to be a bit more open with needing help, though he had become more welcoming of it ever since he'd started working with Gaspar.

"You'll call if you need anything?" Gavin said.

"I suspect you'll know if I do. Besides, if there's anything out here, you would've already activated it. There is not much chance I'm going to be the one who does."

Gavin shrugged. "Maybe not, but we don't know what the Sul'toral still intend."

Jayna had taught them about the Sul'toral and about Sarenoth, but she had not known what else the Sul'toral wanted. Power, Gavin presumed, as that was what he had seen from them so far. But the kind of power they pursued was beyond his comprehension.

He left Gaspar and made his way back toward the city. When he reached the outskirts, he paused for a moment, checking on the enchantments that protected it. Enchanters had placed incredibly powerful defenses around Yoran, and the El'aras had added their own to help layer protection over that. The combination was beneficial, but given what Gavin had just encountered, he began to wonder if it would even make a difference.

Everything looked to be intact.

The outskirts of the city had changed in the days since the El'aras had first arrived. They were nearly five hundred people strong, though Gavin had a feeling from Anna that there should have been more. The El'aras lived long lives, but he also had a sense that when they had been chased from their forest home, something had changed for them. Perhaps the appearance of the Ashara. After Gavin had saved Eva and the other Ashara, Anna had been less willing to share much with him. That had been a recurrent problem for him. He would learn something about the El'aras and begin to feel as if he was a part of them and their future, only for something to come up that made him question it. He was not bound by the same history—or biases—that the El'aras had. Anna struggled with that as well.

The buildings just outside the city were all made of gray stone, and over time, they had started to crumble and decay. They were some of the oldest in Yoran, remnants from a time when the El'aras still occupied it. Gavin had not been surprised that the El'aras had returned, but he *had* been surprised that they started to make modifications to the stone. Their masons added a touch of their power to it, almost restoring it.

It was bizarre to think that stone could be healed, but when he saw what they were doing and the way they were using their control over the material, he couldn't help but feel as if that was exactly what it was. Each time Gavin looked at it, he felt as if the stone itself was starting to become a lighter color.

This part of the city was also protected in a different

way than the others. There were still enchantments in place, and he could still feel the effect of the magic suppression that encircled the city thanks to the enchanters, though Gavin was no longer quite as attuned to it as he once had been. Now that he had a level of control over his power, he could feel his core reserves and the connection to the El'aras far more easily than he had ever been able to before, and he didn't have to worry about the suppression field overwhelming him.

Gavin stopped at a smaller building in the center of the El'aras section.

The stone was a light gray now, as if the magic they were pouring into it had cleansed the dullness from it. It reminded him of nihilar and how it had caused his blade to glow with gray light. He frowned at that thought. Was that what they were doing? Were they somehow pushing out the effects of nihilar from the stone?

He found a pair of masons working at the material, each of them tracing patterns onto the various rocks that made up the building. Neither of them looked up at him, continuing their work as he approached.

Only as he neared the doorway did somebody step forward.

Gavin nodded to the woman standing guard.

He recognized Celine, though he didn't know her very well. She was one of Anna's warriors, skilled with the blade, and probably incredibly old. She had taken up a more prominent position ever since Thomas had perished in the attack on Arashil. Celine regarded Gavin for a long moment. She watched him with suspicion burning in her eyes, like so many of the other El'aras did. They recognized him as something different. And Gavin often felt different, especially around them.

"I'm here to see Anna," he said, standing before the door without pushing his way in. He could try, but in this place, he suspected there were other protections that would make it more difficult for him to do so if they were activated. He didn't want to cause additional trouble with the El'aras, and he certainly didn't want to anger them in any way.

Celine continued to watch him. "I suppose she would welcome your visit."

"You suppose?"

Though Celine frowned, she didn't move. There had been a strange tension between Gavin and Anna ever since he had not only taken on the nihilar but also helped the Ashara. He suspected that was tied to the El'aras beliefs about the Ashara, which were something Gavin didn't fully understand.

"You may pass," Celine said. As Gavin stepped forward, she raised a hand. "You should know that we have fortified these buildings." She nodded to some of the ones around them. "The ancient protections are reactivated. If you try to do anything, you will fail."

Gavin arched a brow. "Are you afraid of the prophecy? You've learned the truth about that, I'm sure."

He hoped that Anna had made sure the others had learned how the prophecy had been manufactured to control the El'aras. It was one more thing that the Sul'-toral had done.

Celine glowered at him. "Do not mock what you do not understand."

"I'm not mocking anything," Gavin said.

He did not wear the El'aras ring anymore, and to some people that marked him as no longer serving as the Champion. He wondered what they would think if they knew he had connected to the bralinath trees and to the true power of the El'aras. It was something he hadn't shared with anybody other than Anna, not wanting to cause any further strife among the El'aras but also because he didn't really know what it meant, nor did he understand why he could do what he could do.

"You may have convinced the Shard that you are the Champion, but not all of us are so sure. I will keep an eye on you."

Gavin nodded once, appreciating the forthrightness. Too often with the El'aras, everything was shrouded in a sort of hidden distrust, which made it more difficult for him to know where he stood. Celine, on the other hand, was open with it, and she made no attempt to conceal her dislike of him.

He stepped through the doorway and felt a tingling sensation that pressed down through him. It reminded him of how he'd had to pull power in the reverse direction when he had been in the prison realm, as if it was trying to suppress some part of his El'aras being.

This had to be the protection Celine had mentioned that was placed on the buildings. They might be effective for most people, but Gavin had been in the prison realm. He understood how that power flowed in the opposite direction, so he thought he knew what it would take to resist that power and overwhelm it if it came down to it.

The entrance hall was empty. It had not been decorated like other parts of the building had, though the stone had been changed to an almost milky white. As Gavin headed through it, his boots thudding across the stone, it seemed as if there was an energy that radiated inside of the hall.

He stopped at a darkly stained doorway and hesitated. It was made of bralinath wood. Why would the El'aras use bralinath wood, which was sacred to their people, for a doorway? More importantly, had it always been here, or had the El'aras brought it with them?

The door opened, and Anna stood before him. She was dressed in a deep blue that made her appear regal. Her golden hair was tied back, leaving her long neck exposed. A silver band encircled her neck, which was a marker of power or perhaps even an enchantment.

She cocked her head to the side and smiled at him. "Gavin Lorren," she said, her voice soft, almost musical. "I felt you coming."

Gavin smiled back at her. "You *felt* me?"

"You aren't so subtle. Not yet. When you come through the protections that are layered around this facility, I can feel it."

"I'm sorry if I disrupted anything."

She grinned more broadly this time. "You did not do anything wrong."

There was still a distance between them, which seemed to have widened even more since his return from the prison realm. For a time, Gavin had believed that they would be able to come to know each other better, but lately he had started to feel her growing apart from him again.

He glanced behind him to the doorway, where he imagined that Celine was trying to hear their conversation. If he knew Anna, she enabled it so that Celine could listen in.

"There was another kind of attack just now," he said.

Anna stiffened.

"Sorcery," Gavin continued. "A kind I've never faced before. I thought it was Toral, but now I'm not sure."

He described the metal enchantment and then the woman he'd faced. Anna gave him a blank stare as he talked, before breathing out slowly.

"Not a Toral," she finally said, "though I would not have expected there to be a sorcerer who serves them."

"Serves who?"

"The vendalat."

Learning that Chauvan had access to some sort of additional power left Gavin even more concerned. How many different allies could Chauvan have found? He obviously had connected to the Sul'toral, and that was a problem for them.

"We have had some experience with them over the years, though none recently," Anna explained. "They manipulate metal and often can use it with their own magic, but it hasn't been my experience that they have any way of controlling magic on their own." She frowned.

"Typically, they do not use sorcery. They only have control over the metal. Nothing more than that."

"What if they have learned to wield some power over it?"

She shook her head. "I don't know."

"Why would they be here now?"

Gavin couldn't let go of the feeling that the sorcerer had been a Toral, so whether this was one of the vendalat or not was a different matter altogether. If it was a vendalat, then why were they even here? He was having a hard enough time with the Sul'toral, and before that the nihilar, and before that the Society. It was all tied to the ancients, he suspected.

"They serve something different," Anna said. "Not an ancient, if that's what you fear."

Gavin shrugged. "Well, a little. This was a difficult power to defeat, and I barely did so."

She watched him. "I can see that."

There was something about the way she said it that left him on edge. "What do you mean by that?"

"It is nothing, Gavin Lorren. Tell me. Why was she so difficult for you?"

"I don't know. Maybe a combination of magic and metal. Or maybe it was just that she had more control than I do."

Whatever it was, Gavin guessed that Anna would tell him that he needed to have a better understanding of his own connection to his El'aras abilities. And she wasn't wrong. He did need that—it was just that he did not know what it would take for him to do so. He didn't have the time.

"Regardless," he said, "I am concerned that others might come with the same sort of power."

Anna smiled again. "There are ways of protecting us, as you are well aware. This city can be defended. You have ensured that, and my people are adding to that."

"But we need to figure out why."

"That is a much different concern," she said.

"Why?"

She motioned for him to follow. "Walk with me."

They stepped out of the building, and Celine started after them, but Anna waved her hand and kept her from joining. Gavin looked over. Celine frowned deeply at him, a look of darkness burning in her eyes.

Anna walked over to Celine and whispered a command in the El'aras language, though Gavin couldn't understand what she said. He caught snippets of a reassurance, but there was something else to it as well.

When Anna rejoined him, Celine wasn't staring at Gavin with the same anger on her face as before. There was still some emotion there—irritation, perhaps—but not quite like what had been there.

"She's not going to like you walking with me," Gavin said.

"She feels it's her duty to defend me," Anna said. She started down the street, nodding to each of the El'aras they passed, mostly masons who were working on the buildings.

"I think anyone who protects you feels that way after what happened to Thomas."

Anna glanced over, a flicker of sadness in her eyes at the mention of her old guardian. She nodded. "That's part of it, but it is also a desire to protect the Shard."

"Can she?"

"Against you? Probably not. I doubt there are any among my people capable of stopping you." She eyed him warily. "Do you intend to harm me?"

"I thought we were well past that by now," Gavin said.

"I thought so too."

"This is about the Ashara."

She held his gaze for a long moment. "You freed what should not have been freed."

"Well, seeing as how I wasn't the one to free it, I don't think I did anything I wasn't supposed to do."

Anna sighed, and she turned away. "It's because you don't understand. You have gained power without the insight necessary. I think that's what sets you apart. Perhaps it's the reason you were able to become the Champion, but perhaps it still separates you from the people you are supposed to serve." She shook her head. "And now you are drawing power to you."

"I'm not *drawing* anything," Gavin said.

"Not intentionally, but power finds you nonetheless." She stopped at the edge of the city, and Gavin could practically feel the effect of the barrier, the faint shimmer that was suppressing everything around them. "You have come into your power quickly."

"Magical power," Gavin agreed. "Though not all of my power."

Anna smiled tightly. "I suppose that is true, is it not?"

"You suppose?"

"Again, I don't fully understand all aspects of your abilities. You are the Champion, but you have acquired a different set of skills than what I think was prophesied." She looked away, staring off toward the forest nearby. "But as I say to you, you lack insight and understanding of what you are to serve."

"Because I'm not El'aras."

She was quiet for a few moments. "You are El'aras, but you don't understand where you come from."

Gavin scoffed. "I understand very well where I come from. It's the reason I am the person I am, and the reason why I fight the way I do. If you'd like, we can go back into the city, and we can find Tristan and have him explain everything I went through."

If Gavin was right, he suspected that Tristan was still in the El'aras hall, trying to read the ancient writings. He believed there were secrets there, though those secrets no longer mattered to Gavin quite as they once had. Wrenlow had already documented everything and was working through them, mostly so he could have access to it before anyone disrupted it and perhaps changed it.

"That is not what I mean," Anna said. "It is not the fighter you become—it is the fighter you should have been."

"And what *should* I have been?"

She was silent for several seconds, then finally looked over to him. "Are you sure you want to know?"

"The way you say that suggests I don't."

"Some people prefer not to know. They would rather not learn secrets that might harm them."

"Will it harm me?"

"Only you can decide that," Anna said.

Irritation flared within Gavin, but he wasn't going to tell her that. Nothing she shared about who he or his family was or where he came from would harm him. He had long ago given up any desire to learn those secrets. Anything that had happened before Tristan had found him was interesting but not of importance.

Because of that, he had never looked into his family heritage. There was no point in it. He wouldn't gain anything from it, he wouldn't find any part of himself, and he would never have to worry about anything more.

"If you're trying to allude to something greater, you might as well say it. I don't care."

He felt her hold on to power, as if to make sure he was aware of what she was doing. She then released it. It was more power than she normally drew, and he realized exactly what it was from.

Her Shard.

She had it on her.

Of course she did.

The magical artifact granted her additional power, and it helped her tie into the El'aras magic in a way that was far greater than what she could use without it. Much like the ring had helped Gavin tap into the El'aras power more effectively than he could otherwise do.

"I would like to show you something, if you would see it," Anna said.

"What is it?" Gavin asked cautiously.

"Your past, and perhaps your future. You have been wondering why power has been accumulating here in the city." She glanced behind her, and Gavin followed the direction of her gaze. She looked upon Yoran, and there was sadness in her eyes. "If you really want to understand, I will show you, but you must come with me. And you have to trust me."

She shared a look with him for a long moment, the crystal blue in her eyes seeming to swallow him. He could feel the power she held, and she wasn't using any pattern as she did. It was merely the depths of her focus on him. Ever since their first encounter, Gavin had felt the connection between them, though it had been a while since he had felt it quite as strongly as he did now.

"I trust you," Gavin said.

"You have to trust that what you see is true."

He frowned. "If there is something I need to see that you're concerned about—"

"I'm not concerned about it, but you must trust me."

Gavin regarded her for a moment, and once again, he felt the power she was drawing on and how it seemed to radiate from her. "I trust you, but that doesn't mean I'm not going to question it."

"As you should. As you always should."

CHAPTER THREE

The stone golem enchantments shaped like wolves rumbled forward, moving with a distinct fluidity despite the stone that bounced beneath Gavin's backside.

He glanced over to Anna, and she clung to the stone wolf's back all too easily. She looked comfortable riding atop the stone enchantment in ways that even Gavin did not. Then again, she was true El'aras, whereas he felt as if he only played at it.

They raced through the forest, and he let Anna take the lead. The stone wolf seemed to enjoy streaking through the trees, though it was odd for Gavin to feel excitement from the enchantment. His connection to the bralinath trees felt even closer here. It wasn't so much that he was distant from that power when he was out of the forest and on the plains, it was more that when he was here, the power he was able to access was direct and happened faster. He didn't have to tap into any of his own core reserves.

Gavin wondered if his core reserves were a means of connecting to the bralinath power without being in proximity to them. Maybe Anna would know, but would she reveal any answers when it came to that kind of power?

As they started to slow, Gavin looked around. He knew where they were. They'd been riding the stone golems through the forest for the last few hours and had encountered nothing. There was a quiet, almost strange energy to the forest.

When they slowed, he glanced over to her. "Arashil?"

"It's a start," Anna said.

"To understanding where I came from?" He smiled. "Before you resettled this place, it had been abandoned for far longer than I've been alive."

"Yes, it would have been. But as I said, this is a start."

They reached the outskirts of the settlement, and she climbed off her stone wolf. Neither of them drew power back out of the golems, leaving them full size. Gavin had taken to doing so, partly because of a strange connection he felt to them, and partly because it no longer took the same amount of energy to activate them.

He leaned closer to his wolf. "Keep watch?" he whispered in its ear.

He scratched behind the creature's ears, and it seemed to perk up. Gavin felt the tremble of energy through his connection to the wolf. It agreed.

Gavin had bonded some part of himself to the

enchantment, and that enabled him to control it in ways he would not have been able to otherwise. He wondered if it bothered Mekel, who had created the enchantment in the first place, though he'd never said anything about it to Gavin.

He followed Anna into the settlement, where they paused at the temple. The door was open, something that had never been the case when he had been staying here while training with the El'aras to understand his power. The floor of the temple glowed, though it was faint. Has Anna done something before he had reached it?

"This place has been lost for so long that perhaps we should have reclaimed it," she said. "There is still power here."

"I don't feel anything."

She stood in front of the temple, watching him. "Focus, then, and you will."

Gavin wasn't sure what she was asking of him, only that she seemed to want him to draw on some deeper part of himself. Perhaps even to connect to the bralinath trees. As he focused, he began to feel power building steadily within him. The power of the bralinath trees stretched deep, connecting to the other trees, and with that power came flutters of images.

A series of visions flashed in his mind. The trees surrounding the settlement. Arashil, filled with life, teeming with the El'aras. Much larger, much more active, but still part of the forest and blended together. The bralinath trees ringed more of this place then than they did now. The visions were brief, hurried, filled with a certain energy. They carried him back in time, from when the settlement was fully occupied to when the buildings were being constructed to a period where everything was gone other than the temple itself.

It was the first structure to exist, and Gavin suspected that it came from a time before even the El'aras. As he studied the visions that the bralinath trees provided, even the temple eventually disappeared, and then the memories faded.

"Did you see it?"

"I did," Gavin said.

Anna gave a tight-lipped smile, and a look of concern flashed in her eyes. "There are some among the elders who would claim that very few can see what the trees offer without having served the El'aras people for centuries." She sniffed. "The trees are a way of connecting to and seeing the past. The elders, of which there are so few left, are able to reach into that and preserve the memories of the people." She looked over. "Until now."

"I didn't mean to somehow connect to your people."

"They are your people as well, Gavin Lorren."

Had he truly been raised among the El'aras, he might've understood what he saw in the vision. Perhaps he would've known what the different buildings were for, but his ignorance made it impossible for him to understand. Instead, he saw the village slowly descend into nothingness.

"The trees allow you to look back in time. They are a connection to the past, but there are connections to the future too." She watched him. "It is those connections that others within the El'aras seek to find."

"You," Gavin said.

"I was tapped as one who had potential. The Shard is a way to see. It traps the kind of power that only a few in this world can possess."

"The Shard was a connection to the El'aras power."

"It is. The El'aras power of the future."

Gavin frowned and shook his head. "I don't really understand."

"The Champion represents the power of the past. The Shard represents the power of the future."

"It doesn't feel like I'm connecting to some power of the past," he said.

"Perhaps not." Anna looked all around her before turning back to him once again. "Perhaps it is something else you connect to. You are the Champion, regardless of how you have come to us. There are those who were concerned about your presence, but they came around… until you bonded to the nihilar."

"I still don't understand the nihilar."

"Neither do the elders. It seems as if you are somehow connected to the power of the ancients. As you know, El'aras magic is but one power. There are others that exist in the world, and they will all eventually reveal themselves once again. The nihilar is likely evidence of that."

Gavin looked around the forest. "The nihilar. The bralinath power that is tied to the ancient El'aras." He looked over to Anna, who did not meet his gaze this time. "I wonder if I should spend more time trying to understand the nihilar the way I tried to understand the El'aras power I possess. It seems like it's important, but I don't really understand what I can do with that power." Despite having taken it from Chauvan, Gavin did not have control over it and did not know what it was. He only knew that it seemed to have some twisted energy to it.

"You should take the time to understand what you have access to," Anna said.

A flicker of shadow in the forest caught his attention. He stepped forward, pushing the thought he had started to have about Tristan into the back of his mind as he unsheathed his sword.

Anna rushed up next to him. "There is no danger here."

"I saw something. The last time we were here, we faced trees that moved. Brandon called them seeker trees."

"They are the progenitors," Anna said softly.

"To what?"

"To the bralinath. They search for a place to settle."

"If they are the progenitors to the bralinath trees, they were still quite inclined to attack me."

Anna frowned deeply. "Unusual. They should not have done so."

Gavin stopped at the edge of the settlement and looked out into the forest. He didn't see anything there, yet something had caught his attention. It was movement of some sort, though he couldn't tell what it was.

He stepped out into the forest. Would the trees be able to help? He smiled at the thought, but as soon as he did, an image flickered in the back of his mind.

Unlike what he had seen before, this one was recent.

He knew that because *he* was in it.

A shadowy form had come through here.

He focused on the power of the bralinath trees and what they had shown him. "Show me more," he whispered.

The image flashed again, but this time it traced its way across the ground. Gavin followed it, and he didn't even need to keep his eyes open in order to do so. He was distantly aware of Anna walking alongside him, only because he could feel the power she held, even though Gavin was buried deep within his own power. He was tapped into the magic of the El'aras and the bralinath trees, using that to connect through him and following the trail through the forest.

It was a strange sensation for him to have, but even stranger still was the fact that he knew it would work. The bralinath trees guided him. He was aware of how many of them there were in the forest, and he could see everything they saw, as if they were granting him a connection to some greater power, something more than what he would have otherwise.

He continued to follow the trail.

And then he saw it again.

A shadowy form in the forest.

"What's up there?" Gavin asked. When Anna said nothing, he motioned to where he detected the movement. "I can feel something up ahead."

"There is an old city there, if that is what is drawing you, though you should not be able to see it. I can take you there."

Why wasn't he supposed to see it? As he looked over to Anna, she did not meet his gaze.

Gavin followed what the bralinath trees showed him while trailing after Anna. It seemed as if there was some presence and pressure up ahead that drew him toward it, and he needed to know why. He took out three paper ravens and tapped on them, pulling on power as he connected to them. He let power flow out from him and drift into the ravens. They took to the air, flying between the trees. In the back of his mind, he was able to see the image they showed him.

"That will not be necessary," Anna said.

"I've been told that before, but I'm not willing to take the chance of being surprised by what's up ahead."

As the ravens flew, they showed Gavin images that blended with what he saw through the bralinath trees. He made out the outskirts of the city. There were aspects of stone and flashes of images that came from the bralinath trees, but the structure of the city up ahead was older than what he had found in Arashil. The forest had begun to become overgrown, and trees not nearly the size of the bralinath were staggered throughout the city.

It took Gavin a moment to realize what they were—seeker trees.

One of them reacted to his presence and started to wave its branches at him. He held his hands up, calling on the power of the bralinath trees to try to push back, wanting to alert the tree that he wasn't here to harm it.

"I've never seen a tree do that before," Anna said.

"I think this one fought me last time."

"You didn't destroy them?" Anna asked.

Gavin shrugged. "Well, I cut through the root system of one, which injured it," he admitted. "I didn't really want to, but it was trying to kill me, so I didn't have much of a choice."

"They should not have done that," she said softly.

Gavin looked over to her. "Because they are precursors to the bralinath trees?"

"The seeker trees are some of the oldest El'aras who have taken on a different form," she said. "For them to have attacked you…"

"They saw me as an outsider," Gavin said.

"I don't know if it's only that or if it's something else."

"Even if it was just that they saw me as an outsider, they weren't wrong. I *am* an outsider, especially when it comes to the El'aras."

Anna frowned. "But the bralinath trees recognize you."

Gavin bit back the retort he had. The bralinath trees did recognize him. He had seen it from the very first moment.

"They do now, but they didn't at the time," he said.

Gavin approached the seeker tree that was swinging its branches at him, and he held on to the power of the El'aras energy within him. He filled himself with it, and the seeker tree began to slow, the branches no longer swinging as wildly.

"They are protective," Anna said. "This place was once a city unlike any others in this part of the world. It faded away."

"But it's not as old as Arashil."

"No," she said, "not as old. But it was treated with a different sort of violence than Arashil. Those who came from here managed to evacuate, but it was more than just getting out. They had to hide who they were and where they came from, otherwise they would've faced a great danger."

Gavin could feel the anger of the trees but didn't know what it was. Strangely, though, it seemed as if the trees wanted him to understand. So he closed his eyes and focused on the bralinath trees around him.

When he did, an image started to flicker within his mind after several moments. This one wasn't as easy to make out as the other. The last image they'd shown him had been crystal clear, as if the trees wanted him to know, wanted him to see.

In this case, Gavin saw things in little more than snippets.

A flutter of an image came to him, showing a vast city made of the same white stone that he now saw reappearing within Yoran. Towering spires blended into the forest, while some buildings looked as if they were flowering trees but made out of stone. Others were actually made from trees, though ancient and old.

Through it all was life.

He saw the El'aras, and he saw the people, and then he saw it begin to dwindle. He never managed to see what happened. It was almost as though the bralinath trees couldn't see it. Or if they could, they didn't want to show it to him.

When the images faded, he opened his eyes.

"How far back were you able to see?" Anna asked.

Gavin looked over, not at all surprised that she understood how he had been looking back in time. "They could not show me what happened when the city fell."

"Because the bralinath trees were not here," she said, her voice soft.

"I don't understand. There are bralinath trees here now."

Anna stared at the ground. "Now. But not before."

"So they took hold after the city was gone?"

"After the city fell, they migrated here to preserve the memory, but only so much can be preserved in a place like this. Unfortunately, too much had been lost. And, regardless of what the El'aras people wanted, they lost those memories."

"How?"

"Because whoever attacked this place knew to target the bralinath trees."

Gavin understood. The attackers had known about the power within the trees.

And his own power was somehow tied to them. Perhaps not entirely, but some part of it was. He had started to question how much of his magic came from his core reserves and how much of it was borrowed from the El'aras elders that had formed the bralinath trees. It had become increasingly difficult for him to separate them.

"So the seeker trees..."

"They are here to defend the forest," Anna said. "They would have come later, much later, and they have managed to preserve some aspect of the memory of this place, though not all of it."

Gavin nodded slowly. "I see." Still, he wasn't entirely sure. It seemed strange to him that there would be memories of this place from before, but not memories of its fall.

Unless...

He peered around, looking back at the bralinath trees that circled the remains of the city. There was crumbled stone, but none of the spires and none of the massive trees he had seen in the images. There was nothing here, other than the seeker trees and the ring of five bralinath trees.

"Those El'aras that would eventually become the bralinath returned here afterward," he said.

"They came back, and they brought their memories of this place, but that is all."

"So what's here is reflected memories of the bralinath trees, but nothing from when it fell."

"Nothing from that time," Anna agreed.

"Why did I need to come here?"

"I don't know," she said. "None of the people even come here. It is too painful."

"Painful because the bralinath trees fell?"

"Painful because they did not protect them," a voice said from nearby.

Gavin looked over, and a flicker in his mind told him that the figure coming toward them was the same one he had seen making its way through the trees. He wasn't surprised to see Tristan.

Anna stepped toward him, anger flashing in her eyes.

"She doesn't want to share that they failed to protect these trees. They retreated," Tristan said, watching her.

"You know nothing," she snapped.

"I was here."

Gavin jerked his head around toward Tristan. "What do you mean that you were here?"

"Do you think I've been in exile from the El'aras all this time? They abandoned what they should have protected."

"But you don't even understand the trees," Gavin said.

"I understand my heritage and the power of what it is meant to do. I understand what they did not do."

Silence fell between them all.

"You and I can talk later," Anna finally said. She turned and strode away from Gavin toward the remains at the edge of the city. She approached the stone wolf she'd ridden on and climbed onto it. Within a moment, she was gone.

Gavin turned back to Tristan. "Did you intend to scare her away?"

"I don't intend to scare her," Tristan said. "I wanted to have a conversation with her, but she obviously does not want to. She wanted to show you the past so you can understand your future, or something along that line?"

Gavin frowned, but he nodded. "Yes."

"Because she can't see it."

"Can you?"

It was a question that had been coming to Gavin while he was talking to Anna, a consideration he initially thought was improbable. The more he thought about what Tristan had been doing, the way he had been planning and trying to find a Champion, the more Gavin started to question whether that was the real reason behind all of it.

What if Tristan had some way of seeing into the future, much like Anna did?

Tristan gave him a tight smile. "It's about time you understand."

CHAPTER FOUR

IMOGEN

The darkness settled in full around Imogen.

She slipped forward in one of her sacred patterns, letting it guide her as she practically floated in her movements. Petals on the Wind made her feet light and allowed her to move easily, while she remained constantly ready for the possibility that she might need to attack.

Her people walked behind her. There were hundreds of them, most fully capable of fighting. Imogen had trained many of them herself, and those who could not wield a sword offered other levels of support using talents honed through countless battles.

But they were tired. Some were exhausted, ready to rest and find a measure of peace, though Imogen no longer knew if peace was even possible for her people. Perhaps it was little more than a dream.

"The scouts noticed something up ahead," Jorend said, emerging from the darkness.

There was little moonlight tonight, though Imogen didn't need to see much in order to know that her second-in-command approached. She could feel him through another of her sacred patterns, one she had been taught from the first day she had gone to the sacred temple—a pattern known as Tree Stands in the Forest.

"Anything to be concerned about?" she asked.

Jorend tipped his head in a bow. "Not that we can tell, but we wanted to alert you."

She nodded and drifted forward, following her pattern and feeling the power within it. There was something to be said about how potent the pattern was and what it offered, but it was also comforting, primarily because it helped her feel connected to what she once had been.

"Have the scouts stay alert, and bring several of the shamans along with you," she instructed. "If there's anything up there, we need the sword and the shield."

"It has already been arranged, First," Jorend said.

She gave a small smile. "I'm sorry. I shouldn't issue commands like that. I know you are prepared."

It wasn't just that he and the others were prepared. It had more to do with Imogen and her own issues than it did with Jorend and the rest of the Leier traveling with her. He knew that—but he also would never tell her that. And he would never tell her not to go and scout, though she suspected he wanted to.

Imogen moved in a different sacred pattern now, Stream through the Mountains, gliding as if she were actually flowing through a stream, until she reached a rocky ridge. She paused and looked back. The campsite spread out behind her, arranged in a series of neat, orderly lines. Small campfires bloomed against the darkened night, though most were only faint fires, little more than embers to offer a bit of warmth against the chill in the air as they made their way through the mountain pass. The mountains themselves rose up on either side, stretching high into the air, creating darkened shadows that had chased them the entire time they'd been traveling. Imogen had guided her people through the mountains, taking the easiest path that she could. With every step they took, it felt as if they were getting farther and farther from everything they had known.

Jorend spoke quietly to one of the scouts as he made preparations. He was a good head taller than Imogen, and his face had more scars than it did when she'd trained with him in one of the sacred temples before it had been destroyed. The man himself was just as scarred. Much like Imogen had been.

Perhaps all of their people had been scarred, given everything they had experienced. This journey was meant to help them find a place of safety, but it had been far more dangerous than Imogen had anticipated.

All because of her brother.

She turned away from the campsite and looked off to the west, staring against the darkness. Jorend claimed the scouts had identified a threat. Imogen attempted to make sense of what was out there, but she could not come up with a clear answer.

She had other ways of searching, though.

Her gaze drifted to the sky, where the darkened shapes circled as they had been for the better part of the last few days. She breathed out a heavy sigh and then began to focus on Tree Stands in the Forest.

It was a simple pattern. Because of that, it was complicated to truly master.

That concept had been difficult for Imogen to grasp when she had first learned about the sacred pattern and what it would mean for her. When she'd first been shown that pattern, Imogen had not known it for what it was. Now it was the basis for everything she did. By holding on to this pattern, she could tap into the power of her people —a power that none of her people had known they possessed until she had rediscovered it. In doing so, she could sweep outward with imagined branches and roots that allowed her to explore beyond what she could find with her other senses.

She trusted herself to do that now.

Most of the time, Imogen closed her eyes as she used the Tree Stands in the Forest pattern, making it easier for her to concentrate. There were other times, though, such as within battle, where she had to remain vigilant. Not many could overpower this pattern, but lately, Imogen had been dealing with those who could far more than she had wanted.

While probing, she began to feel a strange resistance against her roots and the branches she sent slithering away from her. She paused, no longer pushing quite as hard. Anything she might do now ran the risk of releasing too much of her own potential. That resistance was significant, she realized, and she needed to understand it in order for her to know whether there was a danger to her people. So far, what she detected was off to the west, the direction that her people traveled, and did not seem to be chasing them. But that didn't mean it was not a threat.

Imogen couldn't quite tell what was out there, though as she extended her awareness through Tree Stands in the Forest, she knew that whatever was there had to be significant. And likely dangerous.

More than that, she suspected that what she detected was the very thing Jorend had warned her about.

She looked over to the others standing watch and the ones scouting down below, and she decided to explore on her own. She caught Jorend's eye. He gave her a look of irritation, even as she knew that he understood what she was going to do. It wasn't the first time Imogen would be going off on her own.

She darted forward, easily gliding up and over the rocks, faster than almost anyone would be able to follow her. Jorend would be able to keep pace, but he was probably the only one without any enchantments capable of doing so. When she reached the border of where she had detected the strange energy, Imogen stopped.

Once again, she switched to Tree Stands in the Forest and pushed outward, probing to try to understand what was there. The rocky mountains around her made it difficult to determine if there was anything here, other than the overwhelming sense she had of the fact that something had come through this place.

Then it seemed as if the ground rippled.

Imogen braced, immediately shifting to a defensive posture. She didn't unsheathe her sword quite yet, knowing it wasn't necessary. But she glanced up the slope she had descended and saw that the Leier had already started to make their way toward her. They had noticed the same thing.

She didn't want to react quite yet. She needed these creatures—or enchantments, as Imogen didn't know which they were—to be lured in, and needed for them to believe that she would not go anywhere. That would be how she would draw out their master, which was what she wanted more than anything else.

There was no change, though.

She watched as the rock began to unfold, forming arms and legs and even bizarre rock-shaped heads, and she watched as they all turned their attention to her. They were attuned to her.

Dark creatures, or enchantments?

At this point, the difference was negligible, though if they were dark creatures, Imogen would happily strip that darkness from them. She had learned she could do that to try to free the creatures from that influence. If they were enchantments, then the only answer was to destroy them or the one who controlled them.

She held the creatures at bay with her Tree Stands in the Forest pattern. Then she pushed.

The creatures let out awful shrieks that echoed off the rocks.

Definitely dark creatures. Enchantments generally didn't react like that.

By holding her pattern, Imogen thought she might be able to cleanse these creatures of the darkness. There were fragments of power that might still be stranded within them, fragments of some other entity that had been used to taint the creatures in a dark ritual that lent them a different sort of power. But Imogen simply did not have the time.

The creatures swarmed toward her, battering against her sacred pattern, and they made it so that she could do nothing other than try to hold them at bay.

Distantly, Imogen felt the sacred patterns of the Leier coming toward her, along with the sense of magic coming from the shamans. Their efforts would help, but Imogen had to do her part.

She unsheathed her sword. As she did, a bit of moonlight reflected off the slender blade, making it look as if the metal glowed with a silver light. Perhaps it did. This was the blade of the sacred sword master, and Imogen was one now.

With a calming breath, she readied herself. Then she launched forward.

Her blade was a blur. Imogen rushed toward the nearest creature, driving her sword into it. She felt the stone try to coalesce around the blade as if it was going to hold it. Imogen had pushed too much power into it, though, and the stone shattered in a faint burst. That reaction suggested that the dark energy within the creature was finally freed.

She spun and danced with her blade, sliding quickly as she carved in an ever-widening clearing around her, shattering the stone creatures. With each one she cut down, there was another soft burst of energy, until even that became lost in the background. Imogen was aware of how the Leier fighting nearby were using similar sacred patterns as she was, carving through these creatures in ways that only the sacred sword masters once could do.

The shamans used a different technique. Although it was not sorcery like those of the Society, it was still magic —and powerful. The steady buildup of magic that came from them exploded, and a burst of light shimmered all around them.

Then a glowing light streaking down from above drew Imogen's eye, and it landed next to her. Lilah was dressed in a dark gray cloak, her raven hair flowing in the wind. With her dark eyes and slight features, she could have been mistaken for Imogen's sister. One who had learned sorcery rather than the blade as Imogen had.

"You didn't call for help," Lilah said.

Imogen shrugged. "There wasn't a need."

"This would argue otherwise."

Imogen pursed her lips.

Lilah turned in a circle and created a twisting pattern around her, then sent flashes of what looked like silver lightning coursing out from her fingers. The magic streaked into the stone creatures, which then shattered.

"You see?" Imogen asked. "These aren't difficult to topple."

"It's not a matter of difficulty. We can't have you

risking yourself unnecessarily."

"And I don't consider it a risk."

In this case, Imogen had done nothing that endangered her. There wasn't so much power here that she had to be concerned about it. In fact, what she had encountered so far was not nearly as powerful as what they had dealt with prior to leaving her homeland.

Lilah smirked. "At least let others have some fun."

She stepped forward, and this time when she brought her hands down, she looked as if she was trying to push down on the ground. A faint silvery wave radiated outward, rippling through the rock. She followed that by twisting her hands again, which led to a crackling surge of power that flowed out and slammed into the next layer of stone creatures.

Imogen had to admit that the technique was certainly easier than what she had done.

"Now you're the one taking away the fun," Imogen said.

Lilah glanced over, flashing a broad smile. "At least now you know what it feels like."

Imogen let Lilah work and listened to the sound of the Leier carving through other stone creatures. They darted through the enemies and cut them down quickly. Perhaps not as quickly as Lilah worked, but Imogen doubted that they were in any true danger.

When she began to feel a faint tingling sensation along her arms, she realized why that was. All of this had been to draw them in.

She looked around, though she could see nothing.

Not from the ground at least.

She glanced over to Lilah. "Be ready," she said.

Lilah caught her gaze and frowned, but then must have detected the same thing Imogen had begun to feel. As she paused, she created a protective barrier around her that created a ring of energy that could not be easily pene-trated. Imogen held her blade upright, and then she focused on a different sacred pattern, Lightning Strikes. It sent her streaking up into the air, where she shifted into Petals on the Wind again. As she floated there for a moment, she looked down into the mountain valley and saw a singular shape waiting.

Watching. Commanding.

Imogen flew toward the figure.

She streaked as fast as she possibly could and even added one of the newer sacred patterns she had discov-ered that allowed her to burst forward on a lightning bolt of energy. She came to land only a dozen paces from her brother.

Dressed all in tattered black robes, Timo looked nothing like the man he once had been. He'd been injured, his face scarred, and his hair was cut short. His eyes carried a wildness to them that they never had before, but it was more than just the wild energy he possessed. It seemed as if some power hid in the darkness of his eyes.

"Just you?" Timo asked, though he didn't move. He had a pair of blades sheathed at his side, and Imogen knew that in the time they had been separated, he had come to learn to use those blades in ways he never had while training with the Leier. "Even the great Imogen Inaratha would need help, I would think."

"You don't have to do this, Timo."

"Whatever you think I have done is beyond you."

"You have brought destruction to our people. You have betrayed everything we are—"

He took a single step forward. Rage flashed across his face, contorting his brow, making him look even wilder. "*I* have betrayed? Do you not even see what you have done, Imogen? You accuse me of the very thing you have done."

He snorted and flicked his gaze up, and with barely more than a twitch of his fingers, a gale swept out from him.

Imogen held on to Tree Stands in the Forest while turning so she could see just what Timo had done. Lilah battled against the power Timo had used on her and seemed to be struggling with it. She managed to stay in the air, though she was being battered from side to side.

Imogen turned her attention to her brother, and she focused a burst of Lightning Strikes on Timo, sending it toward him while never moving her blade. Timo blocked it without turning toward her. But it distracted his focus briefly enough that Lilah managed to regain control of herself.

Timo turned back to Imogen. "And look at who you protect. One of *them*."

"We are the same people," she said.

It was an argument she'd made to the Leier, but she'd never had a chance to share it with Timo.

"We could *never* be the same people," he snapped.

Imogen shook her head. "I wish it didn't have to be this way, Timo."

She readied her blade. More than that, she prepared all of the knowledge she had gained in the time since she had left Yoran what seemed like an eternity ago. She knew that she had to finally—and definitively—deal with her brother. She had avoided it long enough and could no longer shirk her responsibility to her people.

Timo twisted his head, making him look almost serpentine.

What had he learned?

He had attempted to steal power from many others in the time since he had left their people. He'd used the Sul'-toral. Porapeth. Branox. The gods only knew what else. Imogen had no idea how much success he'd had, but given what she saw from him and the way he looked at her, she was left believing that he must have gained power to some degree.

Timo sneered at her. "Do you really believe you can get there in time?"

"Get where?" she asked.

What did he know? Worse, what had he done?

He grinned. "Oh, don't pretend I don't know where you and your people are heading."

"They should be your people too," she said, but she knew it was a futile attempt. There wasn't anything she could say to him that would sway him at this point. Timo was too far gone.

"You won't make it in time."

"Perhaps not. But you won't be there either."

Imogen did not feel as confident as she attempted to sound. With a heavy heart, she focused on him, on Lightning Strikes, on the power she could summon from the storms through the pattern, and she sent it all toward Timo.

But he did something she hadn't seen him attempt before. It seemed almost as if he folded out of existence, disappearing in a burst of power that sent her staggering back.

Imogen let out a long sigh.

She'd been making her way toward Yoran, knowing that she needed to get her people to safety, and thinking that would be the first place to seek refuge, since she had friends and allies there.

Now she needed to head there for a different reason.

She needed to get to Yoran to help protect it.

CHAPTER FIVE

Tristan guided Gavin around the stone, pausing for a moment and crouching down in front of a pile of debris. The stacked rock had grasses and weeds growing through it, and moss covered much of it. A hint of a breeze drifted through, carrying the smells of the forest, and also a certain isolating energy that Gavin was all too aware of.

"This was my home," Tristan said, his voice soft.

"What happened here?"

Tristan breathed out slowly. "The same that's happened every other place. And unfortunately, the same thing that will continue to happen."

"Because of the El'aras not protecting themselves?" Gavin asked.

"It is more than that," Tristan said. He crouched down and ran his hands along the rocks, as if he was trying to trace a pattern.

Gavin frowned as he watched. He looked up, sweeping his gaze around while trying to understand what Tristan was doing, but he couldn't tell. The forest here looked no different than any other part of it, yet when he focused and tried to make sense of what the bralinath trees could show him, he was able to catch glimpses. There was enough that he thought he might be able to find answers, but only if he could look deeply enough into the past. Otherwise, all Gavin saw were fragments of images, flashes that seemed to flicker in his mind before fading once again.

Tristan lifted a rock, hefting it in his hand, and then he looked over to Gavin with a frown. "What do you see?"

"A rock and other debris from whatever settlement was here. What are you trying to show me, Tristan?"

"You see what you want to see. What they wanted you to see." He shook his head. "I see what once was here. A home destroyed. My city, my people, those that I knew, all lost."

"How long ago was it?"

"This place was destroyed about one hundred years ago. There should have been more survivors than there were." Tristan turned in place slowly, continuing to shake his head. "No. This place should not have been attacked in the first place. We should have thrived here. Instead..." He looked off into the trees. His eyes went distant, as if he was seeing into the past the same way Gavin could by using the trees around him. "They fell victim, as some-body before them did. Many of them wander, looking for a place to call their own. Some of them tried going deeper into the El'aras lands, but they had only known this place. Others went into Arashil," he said, nodding back to the forest. "They joined the settlement there, though it was never home. It could never be. It took me a while to make my way back here. I had been gone for a long time at that point. My responsibilities had carried me away. Had I known..." Tristan let out a heavy sigh. "Perhaps had I known, I might've come, but I wonder if I would've had any way of offering protection."

"You don't think you could have helped?" Gavin asked.

"I doubt I could have. This was beyond even me." He looked up. "I had been searching for evidence of the Champion. I had not found any."

"Chauvan," Gavin said, suddenly starting to understand. "You began working with him because of what happened here."

Tristan breathed out slowly. "I did so because it was necessary. I could see it. I could see only glimpses of what might come otherwise, and when I was closest to the people, I was able to see other glimpses of what needed to be done."

"So you needed to torment Chauvan and myself and try to turn us into your Champion?"

"Not mine," Tristan said.

"You wanted to make us into something we were not," Gavin growled.

Tristan looked over to him and gave a small shrug. "Don't think that I'm going to apologize for what I did or how I worked. Don't think that I'm going to feel bad about turning you into the man you are." He snorted. "It's my curse, and that of those like her," he said, waving to the edge of the forest where Anna had disappeared. "We catch snippets, but we can't see quite as well as those who are born to it. It's as if we have only a little bit of that power."

"Who are born to it?"

Tristan waved his hand again. "The damn Porapeth keep themselves hidden, concealing themselves in the world, as if by offering any sort of influence they will force us down one path or another." He rolled his eyes. "But those of us who have any sort of ability with it have an obligation. We must find a way to share that."

"I don't really understand what you're going on about," Gavin said.

"No, you've never cared to, have you?"

"It's not a matter of caring. Besides, you never trained me to."

Tristan chuckled. "You keep accusing me of that, but you also fail to acknowledge your role in all of this."

Gavin turned away, looking around the forest. He tried to open himself to the bralinath trees, wondering if he might be able to feel something. Even as he did, he couldn't detect anything more than what he already had. The seeker trees were there, and every time he got close to one, it would lean its branches down toward him as if it was going to attack again, but it never did.

He found himself looking over to Tristan. When Gavin was growing up, he didn't know that Tristan was El'aras. He had hidden that part from him. He had pitted Gavin against the El'aras from time to time, though always on the periphery, and always just to test him. It had taken

Gavin learning more about himself in order for him to understand why Tristan had done that. Later, when he'd met Anna, Gavin started to recognize that Tristan had some connection to the El'aras. He had thought his old mentor had no hold over power, but even that wasn't true. Tristan obviously possessed some connection to magic and had simply masked it. And now... Now Gavin realized that Tristan was a greater part of all of this than he had ever realized.

"How did you have that ability?" Gavin said.

"Has she ever talked about hers?" Tristan asked him instead.

"About her connection to power?"

"About herself. About the Shard. About what it means for her?"

Gavin scoffed. "Well, considering that what I have come to understand that means and what she believed that means seem to be inaccurate..." He shook his head. "I don't think any of us really know."

"She knows," Tristan said softly. "There are more prophecies than the ones she has let on."

"You've said that before."

"And there's one in particular that is greater than all of them."

"Which one is that?" Gavin asked, turning to Tristan. He could still feel the power of the bralinath trees, as if they were trying to push their energy and connection through him, like they wanted him to be fully aware of what they were doing. As he looked over at Tristan, he couldn't help but wonder if there was something more that the trees wanted him to be aware of. Was it a warning?

They had certainly alerted him of Tristan's presence in the trees, as though they had wanted to make sure he knew they were watching. But maybe it was something else.

"Is it a prophecy about the Champion?" Gavin asked. "Is it something about you trying to find power? Or perhaps it's a matter of you wanting to manipulate me, Chauvan, and any others you think might be useful to you."

"I have never used you. I *guided* you. Nudged you when it was necessary. I prepared you, but I've never used you."

Gavin snorted. "I have a hard time believing that."

"There are things you need to know about yourself, Gavin."

"And what sorts of things are those?"

"The kinds of questions you should have been asking from the very beginning. Your single-minded focus was what allowed you to become as successful as you are, and it is what made you powerful, but..." Tristan shook his head. "You should have been asking questions."

"About what?"

"About who you were... before."

Gavin gave a small laugh. "Who I was before? I wasn't anything."

Tristan smiled at him. "You were always something."

Before he had a chance to press, a flash appeared in Gavin's mind, and he felt another surge of energy. A warning.

He unsheathed his sword. Tristan frowned at him, but he made no movement.

"The trees," Gavin said. "They're warning me."

"About what?"

"About…"

Gavin focused, and he tried to feel for what the trees were warning him about, but he couldn't see it. He knew something was there, but despite how he concentrated, he couldn't tell what it was. He felt a surge of energy, and as he focused on it, he realized it was hidden from him.

It was power.

He closed his eyes again, then used the bralinath trees. That energy was close, and he needed to draw on it, needed to see something more and try to understand what it was. He felt flashes of brightness but nothing else. It was all most as if the trees were trying to share an image with him, but it was concealed.

The seeker trees began to walk. They shrieked, and the ground trembled as they moved away.

He followed the trees, Tristan at his side, until they reached the edge of the city remains. From there, Gavin could feel something battering, twisting, thudding. And there was power.

He could *feel* it.

Then he saw it.

Twisted metal gleamed dully in the fading light, which drifted down, reflecting off the metal branches snaking through the forest—and around the bralinath trees.

Vendalat power.

Why here, and why now?

Gavin reached into his pocket, grabbed one of the stone skin enchantments, and quickly slipped it on before pushing power out through it. He used his core reserves, but he also called on the power of the bralinath trees.

He detected an injury. The metallic enchantment had somehow damaged the tree, tormenting it. Gavin could feel what was happening, even if he didn't understand, and he could practically feel the tree writhing in pain.

Sword in hand, he raced toward the creature and chopped at the vine winding around the tree. He immediately called upon power to melt the enchantment, then grabbed for the one wrapping around the bralinath tree and unraveled it as quickly as he could. The bralinath tree surged power within Gavin's mind.

Another image formed. The other trees were in danger.

Gavin looked over to Tristan. "We need to help. How much control over your El'aras abilities do you have?"

"I'm not as talented as many others are," Tristan said.

"Then do what you can."

Gavin focused, and he could feel where the next bralinath tree was. He hurried through the forest and came across the next tree that was under attack from the same metallic barbed vine working around it. This one had snaked even higher, and Gavin hurriedly chopped off one end of the vine, which melted it and began to unravel it.

"Go," Tristan said. "I can handle this." He worked at peeling away the vine.

Tristan was right. Gavin might be the only one who

could melt the enchantments, but Tristan could remove the barbed part.

Gavin rushed toward the next bralinath tree. He darted around one of the seeker trees as it swept its branches at something. With a kick, he exploded an enchantment made of stone and metal, and then he jumped again, leaping over something on the ground before landing near the bralinath tree. As he did, he immediately carved through the metal vine and then melted the next enchantment.

Out of habit, he started to rip the enchantment free. Tristan shouted his name, and Gavin turned. Tristan was dangling the metal vine he'd peeled off the other tree behind him, and he came racing forward.

"Go," he said.

Gavin nodded and left the vine to him, then raced for the next bralinath tree. Two more were under attack. Pain surged through him from his connection to the trees, a blinding and acute sensation he had to force away. Without the training he had endured as a child, he wasn't sure he would've been able to ignore it.

Gavin hacked off the vine, melted it, and began to unwind it. This one was buried deeper into the tree, but he was afraid to leave it for too long. It might burrow itself in, re-form, or, even worse, tangle around the tree and ensnare it completely.

Tristan joined him, now dragging two vines behind him. Gavin pulled enough of this vine free for Tristan to grab it, and then he hurried toward the last of the bralinath trees. The vine was tightly wound all the way up the trunk.

Gavin could feel the tree's pain, and flashes of bright light surged in his mind. The tree seemed to be trying to show him just how much agony it was in, but he didn't need that encouragement. He could feel the metallic vine sweeping around the tree, binding it entirely.

He cut off what he could, and then he began to peel it away. The barbed vine had dug in deeply, which meant he had to try to pull it out as carefully as he could. Gavin struggled to remove it, but the tree seemed to push, helping give him additional strength to separate the barbed branches from it.

He had to jump each time he circled around it, jump to try to tear that branch free, jump so he could peel away. Each time he did, Gavin could feel the barbs trying to bury back in. He had to activate his stone skin enchantment and use that to help fortify himself, worried that if he didn't, the metal would dig back in and somehow trap him in it too.

Energy pushed against him, and he could feel the way the tree fought its attacker. He needed to help, but first, he had to get around this.

He needed the ravens.

As he focused on them, the connection to them came in a flash. He called them to him and then pushed power out of himself and into the ravens, which caused them to enlarge. They grabbed him by the shoulders before circling.

While he looked down at the ground, he searched for

Tristan but didn't see him, nor did he see anything through the ravens' eyes at first. That changed once he saw an image of vines wrapped around something on the ground.

Gavin's breath caught.

A body lay constricted in the same metallic vines.

They raced forward. By the time he got there, the vines were snaking all the way around the body, and he could feel the power they were holding on to.

"Tristan?"

Gavin couldn't be sure, but he had a strong suspicion that Tristan was trapped in the center of this bramble of vines. He reached for them, but they were squeezing too powerfully.

"Tristan, if you're in there…"

A bulge formed in the vines, and they flexed away from Tristan for just a moment. It was long enough that Gavin believed that Tristan could get free, but then the bulge disappeared. Whatever Tristan was doing, however he was using his power, it was failing him.

Gavin needed Tristan to flex again, and he realized there was something he could do.

"Tristan, push out, and I'll melt them."

This would involve Tristan using power he could hold out from himself. Gavin had no idea whether Tristan had enough control over his El'aras abilities to do that. And if he didn't, Gavin knew quite well what was going to happen to his old mentor.

The power of what he used might blast through Tristan.

There was something more he could try too. He focused, pushing a thin, razor-like beam of power from himself to shear the vines free. He caught sight of Tristan's legs and torso. He grabbed the vines, twisted them together, and added power through his hand to melt them.

But the vendalat vines had already started to attack Tristan again.

Gavin had to channel that power from himself once more to cut the vines. Each time he did so, the vines regrouped and regenerated faster than he could act. Anything he did was too slow—or it would harm Tristan.

And there was more that Gavin needed to learn from him.

Tristan had some secret he hadn't shared with him yet. It was tied to Gavin's past—who he was, what he was—and he needed to hear it from his old mentor.

He called on the power within him, focusing on the power and energy the bralinath trees gave him, and he waited until he felt a surge of magic.

Gavin tried to time it exactly. He pushed out, heating the vines.

Tristan let out a shriek of pain. In all the times that Gavin had fought with Tristan and alongside him, he had never heard him cry out like that.

The vines started to melt.

Gavin grabbed them, but they were too hot. He ignored the pain and tried to focus on his connection to his El'aras power so he could free Tristan, but the vines continued to constrict. He had no choice but to keep pushing, trying to send that power out from him, needing to use it in order to destroy these metallic vines.

But each time he tried, he could feel something fighting him.

He had to do this. Tristan held answers, and Gavin needed those answers.

He forced his core reserves to draw more and more power as the vines attempted to burrow into him. He cried out, and he could hear Tristan fighting and screaming, but Gavin could not get to him fast enough.

The metal continued to melt, slowly oozing away. Gradually, the vines began to disintegrate, and Tristan was left lying on the forest floor. He was badly burned, but it was more than just the burns.

Something had changed. Some part of Tristan was missing.

Gavin tested for a pulse. He was still alive, but barely there.

Gavin looked around the forest, around the remains of the city, and he could feel the bralinath trees. He wished there was some way for him to add power through himself in order to heal Tristan, but he didn't know enough about how to do that.

Yet there were those who did.

He grabbed the paper dragon from his pocket, pushed power through it, and watched as it unfolded. Wings began to spread, growing larger, and a tail flowed outward as well. The head unfolded last, forming a long snout with teeth filling its mouth. The paper seemed to grow thicker and warmer as it was filled with power.

He turned his attention to the paper ravens. "Scout," he whispered, "and find Anna."

The ravens took off, soaring above the forest.

Gavin could reach her through the enchantment, and he might need to do so, rather than waiting on her to come to him. When he tried, there was no response. Still, she would need to know what had happened and that he could not wait long for her. Tristan's life might depend on it.

He glanced around but didn't see anything else of danger. The metal vines had been nothing more than enchantments. But they had come here, and he didn't know why they had. Was it tied to him, Tristan, or something else? Anna had known about the vendalat power, but why did it come after them here?

When they'd been attacked outside of Yoran, someone had controlled that power. A Toral, or possibly even a Sul'toral. Perhaps the same had happened here—but if so, where were they?

He climbed onto the paper dragon, carrying Tristan with him.

As they took to the air, he focused on the stone wolf that had remained. "Return," Gavin whispered.

The wolf darted through the forest and would return to Yoran before Gavin.

The paper dragon headed north. Gavin had to hope they could reach Nelar before Tristan died.

CHAPTER SIX

The city of Nelar was enormous, and it was hot and humid in a way Yoran was not. Gavin paid little attention to anything within the city as the paper dragon came to land just outside of it. They streaked through the air faster than he had ever flown on the dragon, as if Gavin's sense of urgency pushed through his El'aras connection into the dragon and guided the enchantment so it could move more quickly than it could otherwise. When they reached the edge of Nelar, Gavin jumped off the paper dragon, leaving it fully unfolded and enchanted, and he raced toward the Sorcerers' Society outpost. He leapt over the wall leading into the outpost, hurried toward the door, and pulled it open.

He had been here twice before, once when he had needed help, and then when he'd needed to find answers. He had no idea if the sorcerer he was searching for would even be here.

Everything about the outpost felt wrong, and there was an air of disuse to it. He didn't see anybody around, which was unusual. Even the sense of magic that was normally present didn't seem to be here.

What had happened?

The outpost in Nelar had always been a place of considerable power, and Gavin had not expected that to have changed. Why would it have now?

He made his way down the hall and looked in different doors, everything telling him that there was no one here. He was about to reach for his communication enchantment and talk to Gaspar when a youthful face poked out of the doorway.

"Can I... Oh. You."

Gavin held out Tristan's injured form. "I need your help."

Char looked as if he wanted to snap at Gavin, but he apparently resisted the urge. He motioned, and Gavin followed him down the hallway. He was a few inches shorter than Gavin, with serious eyes that seemed to take in everything around him.

They hurried to a door at the end of one hall, and Gavin paused and looked in the room. It was the same place Char had brought Gaspar when he had been hurt.

"Come on," Char said. "I have other things I need to be doing."

Gavin nodded. He wondered how much of that had to do with Jayna and her pursuit of dark magic users. Char was friends with her, and from everything Gavin had seen, he was a powerful sorcerer in his own right, though focused primarily on healing.

"What's going on here?" Gavin asked.

"We have decided to leave the outpost for now and have called everybody back to Ishan."

That didn't fit with Gavin's experience with the Society. Once they were in a city, they never abandoned it.

"Oh, don't look at me like that," Char said. "The city has its protections, and plenty of healers. Besides, we have an easy enough time getting back here."

He didn't explain more, though Gavin was curious. This didn't strike him as the same person he had met when Gaspar had been injured. Something about him was different. More confident in some way.

Gavin carried Tristan's body into the large healing room and set him on the bed inside. Cabinets ran along the opposite wall, and there was a counter with different medicines and enchantments. He had to hope that Char would be able to heal Tristan quickly.

"What happened to him?" Char asked.

"Some strange enchantment," Gavin said, and he described the barbs and what he had needed to do to remove them. "I've never seen anything like it before, but it's a kind of power the El'aras apparently are familiar with."

"Enchanted power," Char muttered, though it was mostly to himself. He hurriedly traced a pattern across Tristan's chest and then pushed down, pressing power into the spell. His eyes widened. "He's El'aras."

"You can tell that?"

Char nodded, though he didn't look over to Gavin. "There's a distinct signature to somebody with magic, and I have had increasing experience with those who are El'aras lately…" He paused and didn't say anything more for a few moments as he moved his hands. "Well, he's alive. He's breathing. His heartbeat is rapid, but I think that's just from the burns." He grabbed several ceramic enchantments from the counter and set them around Tristan's body. "I'm going to have to be left alone to work. I know you want to help him and save him, probably the same as you wanted for your other friend—"

"He's not even a friend," Gavin said.

Char frowned at him, but he continued to arrange the enchantments, placing them around Tristan. "An enemy, then. Do you need him to be tormented?"

"No. He was my mentor. He…" Gavin shook his head and started to walk away. "Just send word when he comes around."

"If."

Gavin stopped and turned back to Char.

Char looked over and nodded slowly. "I can't make any promises here, Gavin. I don't know if I'm going to be able to save him. The burns are quite extensive, and there are certain things I can do magically to help with that, but there's something else that's wrong with him. I can't quite put my finger on it, but I'm going to keep working on him."

"Do what you can," Gavin said.

"I told you I would. I will get him to Ishan for healing. You don't need to bring him yourself, as I have transportation." That took away one concern for Gavin to deal with. "And I will take good care of him."

"I know you will." Gavin glanced around. "I'm curious about what happened here."

Char blinked. "Jayna happened," he said, shaking his head. "She headed to the capital because she wanted to get more deeply involved with the Society."

Gavin raised a brow. That didn't strike him as Jayna's interest at all.

"She ended up discovering that the Fates were something terrible," Char said.

"I've dealt with them," he muttered.

"Have you? Well, then you may be pleased to hear that they were Sul'toral."

Gavin's breath caught. "They were?"

"No need to worry. Jayna took care of them."

At one point that might've surprised Gavin. He had known that Jayna was skilled, but he had not known just how powerful she was until he'd been trapped in the prison realm with her and had come to appreciate her strength. He found it odd that she hadn't shared what she had done with him. Then again, they'd been more focused on getting out of the prison realm than talking.

"Thank you."

Gavin glanced over to Tristan one more time before he turned and headed out of the room. He felt as if he was leaving some part of him behind. It was odd, but he didn't know if it was because Tristan was dying or because he had some secrets to Gavin's past that he was keeping from him. Either way, Gavin knew he couldn't linger here any longer.

Instead, he reached the door and pulled it open.

"Have you seen Jayna recently?" Char asked.

Gavin paused. "Not long ago."

Char let out a long sigh.

"You haven't?"

"She's been gone for a while. So has Eva. I think it's related—"

"It's related. They're both well. At least, they were the last time I saw them. We took out two Sul'toral, though there was one who got away."

Char nodded again. "Okay. If you see her before I do, let her know I just want to know how she's doing. I used to know where she was…" He sighed again, and he continued to arrange the enchantments around Tristan. "It doesn't matter. Let her know, if you would."

"I will," Gavin said.

He hurried out of the outpost and took flight on the paper dragon. He had the dragon circle above Nelar, giving him a chance to look down upon it. About as large as Yoran, the city was an old place of power, though he had never really spent much time here. Jayna had come to hunt dark sorcerers, but Gavin didn't really know much more about what she had done other than that. He again noted the seven massive mansions at the center of the city that surrounded a courtyard. Something about it was different than the last time he was here. The courtyard looked to be even more destroyed than he remembered.

He frowned for a moment before tearing his gaze away.

It was time to get back. Partly, he wanted to return because he had to ask Anna what had happened, but he also needed to ensure that the other bralinath trees had not been attacked while he was gone.

He would've expected to feel something if they had been—at least, Gavin thought he would, but maybe he wouldn't. The only reason he thought he felt something when he had been in the forest before was because of his proximity to the trees. What if others had been targeted the same way? What if he wouldn't be able to help them?

Gavin turned the paper dragon back toward Yoran, and with a tap and a quiet command, the dragon streaked across the sky.

The wind whipped around him, and the temperature went from warm to cooler, though not cold. As they neared the city, they began to descend.

He could feel that the stone wolf had arrived ahead of him. It was only then that Gavin remembered that the ravens were still enchanted. He called them back to him, tapped on them, and folded them back up before stuffing them into his pocket. Once he landed, he touched the paper dragon on the side, which caused the power to leach out. The dragon folded back up into a small enough size that he could tuck it into his pocket.

He turned his attention back to Yoran. Gavin wasn't sure he wanted to return like this. He was troubled by what he had encountered and by the strange power he had seen, but he also felt strongly that he needed answers that may not come from anyone but the El'aras. Maybe he could see what Anna knew.

He headed toward the El'aras section outside the city, but before he reached it, a small, dark-haired girl walked toward him.

"I felt what you were doing," Alana said. "You have to focus on these enchantments. My paper doesn't like you to be so distracted. Somebody else might take over them."

"I didn't realize it was possible to take over your enchantments," Gavin said. "I've added my own magic to them. That should be enough for me to maintain a connection to them."

Alana bit her lip as she looked past Gavin, toward the stone wolf prowling nearby. "I can feel your touch, but I think if you leave too much of it, others might still be able to overpower it. You just have to be careful. I can feel everything you do, and so can Mekel, so we just want to make sure you aren't leaving them unprotected."

Gavin patted his pocket. "I shouldn't do that to you. I'm sorry."

"You don't have to apologize, Gavin. I know that you're doing... Well, whatever it is you do. I keep asking Zella to tell me more, but she tells me she doesn't know, even though I suspect she does." She looked down the street before turning back to him. "She tries to act as if she isn't connected to the rest of the constables and doesn't hear all the rumors, but I know she does."

"Oh, I know she's connected to them too," Gavin said.

"Are you going to come visit again?"

"Eventually."

Alana frowned. "Why just eventually?"

"Do you want me to come by sooner?"

"I always enjoy your visits. And don't let Zella tell you otherwise. She likes it when you come by too. She always saves the good enchantments for you. Especially lately," she said. "After what happened outside the city recently, she's been really working with the others to try to make the enchantments as strong as she can. She's been experimenting, but some aren't working the way she wants them to. She has me experimenting too. I'm not reaching my *full potential* yet," she said, as if mimicking Zella's tone. "And then we can feel that there's something else going on. I don't know what it is, only that I can feel it too. I don't have any enchantments involved in all of this, not the way people like Mekel do, mostly because I've been told that my enchantments aren't that *useful*." She rolled her eyes.

Gavin patted her on the head. "Your enchantments are incredibly useful. They're also different than what most others make. That's why I like them."

Alana smiled. "I'm going to have to tell Zella you said that."

"You go ahead and do that. I wouldn't have been able to save a friend of mine without your enchantments." It was more than that. He wouldn't have been able to reach the city to defend it were it not for them either.

"I think they don't really understand the full benefit of what paper can do," Alana said, winking at him. "They see it as flimsy, but when you add part of yourself to it, it gets thicker."

Gavin chuckled. "Like a dragon."

She grinned at him. "Exactly. Like a dragon. Like *your* dragon." Her grin turned into a frown. "Although your dragon has become different. Whatever you did to it changed it."

"In a bad way?" Gavin asked. He had no idea whether he was harming the dragon with his magic, but each time he added an augmentation of power into the dragon, he had felt something shift.

"Not in a bad way," she said, "only different. I don't really know. I can feel it, but I can't tell what it's doing or how you might have changed it. I think if you give me a little more time, I might be able to come up with it, but..."

"If you want to test the enchantment, all you need to do is ask."

Alana waved her hand. "No, I don't need to take it away from you. I was just saying that I might be able to understand a bit more. Maybe I could do some of the same things if I had a chance to experiment. I might have a few things for you soon."

"What kinds of things?" Gavin had always found Alana's enchantments to be quite useful, so if she had something else, he was eager to find out what it was.

"This one doesn't even have wings," she said, smiling at him again. "But I don't know if it's going to work. I've been trying to test it, but it's hard to do inside the city, and Zella doesn't like it when I leave. I only go to the trees, where it's mostly safe."

"It probably is safer if you have somebody else with you."

"Would *you* come with me?"

Gavin forced a smile. "When I have time, I'd be happy to go with you."

He still wanted to understand her power. Her enchantments were different than those of other enchanters, something he thought was significant, but he didn't quite know why. Increasingly, he thought he needed to learn the reason.

"You just send one of the ravens to me when you're ready," she said. "I'll know what it says." She continued on down the street, leaving Gavin alone.

He turned a corner and was unsurprised to see the other stone wolf walking with Anna. He had felt the stone wolf coming, but it had stopped. Had Anna known he was talking to Alana?

"Why did you leave me there with Tristan?" he asked her.

"I am not certain of him. I felt it best to give you time. You have your own issues that must be dealt with in order for you to reach your own potential."

"You missed the attack. We nearly lost the bralinath trees."

He shared with her what happened and what he had to do, even about taking Tristan to receive healing, though he left out where he had taken him. Gavin understood Anna's dislike of Tristan, a feeling that a part of him shared. But Tristan had knowledge that they needed. He had known the truth about the prophecies and had worked to ensure that they would benefit the El'aras. That was something Anna still did not acknowledge the way Gavin thought she should.

"I'm sorry I wasn't around to help. You saved the trees?" she asked.

"As far as I know. Were any of the other trees near Arashil attacked?"

"Not that I saw."

"Would you have known?"

"I would have been aware of it," Anna said.

Gavin focused, calling on the power of the El'aras magic within him, which he knew was bound to him because of the bralinath trees. He didn't detect anything dangerous, though he wasn't sure if he even would. Gradually, he began to feel a strange emptiness between him and the trees that he had not noticed before.

At first, it was a subtle change, just a shift of a connection that came from the fact that he had separated from the trees. But it also came from the fact that there had been some injury to them he had not yet understood.

"I can see from your face that something is wrong," Anna said.

"It's just that when the vines attacked, I didn't think there was anything else that happened, but now I can't be certain."

"What makes you think anything else happened?"

"Because I can feel the way the bralinath trees still lingered within me, and I can feel that there is some part of what happened there that remains separated."

He wasn't sure what it meant, only that he could feel that power, and he worried about the source of it.

Anna regarded him for another moment, and Gavin realized that there were other El'aras arranged around her.

"They targeted me," Gavin said. "And the trees. Was it because I'm the Champion?"

"It may be because you have started to detect something else."

"What else is there?"

"What you may find of the past."

The past. That was the only connection he had with the bralinath trees, though Anna knew that. Increasingly, Gavin believed that she hoped for him to search that connection, but for what reason?

She wanted something from him.

"When I was in the El'aras city and in Arashil, the only thing I was able to tell was that the past eventually brought it back to nothing," he said.

"Don't you think there are answers that can be found in that?"

Gavin laughed softly. "Lessons that can be found in the nothingness? I don't think there's anything to learn there."

He'd been trying to figure out just what it was that Chauvan was after. Power, but what kind? He had been angry that Gavin had the power of the El'aras through the bralinath trees, but he'd also been upset that Gavin had access to the nihilar.

Between Chauvan and the Sul'toral after him, he couldn't shake that it was all somehow related. He doubted that Chauvan would be able to take his connection to the bralinath power, but could he take Gavin's magic from the nihilar? He didn't think so, but it was a power he didn't really understand.

And unfortunately, it was one he increasingly felt like he needed to try to better understand. There was some aspect of it that didn't feel quite right. He had not been drawing on the nihilar all that much, especially since he had such a stronger connection to the El'aras magic through the bralinath trees, but he did wonder if he should have taken the time to master the nihilar power. Now he didn't know how he would go about it.

"There are other places you could go," Gavin said, "other places that the power exists where you can—"

An explosion thundered in the distance, a powerful burst of energy that trembled inside of him.

Gavin jerked his head around. It was not from within the city.

He immediately started to turn, but Anna grabbed him. "I don't think this is for you to do," she said.

Gavin glowered at her. "You aren't stopping me from going to help these people."

He didn't hear another explosion, but he could feel something changing. Power was building.

Anna released him. "It will be dangerous, Champion."

"More dangerous than what I've faced before?"

She frowned, then looked off into the distance. Her eyes grew pale, something Gavin had never seen from her. It was almost as if the color within them shifted, like she was seeing something only she could.

When she was done, she turned her attention back to Gavin and shook her head. "I cannot say. All I can tell you is that what's out there is going to be dangerous for you. If you follow this path…"

Gavin smiled at her. "You're afraid of what you can see?"

"I am aware that what I can see may prove dangerous for you, Gavin Lorren. And if it does, there may be no way to protect you from what is to come."

Gavin snorted. "I don't need protection from what's to come. I intend to protect the people I have vowed to protect."

He reached into his pocket and pulled out one of the stone skin enchantments. He had needed them far too often these days, so he wanted to be prepared now. When he reached the edge of the city, he slowed. He couldn't see anything amiss.

"I assume you're somewhere nearby?" Gaspar said, his voice coming through the enchantment clearly.

"I'm back," Gavin said.

"Back?"

"I journeyed out of the city with Anna earlier today to learn more about my El'aras background. Can't say it helped much, but Tristan may be dying, so…"

Gaspar stayed silent.

Gavin felt somebody move behind him. He spun to see Gaspar darting toward him, moving quickly—and enchanted.

"That kind of statement calls for you to talk in person," Gaspar said. "I've heard some of your conversation, but not all of it. Is everything all right, boy?"

Gavin appreciated his concern. He was one of the

people who truly understood what Gavin was going through and seemed to truly care about how he felt.

"He was about to tell me something," Gavin said. "I think that's what bothers me the most."

Then again, his feelings toward Tristan were complicated. When he thought about what Tristan meant to him, Gavin no longer knew whether it was simply about the things Tristan had taught him and the way he tried using him, or whether there was anything more to it. Gavin had thought he was done with his old mentor and that he no longer felt any sort of connection to the man, but he still *did* feel something, despite what he told himself.

"We don't necessarily have time for that," Gavin said, surveying the landscape outside Yoran. He didn't see anything, but he needed to find out for certain.

"What do you think is out there?" Gaspar asked.

"Can't say. Enchantments?"

"Well, you have your own enchantments. Why don't you send them out there to scout?"

Gavin chuckled. "I think you just want to see these stone golems hunt for us."

"I can't deny that it's entertaining to watch them lumber around."

In the back of Gavin's mind, a stone golem existed as an energy he could practically feel humming, even as the massive monster lay motionless. He activated that connection and felt it as the golem got to its feet and started moving off in the distance. He could almost see through its eyes, though not the same way as the paper ravens. Gavin pulled the ravens out of his pocket, tapped on each of them, and sent them soaring into the sky. As they took flight, he focused on what they could see.

"Maybe it was nothing more than just another enchantment that triggered," Gavin said.

They had certainly felt enough of those, and with the unusual metallic vine attack they had encountered here, along with in the forest, Gavin couldn't help but question if maybe there was something else they needed to find.

The ravens circled, though they were larger than they had been the last time he had used them. Had pushing power out of himself and into the ravens changed things for them so much?

"See anything?" Gaspar asked.

"Nothing so far."

Gavin focused on the ravens and stared off across the landscape. Images flashed in his mind from them, gradually piecing together as he managed to bring those images into a singular form that he could see more easily.

Shapes appeared in the distance. Hundreds of them.

They were swarming toward Yoran.

Gavin looked to Gaspar. "We are under attack."

CHAPTER SEVEN

I took Gavin a moment for him to process everything he saw.

There were tons of enchantments. That was the easiest thing to see, even though he wasn't able to make out much of anything from where he stood behind the city barrier. It was almost as if the enchantments were obscured in some way, designed to prevent him from being able to see them.

But as he stepped through that protection, he could make out those dangers surging toward them across the rolling landscape, heading directly toward Yoran. Gavin wasn't sure what was coming at them, but as he stared through the connection he shared with the ravens, he could make out the distinct shapes of creatures swarming.

Gaspar stepped up next to him. "What is it?"

"Enchantments," Gavin said. "Hundreds of them."

"You can't have that many enchantments without..."

Gavin nodded. "Right."

Neither of them needed to say what they were thinking. Not only were there enchantments, but the sheer number meant that there was a sorcerer—or many.

"Wrenlow," Gavin said into the communication enchantment, "if you're there, I'm going to need you to sound the alarm. Alert the constables, along with others, that the city is under attack."

From what Gavin could tell from the ravens, they were going to be assaulted from the north and the east. He couldn't see anything from the other directions, but he didn't want the city to be surrounded.

He tapped on the enchantment again. "Anna, if you're listening, I'm going to need your El'aras to help."

Gavin didn't know if she would agree to helping. He had welcomed her and the El'aras to Yoran and believed that they would step up to help defend it, but he had never tested that.

"That leads down a dangerous path, Gavin Lorren," Anna said through the enchantment.

"Any more dangerous than not fighting?"

"You could draw them away."

"I could do *what*?" he said.

"They are here for you. If you were to draw them away..."

She wanted him to leave? Gavin had no intention of doing that. Not when his people, and his city, needed him.

But why would Anna have even suggested that?

Because she had *seen* something.

There would not be much time. When the attack struck, with as many enchantments as he saw, Gavin suspected it would be a brutal and violent assault. He could handle quite a few of them, and he knew that the others who would fight alongside him would be able to take care of some as well, but the real issue was the sorcerers who were part of it.

What if there was a Sul'toral coming?

"Anna thinks I should draw them away," Gavin told Gaspar. "She thinks I can lead this attack away from the city."

Gaspar pulled out a pair of daggers that had much longer blades than his usual. "Do you intend to run?"

"Not exactly." Gavin glanced over his shoulder. "Partly because I can't help but feel as if the El'aras want to use me."

"You had better be careful, boy. Making comments like that is a sure way to attract danger to you. There are enough people who would rather see the El'aras anywhere but in Yoran. If it seems like the El'aras are starting to take advantage of Yoran's citizens, that's not going to go over well."

"Am I one of Yoran's citizens?"

"Not particularly, but they find you useful enough. That's why no one really minds you being around. You're a bit like a puppy dog, anyway, always coming bounding back, looking for a treat."

Gavin snorted.

He noticed movement behind them, and he looked

back to see dozens of constables and enchanters marching forward.

Davel Chan was among them. He was dressed in the dark gray of the constables, and enchantments worked up his wrist, glimmering under the pale sunlight. He had several on each hand, and then there was a giant band of metal around his neck. He strode up to Gavin, arms crossed over his chest and a glower on his face. "What now?"

"I don't know. Enchantments. Probably sorcerers."

Davel looked out, away from the city. "The protections should hold for enchantments. You said you tested them yourself."

The problem was that they hadn't been fully checked. It was entirely possible that the defenses would maintain and protect against an onslaught of enchantments and even a sorcerer or two, but if there was a more powerful attack, then they might be in more danger.

"I've tested them…" Gavin trailed off and frowned.

"Well?"

"Well, testing something against me is very different than testing it against sorcerers. We don't really know how it's going to hold up."

Davel nodded. "I have my people taking up positions around the city."

"We may need to take the fight to them."

"No," Davel said. "We let the defenses do the work. If they fail, then we need to be within the line of the suppression so that we can defend ourselves."

It wasn't a terrible plan, but it didn't fit with the way

Gavin had been taught to fight. Maybe that was part of the problem.

He looked over to Gaspar. "I'm going out there."

He reached into his pocket and grabbed one of the smaller paper dragons. He didn't use the small ones often, but for what he had in mind, he might need something that was a bit nimbler in the air. The enormous paper dragon flew faster and certainly offered an added layer of protection because of that speed and the thickness of the paper skin when it elongated. It was also filled with power. But a smaller paper dragon had a different advantage.

Gavin tapped on it, and it began to unfold.

"Care to tell me what you intend to do?" Gaspar asked.

"I'm going to go flying. Want to come with me?"

"I'm not so sure I should," Gaspar said, looking at the unfolding paper dragon enchantment. "Can't say that I care too much for flying."

"First, it was snakes, and now it's flying? What else aren't you going to like?"

"A man has to have his quirks."

"I will go with you," a voice said. A figure bounded out of the crowd that had formed at the edge of the city. Most of the people there were enchanters and constables, though a few laypeople had come out of curiosity for what had drawn all of the attention.

Brandon was tall, with dark hair and features that were distinctly El'aras. Gavin had not spent much time around him lately, though he had been helpful when they had dealt with Chauvan and the nihilar. He grinned. "I heard you had something fun going on."

"I'm not sure I would call it fun," Gavin said, "but I'll accept help."

He grabbed another paper dragon. Alana had given him five, and though he had his favorite, there were four smaller ones he could use to hunt. As the paper dragon unfolded, Brandon barely hesitated before jumping onto its back.

"It might be easier if you go on your own," Gavin said, activating a third paper enchantment.

Gaspar looked at it with suspicion. "Don't let it drop me." The old thief grunted, and he tapped on the top of the enchantment before it began to unfold, though it didn't grow large enough to safely ride on.

"Let me see if there's anything I can do," Gavin said.

He touched the dragon, which looked scarcely larger than a horse, before focusing on Gaspar. He pushed a little bit of his core reserves out, and a faint stream of power connected the paper dragon to Gaspar.

Gaspar grunted. "Well, I don't really care for that, but you are getting better with your enchantments."

With that, Gaspar climbed onto the dragon's back, and they all rose in the air.

Gavin tapped on his communication enchantment. "Wrenlow, I'm going to need updates from you."

"You got it. You want me on the front line or—"

"Not on the front line, but near enough that you can give me an idea of what's taking place. That is, if you don't mind."

"I'm not going to sit back and do nothing, Gavin."

Gavin nodded to Davel, who had already started to move away to join the rest of his constables and prepare the line around the city.

Davel wasn't completely wrong about needing to ensure that they had adequate support around the perimeter, but there was a part of Gavin that worried they wouldn't have enough defenses even with that.

He took to the air and focused on the stone golem in the distance, which moved as they flew outward. The ravens circled, giving him the ability to see through their eyes, though he was reminded of Alana's warning about how much he could split his focus. How many different enchantments could he connect to before he became overwhelmed?

Gavin looked over the side of the dragon, watching for movement. A mass of undulating enchantments were making their way toward Yoran. They were not coordinated like an army, but there were numbers to them. If he could find who commanded them, he might be able to stop them.

He tapped on the enchantment. "Do you see anything?" he asked Gaspar.

"Only thousands of enchantments."

"And more than we faced when three Sul'toral came to the city."

"Think it's another Sul'toral?" Gaspar asked.

"Maybe more than one," Gavin said.

The pressure he felt building around him suggested that they were going to have to fight soon. But if they could get past the enchantments and find out if there was somebody here who was guiding them, then it might not even matter. Destroy the sorcerer holding on to them, and from there they could deal with the remnants of the enchantments.

They streaked forward, though not with the same speed Gavin was accustomed to from traveling on the larger paper dragon. This one was far nimbler, though. When he tapped it on one side, the dragon banked. When he tapped the other side, it turned in that direction. It remained connected to him in a way that allowed Gavin to control how fast it went and what direction they were flying, and they moved with enough speed that he thought he should be able to stay ahead of the oncoming enchantments.

He couldn't only stay ahead of them, though. He needed to know what the city would have to face. There was a danger down there. He could see it, even if he didn't really understand its origin. He could feel something with it as well. And what was more, Gavin knew that whatever else happened, he would have to ensure that he found answers so he could protect the city.

On top of everything, he could feel energy shifting below him.

"Where are you going, boy?" Gaspar asked through the enchantment.

"I'm just testing something Anna said," Gavin replied.

"You want to see if they are after you specifically."

"I need to know."

"Don't you think that's a little arrogant?"

"I never said *I* thought they were after me," Gavin said. "Still."

It did seem a bit much for these enchantments and the sorcerers commanding them to be here because of him. There had to be something else that drove them here. But if it was him, he might be able to draw them away as Anna had suggested.

Gavin circled back, getting close to Gaspar. His paper dragon was all sharp angles, and Gavin couldn't tell if it was thick-skinned now that it had turned into a full-sized dragon or whether the paper was soft. Gavin's dragon had thicker skin, but that was partly because he had pushed some of his power into it to offer a level of protection. Brandon was still out there too, though he was circling farther away. With sword in hand, hair whipping in the wind, and his cloak flying behind him, he had a look of a powerful warrior charging into battle. Only, there was nothing here yet to battle.

Gavin guided his dragon forward, and they pushed farther to the northeast. As they traveled, he could feel the energy continue to shift.

"Damn, boy."

"You can see it?" Gavin asked.

"It's slow, and I can almost feel it more than I can see it, but they shift, don't they?"

"They do."

"So does that mean they actually *are* after you?" Gaspar asked.

Gavin sighed. "That's what I'm starting to fear."

"What do you intend to do?"

If they were here for him, wouldn't the sensible thing be to run? For him to draw them away? But where would he even lead them?

They couldn't stay too close to the city. He had to guide them somewhere else.

Gavin cursed himself that he had no supplies on him.

"I have to take them away from Yoran."

"I'm coming with you," Gaspar said.

"I doubt you'll be able to do much."

Gaspar laughed, waving his hand toward the ground. "And you will? I realize that you're the great Chain Breaker, but you aren't going to be able to do anything here, boy."

Black streaks flew toward them.

Several of them.

It looked something like the renral that had attacked him in the prison realm, but this was moving at a different pace, shooting across the ground. The creature was nearly as large as the paper dragon he was on and appeared similar to a bird, but it had a head that didn't seem like it was designed for it. Not a wolf, not a dog, but something almost feline.

"What is *that*?" Gaspar said.

"Grapaln," Brandon replied, getting close to them. His voice was hard and his tone serious. "And if there's one, there will be more. They are dangerous."

"Dark creatures?" Gavin asked.

"Not dark, but they don't care which side they fight for."

Gavin didn't really know the difference between a

dark creature and something that was not, only that dark creatures tended to be more inclined to harm him. All he knew was that they didn't have much time before these grapaln were on them and they would have to fight them.

The grapaln opened its mouth, and the loud shriek that came out gave him chills. It was the sound of the sky tearing.

Gavin ducked just as a bolt of green energy rushed toward him from the creature.

"I would've liked a warning about that," Gaspar said, leaning toward him.

"I think you need to get going. I don't know if you can help against something like that."

"And you think you can?"

"I think—"

Another green bolt streaked toward them, and Gavin used the connection he shared to the El'aras side of him, drawing on the power of the bralinath trees and what made him the Champion. Doing so would provide him with power, but would it be enough? Maybe he needed the nihilar power as well.

The grapaln opened its mouth again, but Gavin unleashed a tight band of power, a bladelike energy, and it struck the creature. It immediately shifted course, avoiding Gavin's attack.

"Agile little bastards, aren't they?" Gaspar said.

"It seems that way. I think it's time for me to do something stupid," Gavin said.

Gaspar looked over to him. "Not again."

"Well…"

Gavin focused on his paper dragon and sent instructions as the grapaln closed in on him. He needed the paper dragon to stay close to him. He climbed onto its back, then leapt. He tried to time it as best as he could, using every bit of his skill and training to coordinate it.

The grapaln banked, as if afraid that Gavin was coming to stab it, but that wasn't his intention. Still, he didn't quite get atop the creature the way he intended. He had to grab one of its wings, which was made of thick, almost oily feathers that tried to force him off, but Gavin scrambled onto the creature's back. The grapaln writhed, but Gavin squeezed its wing tightly and brought his sword up, shoving it down as hard as he could into the grapaln's back.

The creature shrieked, and another green bolt came from its mouth.

Then it started to flounder.

Gavin jumped again.

He focused on the paper dragon. As the dragon started to swoop toward him, another grapaln flew at Gavin. He twisted in the air, sweeping his blade toward it.

The grapaln hooked Gavin with one talon, forcing him to fortify his skin using the stone skin enchantment. He kept the talon from piercing his flesh but had no idea how long he'd be able to do that. He felt the force of the talon as it squeezed him and gripped tightly.

He spun, trying to bring his sword up to cut through the grapaln, but it evaded him. He then tried to swing the blade around to catch its belly instead, managing to get his sword up, but when he stabbed, his blade bounced off. The creature was somehow enchanted as well.

Gavin flipped himself around, yanking free of the talon, and grabbed on to the grapaln's wing. He landed on the creature's back and hurriedly stabbed, driving his blade into its spine.

From this angle, there was no resistance, and the grapaln immediately dropped.

Gavin jumped and landed on his paper dragon. He looked over to see Brandon struggling with another grapaln, though he was using a similar technique to what Gavin had done. There were three others coming at them.

Where was Gaspar?

He found him nearly on the ground. The grapaln had grabbed a hold of Gaspar's paper dragon and was shredding it first. Now that he was aware of it, Gavin could feel it.

He focused on the paper ravens and sent them a command.

"Hold tight," he said through the enchantment.

"I'm about to hit the... Oh. Dammit, Gavin."

Gavin reached for another paper dragon and tapped on it, pushing his core reserves into the enchantment as he activated it. The paper dragon unfolded and swooped toward Gaspar, catching him in powerful paper talons that clutched him out of the air and pulled him free of the grapaln's grasp.

Gavin dove toward that grapaln. As his dragon came close, he thrust outward with the blade. The grapaln tried to grab him with its long, sharp talons, but Gavin flipped himself around and swept his blade through the creature's back.

The paper ravens caught him, lifting him back to the dragon.

As soon as he took a seat, he focused on the three other grapaln.

Two. Brandon had already dispatched one of them.

"Maybe you should take care of them," Gaspar said. "I thought if you could do it, I might be able to do the same thing, but the technique is not the easiest."

"Well, you *are* a little older," Gavin said.

"And you are stupider."

Gavin jumped toward the grapaln, then brought his blade up and stabbed it in the eye. The creature screeched, and a bolt of lightning shot from its mouth. He tried to twist, but he was not able to in time. Instead, he was forced to push power out of himself. He drew on the El'aras energy, his own core reserves, and everything he could, while also trying to use the stone skin technique.

Everything went numb. It felt as if he'd grabbed a lightning bolt in midair.

As he hurtled toward the ground, he tried to turn, but he couldn't. His body didn't react the way he thought it should. He struggled to move, to twist, but nothing worked.

"Gavin?"

He could hear Gaspar, along with the air whistling around him, but he couldn't do anything. He continued to drop. Wind rushed toward him, and for a moment, he thought maybe one of the paper dragons would catch him.

But then he was lifted up, and another shriek echoed.

The other grapaln.

Gavin still couldn't move.

It had not just been a green bolt of lightning, then. It was some sort of paralyzing force.

And he was trapped.

CHAPTER EIGHT

"The damn creature has him," he heard Gaspar say, and Gavin suspected that the old thief was talking to Brandon. "I don't know. I can't get over to him. What about you?"

There was no answer from the other end, and Gavin wished they had an enchantment that would allow him to hear what Brandon was saying.

The creature moved rapidly. It shrieked every so often, the sound tearing at the sky.

Pain surged through Gavin. He was fully aware of that pain and how the grapaln held on to him and dragged him, but even so, he couldn't move. His body did not react. Other than pain, the only other thing he felt was wind whipping past him.

But there was power within him as well.

Bralinath.

He focused. That energy was still there within him,

and he had to call on that. He had his core reserves, but it was more than just that. That power was a part of him and filled him. He could use it.

Gavin found some part of him able to move, and he thrashed as hard as he could. The creature pinched down and held him.

He had to find some other way to get free. He'd always healed quickly, and now he had to somehow force himself to heal from whatever was paralyzing him. He knew that recovery had come from his connection to his core reserves, power he now knew was El'aras in origin, but he had never attempted to direct it the way he did now.

Gavin had to force that power through himself.

It wasn't how he normally used his El'aras connection, and it was more like how he called on power when he had been in the prison realm. It forced him to draw it in a way that was inverted rather than out through his body.

Pain shot through him again. In this case, Gavin suspected that was a positive outcome.

At least he was feeling something.

"You still there, boy?"

Gavin tried to move his mouth. His tongue started to work, so that was good. "Here," he muttered.

"The damn thing is flying you away. We have the other dragons following you, but it's moving too fast for us. We need you to help."

"Trying," Gavin said.

He laughed bitterly to himself. They wanted him to get himself free? That was what he was trying to do. He could feel the creature carrying him, and he could feel its strength, as well as a dangerous energy.

Gavin called power through him again and sent it downward.

The grapaln shrieked again. This time, as the sound erupted from its mouth, he could feel the irritation within it. Irritation was a good thing, he suspected. If he had angered the grapaln in some way, then he had to think that he might be able to get free.

Some part of the energy began to change.

He connected to his El'aras power, channeling that through the bralinath trees. What if he called on the nihilar now too? Maybe it wouldn't do anything. Against this kind of creature, Gavin had found that the El'aras magic had been effective, and only when he stabbed at it.

Energy came from the grapaln. Gavin needed to draw on more. He had to restore himself.

The creature cried out again.

"You're getting farther away," Gaspar said.

"Which way?"

"Northeast. And…"

Gaspar trailed off, and Gavin waited for him to say something else, but he didn't.

Instead, Gavin had to focus, but he could feel the energy around them and the power of the creature as it flew away. The only option he had was to try to call on even more magic.

He tried to move his hand. It worked, and he discovered that even though he'd been paralyzed, his hand was wrapped around the hilt of his sword so that he was still gripping it. He figured that was a positive development.

The wind howled around him, and he realized that he was dangling upside down, his feet clutched in the grapaln's talons. Gavin could stab at the creature, but it would not harm it. Not from this angle.

"Send the paper dragons," Gavin said. His voice had started to loosen up, and it was easier for him to talk now.

"They're trying, but they aren't quick enough. This creature is faster than I would've expected it to be, given its size and—"

"I can help."

Gavin focused on the paper dragons, able to sense a connection to the dragons, though he felt the strongest connection to the one he had powered the longest. He maintained that link, and then he channeled the ravens, using them to help him see.

Below him were the hundreds of enchantments they had spotted from afar. Some were stone monsters made of massive mounds of rock and earth, others were trees or lumps of dirt, and still others looked as if they were actual creatures that prowled through the land.

But it was the gleaming metal that worried him most of all. There had to be several dozen of those metallic vines shooting through there. Even a single one was difficult to fight, but dozens of them?

He shifted his focus, and he looked through the ravens' eyes so he could see the sorcerers controlling them. The ravens circled and swept away from him, and through their eyesight, he caught a glimpse of himself dangling from the massive grapaln. This bird had seemed smaller when it had been flying toward him, but from the ravens' vantage, the creature was enormous, easily more immense than any of the others Gavin had seen. He could feel the power coming from the grapaln up close, and the ravens seemed terrified of it, even though they were nothing more than enchantments. But then, the ravens would've seen the grapaln shredding one of the paper dragons.

Through their eyes, he saw the grapaln holding him upside down, his body bloodied. His clothing was singed, likely from the lightning bolt that had struck him. He could not tell where the grapaln was carrying him until he saw a ring of enchantments that formed an opening on a flat section of rocky earth. It existed on a road leading away from Yoran, perhaps even heading toward Nelar, though Gavin couldn't really tell. Not from this vantage.

A dozen people stood on the road. Toral, he suspected, and probably even Sul'toral.

A red-haired woman among them reminded him of Jayna, though it was not her. She was the one who controlled the metallic vines. Probably Sul'toral, he decided. But she was not alone. There were four others alongside her.

"I think we have five Sul'toral here," Gavin said, speaking to Gaspar through the enchantment.

"Five?" Wrenlow's voice jumped in. "Gods, Gavin, you have to get out of there. If there are five Sul'toral—"

"I'm having a hard time escaping from this, Wrenlow, so I'm going to need you to stay quiet until I manage to succeed."

"What happened? I heard—"

"I need Gaspar right now," Gavin said, trying to be as kind as he could, not wanting to snap at Wrenlow.

"I'm not sure I can disagree with the kid," Gaspar said. "If there are five of them, it's more than what we can manage. You barely survived when there were three, and that was with the help of the Toral and the Ashara."

It would just be Gavin. Well, plus Gaspar and Brandon, if they could reach him. They were not enough to take on five Sul'toral.

Gavin had access to his El'aras abilities in a way he hadn't before, but even that wasn't going to be enough to take on five powerful magic users, all filled with the kind of energy he could not even fathom.

Anna's warning came back to him then, her advice to avoid all of this.

She had known.

She had *seen* it.

The grapaln screeched again, and it jostled Gavin enough that another bolt of pain shot through him.

He tried to move his arms, and as he continued to press his power through himself, he started to find a way to move, nearly enough that he could feel his way past it.

Even so, he was still weak. In order to break free of the grapaln, he needed to have complete control over himself. But it was more than that. He had to brace himself if the grapaln took him toward the Sul'toral. He needed be ready for that attack and had to be prepared for the possibility that he was going to have to face five—no, more than five—powerful magic users.

"Get out. Now," Gaspar said.

"I'm trying," Gavin muttered.

One of the ravens went dark, like blackness faded from Gavin's vision. He felt like a string snapping, almost as if it was separate in the back of his mind. With a sudden realization, he knew exactly what had happened.

One of the Sul'toral, or even a Toral, had somehow managed to sever his connection to the raven. Gavin tried to call that power back, but doing so shifted some connection that he had to the dragons, and a battle for control began to wage.

"Go back," Gavin warned.

"What was that?" Gaspar said.

"Go. *Back.*"

He redirected his focus. He took the power he had, the connection he shared with the paper dragons—not only his but also Gaspar and Brandon's—and he forced his connection through them.

"Return," he commanded them.

Gavin could feel the sudden change, and he let out a relieved sigh.

"What are you doing, boy?"

"They're taking over the enchantments," he said.

He could still feel the ravens, but if he lost some command of the dragons, he knew what would happen.

The Sul'toral would gain control.

Another string snapped in the back of his mind, and another raven was lost.

Gavin felt the pain of it. What must Alana feel when

that happened? Probably the same sort of pain, he assumed.

He realized he had something he hadn't even considered trying, but he needed another moment. First, he had to make sure the others were safe before he attempted his own rescue. He had a sense of how far he had to go before the grapaln reached the Sul'toral. He had some time, but not as much as he wanted.

Distantly, Gavin was aware of the dragons getting free of anyone else's control. They made it behind the suppression border around the city, so he severed his connection to them, hopefully deactivating the enchantments.

And now he had to worry about only himself.

He reached for his sword but found his usual paper dragon instead. Maybe if he used that, he could get free.

When he pushed power out of himself and into the folded paper dragon, it stretched immediately as power flowed from him into it. He clung to the creature and then cleaved with his blade, carving into the grapaln's talon and ripping through it until he was fully freed.

As the dragon carried him, Gavin jabbed the blade up into the grapaln's belly and poured the power of the El'aras out through it. The creature fell onto the dragon, and he kicked it, sending it off the paper dragon's back.

He noticed that his sword was still crackling with energy.

That was new.

Had he somehow absorbed the green energy from the grapaln?

He'd have to think about that later.

Gavin clutched the dragon's back, thankful to have it with him. He leaned over the edge of the dragon and stared. They were high enough that he was able to see the plains below him. Hundreds of enchantments had followed him toward the Sul'toral.

The dragon circled upward into the air. As it did, he saw that there was more movement off to the northeast. For a moment, he thought there were more enchantments coming, but he soon realized they were people.

Did the sorcerer suddenly command an army?

Dark specks streaked toward him. *Renral.*

The only other time Gavin had seen them had been in the prison realm, where he had killed one after it had poisoned him. If he had to face those as well, he wasn't sure he would survive. Which meant he had to take on the Sul'toral.

More and more renral began to appear. There had to be a dozen. Maybe two dozen.

And they were heading toward him with tremendous speed.

"Gavin?" Gaspar said, his voice coming through the enchantment.

"Not now," Gavin said.

"You're going to need to hear this."

Gavin tapped on the enchantment, muting it. He didn't need Gaspar interrupting him and distracting him while he was trying to figure out how to deal with the renral. What he wouldn't give to have a real dragon, something that could breathe fire like in the stories he had heard when he was younger. Something that would be able to defend itself against creatures like this.

Gavin took a deep breath and winced.

He hadn't fully recovered. He could still feel some of the effects of the lightning bolt that had shot through him. The power continued to crackle within him, and he needed to get past that. If his movements were slow by even a little bit, he wasn't going to be able to fight as effectively as he needed to.

Gavin slipped on a pair of rings for speed and strength before grabbing another one for stone skin. And then he braced himself as the renral flew toward him.

Down below, he could feel magic beginning to build from the Sul'toral.

Everything was coming to a head.

And Gavin was caught in the middle.

CHAPTER NINE

IMOGEN

Imogen's people had been moving quickly, with her pushing them as hard as she could to try to make haste toward Yoran. But even as she urged them on their trek, they had been delayed by an almost continuous stream of attacks. The attacks hadn't stopped them—at least, not really—but they had made the journey far more difficult.

"We haven't seen anything for the last day," Jorend said, sidling up next to her.

"I'm aware," Imogen said.

He nodded. "I don't say that to anger you, First."

Imogen took a deep breath. "I know you don't. It's just that this has not gone the way I thought it would." She looked over to him. "When I left Yoran, I did so because I wanted to help my brother. I thought he needed to find his purpose." She smiled to herself at the memory, one of the last few happy memories of Timo that she had before he had betrayed her and everything she had believed. "Only, I was the one who needed to find my purpose, probably just as much as Timo."

Jorend remained silent as they continued their march. Given the size of the caravan making their way west, they could not go faster than the slowest of them. Even if Imogen wanted to move on ahead, to get to Yoran to see if it needed her protection, doing so would abandon some of her people—something she was not willing to do. As difficult as it was for her, she forced herself to keep pace with the caravan.

"Have you ever considered that the two of you were always destined for this?" Jorend eventually asked.

He looked up ahead to where Lilah was working with several other shamans even while they walked. There was no real downtime, so every moment was spent training and preparing, wanting to ensure that everyone was as skilled as they could be. Lilah, having trained with the Porapeth the way she had, was the most adept sorcerer, and she used that skill to help others begin to find their own way.

"I've often wondered if there were specific paths and patterns that were always destined," Imogen said, watching as Lilah demonstrated one of her defensive techniques. There was no time for subtlety with magic. Everything was needed to fight. The Leier warriors served as the sword, but the shamans served as the shield, using their connection to sorcery to offer defenses that their people wouldn't have otherwise. "There have always been different possibilities for us."

"There might have been possibilities, but didn't you say that everything about you was hazy to the Porapeth?"

Imogen smiled. "Hazy, yes, but not impossible to see."

If she had learned one thing in her time with her new abilities, it was that there were aspects that remained difficult to observe—hazy, as many of the Porapeth called it—but there were other ways of looking at that haze. If one angle remained obscured, you had to come at the problem from a different direction. That had been Imogen's experience.

"You never said that before," Jorend said.

"I'm not sure if I believe it," she said, smiling tightly. "It's just that I also have a hard time thinking that Benji the Elder knew nothing."

He had been more than just a Porapeth. He had been a friend who had gifted her with some of his magic when he passed on, so Imogen still found herself thinking of him often. Of the lessons he had taught her, along with some of the things he had implied. The fragment of power that remained with her still carried some aspect of him and his personality, so there were times when he emerged and she had conversations with him, even in what she had once believed had been his death. Now she knew it was little more than the next stage in his existence.

"What can you see?" Jorend asked.

"Everything is hazy," she said.

"So you're trying to look at it from a different angle?"

Imogen nodded. "Trying, but unfortunately, I'm not doing as well as I would like. I see glimpses of brightness. I don't know what those mean, but I have my suspicions."

"Do you care to share with me?"

Imogen chuckled. "Where is the fun in that, Jorend?"

"The fun comes in survival, First."

"There is one who I suspect I am catching glimpses of. He shouldn't be in Yoran, but perhaps he's remained nearby. I'm hopeful that he has, as we may need his help in stopping Timo." Admitting that she might not be the one capable of bringing down her brother was difficult. Since he had betrayed her and their people, Imogen had believed that she was going to be the one to stop him. And she still might. But having help would make the task that much easier. "If he is, then the bright burst that I can occasionally see when I attempt to follow the different possibilities makes more sense. If he's not, then I have no idea what I am seeing. Maybe it's nothing more than Timo."

If it was her brother, Imogen wasn't sure she understood why he would suddenly appear the way he did to her, and within this vision. Any time she had seen him before, he had been less clear and not nearly so bright. It made her worry that perhaps there was some entity and energy that she did not fully understand. One that might create additional challenges for them.

"Do you have any idea how much longer it will be before we reach this place?" he asked.

Imogen sensed some trepidation from Jorend, though most of their people had some trepidation these days, especially as they traveled farther and farther to the west. It was an uncertainty about what they might find and experience, but more than that, the unease stemmed from where they were heading and what they might discover when they got there. For most of the Leier, and the people who had once been known as the Koral, they were heading beyond the homeland for the first time. That was enough to frighten any of them. Imogen understood why, as there were aspects of leaving the homeland that troubled her even though she had done it before. Still, she understood that doing so was necessary. If they did not make this journey, she did not know what else they might be able to find, and she didn't know if they would be able to protect their people the way they wanted to.

She waved her hand off into the distance. "What do you see out here?"

Jorend looked over. "Is this some sort of test?"

"Not exactly," she said. "It's more a matter of asking what you see and feel so you can look around and get a sense for what is here. If you'd like, we could take to the sky and—"

"I have no interest in taking to the sky." He flicked his gaze toward the clouds overhead before turning his attention back to her. "Besides, we have seen far too many grapaln these days, and I don't like the idea that they might come at me. I'm far too tasty of a treat for those creatures."

Imogen laughed. "*You* are too tasty? Are you sure about that?"

"You don't think I am?"

"I just think you'd be little more than a snack to them, and they probably would not care to waste their time hunting for somebody like you."

He chuckled. "You might be right. Grapaln are more

interested in larger prey." They had seen evidence of what the grapaln were hunting, such as carcasses of deer and a few larger creatures like bears. "You keep mentioning this swamp you passed when you came through here before."

"Because I did pass by one," Imogen said. "If you look off into the distance, you can see signs of it, and even smell some of its stench."

"When you talk about it like that, it sounds amazing," he said, laughing.

"I still thought I could help Timo when I came through here last time."

The landscape had become more forested, and they followed a narrow path, taking it between the trees and weaving ever forward at an increasing pace. Their procession was long enough that the forest itself slowed them. It frustrated Imogen, as she wanted to speed along, but it was difficult to go any faster through here than they already were.

It forced Imogen to take different steps to explore and see if there was any evidence of danger nearby. Every time she scouted, she found nothing other than the memories of when she had traveled through here before.

She and Jorend fell into a silence as they continued their trek. They had to stop and set up camp each time a day passed, with Imogen feeling as if she had given Timo far too much time to accomplish whatever his goals were, but she knew there wasn't anything else she could do beyond what she already was. She was pushing her people as quickly as she could. Short of having them ride enchantments, she didn't know if there would be a way she could move them any faster, and enchantments would still be unlikely to carry them as quickly as what she wanted, anyway.

By the time they reached the other side of the forest, nearly a full week had passed from the last time she'd seen Timo. The rest of her people felt relief at leaving the confines of the trees, coming out into the open plains beyond it, which Imogen understood. Living within their homeland provided a different experience than being within the trees and feeling trapped.

"Is there anything I can help you with?" Lilah asked.

"There's nothing we need to do other than to speed this along," Imogen said. "Unfortunately, I don't know that we can do that any faster than we already have."

"There may be something I could offer. Enchantments may provide a measure of speed that we don't have otherwise, so—"

"Even if we had enchantments, I doubt there'd be anything that would expedite this journey," she said. "We will keep our pace."

Imogen looked over to Jorend and the other Leier. She knew they needed to move more quickly but also that there was a limit to how fast their people were comfortable pushing themselves.

As the next few days passed, Imogen noticed more and more grapaln circling above. They were dangerous creatures, and though they had wrestled with them a few times before, they also didn't have the same protection from being in the mountains.

As they traveled, she noticed signs of power. When she

felt it, she knew immediately what it was. Sul'toral. At least, something akin to a Sul'toral. Imogen no longer knew how many of the original Sul'toral remained and how many had gained power through secondary means, much like Timo had. At this point, the difference was probably moot, as the power they had acquired was consistent either way.

They chased after the power of fragments, and it did not surprise her when she learned that others had come to know that same power, probably gifted the same ability her brother had been. Power that was stolen and, in some way, corrupted.

"What do you see?"

Imogen looked over to Eleanor, one of the original shamans who had traveled with her. Eleanor was holding a pair of enchantments in either hand, which Imogen suspected allowed her to see the different dangers that were off in the distance more clearly.

"I see nothing," Imogen replied. "Well, nothing quite yet. It's what I feel that troubles me."

"What do you *feel*, First?"

Imogen smiled at the honorific. "I don't know. Perhaps it's nothing more than a sorcerer, as sorcery is quite common in these lands." At the slight arch in Eleanor's brow, Imogen nodded. "You will come to see that. It is why I left my homeland in the first place. I thought I might find something here."

"From what you said, you did find something here."

"I did, but I didn't find what I thought I would. And now I wonder if perhaps I ever would've been able to."

"If there is something of power up ahead, should we be worried?" Eleanor asked.

Imogen nodded. "We should be ready."

They continued on, with scouts leading the way. Near evening, there came another burst of power, followed by an attack. These were enchantments. Hundreds of powerful ones. Many of them were similar to ones she had faced before. Too often, sorcerers defaulted to what they were familiar with. There were massive stone monsters and creatures made of grass and mud. Some were birds, though she couldn't tell if those were living or merely enchantments. She saw a strange vine slipping across the ground, but even that was merely another form of enchantment, and not nearly as terrifying as some.

Imogen immediately reacted, as did the Leier warriors and the Koral shamans, all heading into battle with the enchantments. None seemed afraid, though none should have been, as they had all faced this kind of power plenty of times now.

They carved through the enchantments easily, and when it was done, Imogen noticed several sorcerers off in the distance. Using Petals on the Wind, she hovered in the air and floated toward them.

She didn't chase them, knowing she could not abandon her quest, so she returned to her people. They regrouped and set up camp, then set out in the morning.

Around the middle of the following day, they encountered the sense of sorcery again, and this time Imogen felt something different.

Not only that, but she *saw* something different. She

shot into the air, holding on to the power she could now possess through the sacred patterns and using it to keep her aloft. The various possibilities echoed in her mind, showing her what could be. And as she focused on it, Imogen stared until she understood what she was seeing.

"You found something?" Jorend asked, striding over to her.

"A friend," she said.

"Who?"

"He's known as the Chain Breaker, a man of considerable power and talent."

"And you're not a woman of those same traits?"

Imogen chuckled. "There was a time when I would've said I was not, but now I feel otherwise."

"You should never question what you are," he said.

"Now who's the one trying to provide advice?"

Jorend let out a small laugh. "I thought it was useful, especially given that it was the same advice you once gave me."

Imogen watched as Gavin fought. There was a certain fluidity to his movements. She had always seen that from him and had always known he was skilled and powerful, but she had forgotten about it. Perhaps it was unfortunate that she had allowed herself to forget how capable he was.

But now she found herself observing him, all too aware of what he was doing. She had long felt that he was far more talented than she was. She had known that if she were to need to stop him, she would likely die in the process.

Now she no longer believed that.

124 | D.K. HOLMBERG

What would it be like if she sparred with him now? Seeing him fight, seeing his skill, Imogen knew that he was capable, but she also recognized something else—he was not more capable than her. The idea seemed strange and surprising, but she couldn't help but feel that way.

Other enchantments were approaching from afar.

Maybe they *had* been fast enough in getting here. Perhaps just fast enough to stop Timo.

"I think it's time that we take those who can move quickly and provide our help," Imogen said. "These people are my friends, and they will need us."

She whistled. Off in the distance, there came an echoing call, a loud shriek, and the overwhelming sense of power that began to build and sweep toward them.

They would go, they would fight, and they would defend Yoran.

CHAPTER TEN

E nergy flowed all around Gavin.
Several renral dived toward him, moving faster than he thought they should be capable of. It seemed as if they flew on a storm cloud with lightning crackling within it. He'd never seen anything so terrifying in the sky before. They were swarming around him, flanking him.

As they did, he could feel something.

Another shriek was building.

More grapaln.

Balls.

Facing multiple renral was bad enough, but dealing with the grapaln on top of that was more than he thought he could withstand. Especially when adding in the Sul'-toral threat.

Gavin patted the paper dragon. He started to focus on power, pushing as much of it as he could into the dragon. He could feel a reserve of energy beginning to form within the creature, holding tightly deep within it. As he did, he realized that the paper dragon was trapping that power. Could he use that?

He tapped on the dragon. They shot upward, and he clung as tightly as he could to it. The dragon was calling on all of his core reserves, on his connection to the bralinath trees and the El'aras power, on everything Gavin could summon, lifting them into the air as high as they could go.

He hazarded a look over and noticed something—the renral were attacking the dozen grapaln coming toward him. They were fighting one another?

As that thought came to him, another realization hit him. There were *people* sitting atop the renral.

They were domesticated?

The dragon was fast enough and powerful enough that he would be able to escape, but something didn't feel quite right. And if there was anything Gavin had learned over the years, it was that when something didn't feel quite right, it probably was not.

Each person seated atop the renral had dark hair and pale skin, and they reminded him of Imogen.

Leier.

That was who they had to be—but it meant the Leier had tamed renral. How was that possible?

Maybe they knew something about the Sul'toral.

He flew down, and he caught sight of a Leier man, one with dark hair, dark eyes, and a black cloak fluttering behind him. One arm looked to be injured, but he was gripping on to the renral and sneering at the grapaln.

The man looked over to him. "Are you the one called the Chain Breaker?"

Gavin frowned. "You know me?"

"The general does."

"General?"

The Leier general had to be somebody with Imogen, which meant help.

His frown must've given away his confusion, and the man pointed behind Gavin.

As Gavin guided the dragon in that direction, he pressed on the communication enchantment. "Gaspar, I think I found—"

"Dammit, boy. I've been trying to tell you that Imogen is coming. Just give her a moment."

"Well, I think I found her people."

"You what?"

"There are a dozen, maybe two dozen, riding atop renral. Remember that creature that poisoned us in the prison realm? They're fighting the grapaln."

The old thief gasped. "They're *riding* them?"

"I'm trying to get to Imogen now. She's to the east. You might be able to circle around the enchantments and reach us."

"Now you'd allow me to do that?"

"I wasn't trying to keep you from fighting," Gavin said. "I wanted to protect you."

"You were just trying to protect the enchantment," Gaspar said.

Gavin chuckled because he wasn't entirely wrong.

The paper dragon surged toward the Leier. When he

landed outside the line of people marching toward him, he stayed on the dragon and looked around. Several people stepped closer to him, but only one of them was familiar.

Or had been.

Imogen had changed in the time she'd been away. She'd always had a graceful confidence to her, and she had power within her, but now there was something Gavin couldn't quite place. *More* confidence? She practically flowed, reminding him of the patterns he had seen her use when she fought, but there was something different to them this time.

When she walked up, she rested a hand on the paper dragon and looked up at him. "Gavin."

He laughed as the realization struck him. "The general?"

She glanced behind her, then turned back to him and shrugged. "I returned to my people."

"It seems you've gotten a promotion."

"Out of necessity, not desire," she said.

Gavin nodded. "We don't have much time. There are five Sul'toral and hundreds of enchantments, all of them marching on Yoran."

"I know. We've been following many of them, though not all," she said, and she tipped her head to the side as if trying to work through a problem. That was a new gesture for her. When she turned her attention back to him, she looked over to the people behind her. "The Sul'-toral. How many Toral are with them?"

"I don't know. I saw a dozen altogether, so I'm assuming there are about seven Toral."

"More sorcerers have joined them than I was expecting," she said. "But not unmanageable."

"Not unmanageable?" Gavin snorted. "Imogen, I don't know what you've dealt with since you left, but I can tell you that we faced three Sul'toral and killed two of them, and I had both the Toral, and Jayna and her friends helping me."

Imogen frowned. Her eyes were dark, and for a moment they flashed with something that was almost silver. Gavin wasn't sure if he had imagined it, but that silver soon faded. "I wasn't aware that two more were gone. It's difficult to know whether the numbers matter any longer. I think the Sul'toral we're fighting are different than the ones who once existed. Regardless, we should finish what we have started."

"What are you talking about?" Gavin asked.

"Can you take me to them?"

"Are you kidding?"

"Not about this," she said.

"I'm not going to put you in the midst of five Sul'toral and seven Toral and risk you getting injured."

"My people will take care of the enchantments," she said, motioning behind her. "And the others can take care of the grapaln. I imagine you encountered them?"

Gavin wrinkled his nose and nodded. "I did. They are particularly dangerous."

She gave him a tight-lipped smile. "'Particularly dangerous' is an understatement. We lost quite a few to their attacks, but we learned that the renral are immune to them." She chuckled. "Everything has a counter, doesn't it? Each move has a countermove. You just have to find the right defense."

There was the Imogen he thought he remembered, but the rest wasn't at all like the person he knew.

"What happened to your brother?" he asked.

Her face became clouded. "He chased power."

She stepped forward, and she climbed up onto the dragon's back. Gavin hadn't been sure whether the dragon would even allow her to, but she simply scrambled onto it and touched her hand to its side in a way that left Gavin thinking she used magic on it, but that couldn't be right.

The dragon immediately took to the air, almost as if Imogen was the one commanding it. Gavin focused, pushing power through him, and he realized that something had shifted. Some part of the dragon had changed, as though Imogen had connected to it.

He looked over to her, a question burning in his mind. "What happened?" he asked.

"I found my path," she said.

Before he had a chance to ask what that meant, Imogen jumped off the dragon's back.

Gavin was too startled to even react.

He looked down. She was sweeping her sword around, creating a pattern that slowed her descent. She was heading straight toward the Sul'toral and the Toral.

Gavin groaned, and he tapped on the dragon before reaching for his communication enchantment. "You should've warned me that Imogen has gone suicidal," he said.

"I'm trying to circle around to get to you, but it's slower this way," Gaspar said.

"I don't know that it matters. Imogen just jumped into the middle of the Sul'toral. I guess I'm going after her."

Gavin focused on the dragon, and then he jumped.

It was probably foolish for him to do the same thing as Imogen, but he mimicked her pattern. As he did, he noticed that there was something within the pattern that allowed him to fall more gently. It reminded him of his hands floating on the wind like a bird, or of a flower dropping its leaves.

Once he landed, he spotted Imogen moving with far more fluidity than he expected.

Toral darted at her, using power she seemed to anticipate with a blur. She stabbed at one Toral, carved through another, and somehow blocked magic with her blade. She brought down all seven Toral without even killing them.

She spun toward the Sul'toral.

Gavin stayed with her, curiosity nearly overwhelming him. When Imogen had fought alongside him before, she'd been talented with a sword, but this was on another level. This wasn't just fighting skill—it was almost like she could anticipate what would happen and where.

One of the Sul'toral turned toward her.

"The general," he said, a sneer on his face.

Imogen rushed toward him blade-first. She shifted, spinning her fist around, catching him under the jaw in a way that made it seem as if he'd turned *into* the punch. He collapsed, and as he went to the ground, she drove the side of her fist down on his chest with a loud crack.

She stood again. The other four Sul'toral watched her.

Gavin couldn't help but stare.

"You will abandon your pursuit," Imogen said, her voice soft, but the command evident within it.

That was what had changed. Gavin had been trying this whole time to figure out what was different. He had thought that maybe it was tied to some new ability, and perhaps it was, especially given how she had disarmed the Toral and incapacitated a Sul'toral in little more than the blink of an eye. But that wasn't the full extent of what had changed about her.

It was her command. She was in charge.

Not only that, but she *knew* she was in charge.

"Do you think we fear you, little one?"

The Sul'toral spread out. Then they seemed to ripple and duplicate.

"I haven't seen this kind of sorcery before," Gavin said.

He was speaking more calmly than he felt, which he realized came from the fact that he wasn't entirely sure he was even needed here. Imogen had acted as if she could manage this all on her own. Given how he had seen her incapacitate the Toral, he realized that maybe she could.

"They think they can mask their presence," she said.

She held her blade up and did nothing. Instead, she simply stood there, rigid.

A flash of power surrounded Gavin, leading to a sense of tension that built on his skin. He called on his El'aras abilities and let that power fill him, but then he noticed something else.

It seemed as if lightning crackled out from her. The energy struck down, shooting beyond a space Imogen had created in a ring of power that circled her and Gavin. The magic shot down toward the Sul'toral.

The duplications faded, and he saw the four Sul'toral. The fifth one got to his knees, not dead but holding his chest. He watched Imogen, anger burning in his eyes.

"I don't know what you have learned, but I think it's better just to kill them," Gavin said to her. "If they're serving Sarenoth, there's a real danger in what they intend."

"It's less that they serve Sarenoth and more that they use him."

"I don't understand."

"I can see that."

There again was another comment that struck him as strange and similar to what he had heard from Anna. Not only from her but also from Tristan. Did she have some power of prophecy? That wasn't the Imogen he knew.

Then again, she wasn't anything like the Imogen he had known.

The Sul'toral continued to circle her. A power radiated from her, and she simply stood in place, holding her blade. Power crackled, this time shooting toward her, but it seemed to strike an invisible barrier and was blocked from hitting her.

She shook her head. "You're making a mistake," she said to them.

Magic shot out from her, crackling in the air and striking the others before radiating outward. The Sul'toral stepped back from her.

Imogen simply stared. "You cannot win," she said. "Lay down your weapons."

The Sul'toral shifted their attack again, and another wave of power swept toward Imogen, which she deflected. She was demonstrating control over power beyond what he believed her capable of.

Imogen shrugged. "I gave you three warnings."

With that, she surged forward. Gavin reacted too. He leapt toward one of the Sul'toral now that Imogen had unleashed whatever fury she was going to and no longer seemed to be holding a barrier around her.

As he darted toward one attacker, he brought his blade up and then twisted, able to feel the Sul'toral turn his attention toward him. Gavin brought his fist around, pulling the power of the bralinath trees through himself and connecting with the Sul'toral's temple. He swept his leg around in a kick, then brought his sword up and stabbed down.

Magic pushed against him and resisted him, and Gavin forced his own power through the blade. Energy built within him as he used both his El'aras abilities and that of the nihilar. He could also still feel the crackling energy of the grapaln flowing in his blade.

As he shoved all of it through the barrier spell the Sul'-toral held on him, he glanced up and saw that the man was gone. Not dead, just simply vanished.

Gavin twisted, turning to the next. Three Sul'toral

attacked Imogen, but she was flowing from position to position, darting and dancing, her blade moving in such a blur that Gavin couldn't even follow. He threw himself toward the nearest Sul'toral. His blade met a feeling of resistance as he attempted to carve through them, but he was finally able to part it. The Sul'toral crumpled.

He spun, looking toward Imogen. The other two who had been attacking her were gone as well. They weren't dead as far as he knew, though Gavin wondered if she had injured them. She strode toward the first Sul'toral she had fought. He was still on his knees, hands up in front of him, energy radiating outward. Gavin could feel the power coming off him as he moved his hands in a rapid pattern.

Imogen simply reached forward and grabbed each hand with hers, separating them. The Sul'toral looked up at her, eyes flashing with anger.

"You have failed your master," she said.

He sneered at her. "Do you think we can be so easily stopped?"

He started to ripple and then began to fold.

"Imogen!" Gavin shouted, though he hadn't needed to.

Imogen squeezed and seemed to pull the Sul'toral back toward her, as if she was fighting whatever power he tried to summon. It wasn't just that she managed to fight that power, it was how she did it. She barely moved, but it seemed as if she was summoning magic.

The power strangely reminded Gavin of the bralinath trees. It seemed like it shot up and arced over her but also streaked downward as though rooting her to one spot.

She gripped the Sul'toral and held him in place while he trembled. "Where is he?"

Power pressed out from her, though Gavin had no idea how she did it. Somehow, she was taking on the Sul'toral all by herself. He was unnecessary in this fight.

"You will never find him until he wants you to see him."

"Where?" Imogen demanded.

The Sul'toral grinned, and Gavin began to feel power building from him.

He sprinted toward him, but there was no point. Imogen seemed to erupt a bolt of lightning out of herself, which shot into the Sul'toral and caused him to collapse. Finally, she stood and sheathed her sword. After turning to look at him briefly, she glanced behind her. Her Leier were sweeping through the enchantments, cutting them down.

"It really is good to see you, Gavin."

He had rarely felt so dumbfounded as he did now. This was not the same person he had known before she'd left the city. "It's nice to meet you, Imogen."

She regarded him for a long moment, then tipped her head forward in a slight bow. "I could use a mug of ale."

Gavin snickered. "I might know a place."

CHAPTER ELEVEN

Gavin tried to get Imogen to talk as they made their way back toward the city. She and the other Leier with her were taking care of the remaining enchantments, doing so far more quickly than Gavin would have been able to do, and more quickly than he would've expected Imogen capable of doing. They were fluid, fast, and deadly. She moved with a grace that Gavin no longer knew if he could even match. Above him, the renral were flying and circling them, but none of them landed.

"How did you tame the renral?" he asked. "Gaspar and I had an experience with them recently. It wasn't pleasant."

Her brow furrowed and darkened as she looked over to him. "Gaspar should not have dealt with renral."

"It wasn't intentional," Gavin said. "Neither of us intended to take on the creatures, but we were faced with something we were not thinking we would have to, and..." He shook his head but then decided that he needed to tell her everything he could. Given what he had seen from her already, he suspected that Imogen might have answers he wanted. "The Sul'toral sent us to a prison realm. Someplace connected to magic but also one that separated us from magic."

She paused. There was a rolling hill in front of them, and her Leier were carving through several enchantments up there. Gavin hadn't seen any of the metallic vines, so he had no idea who of the Sul'toral, or even Toral, were responsible for them. Had they withdrawn? That would suggest there was more control to them than what he had known.

"What do you mean you were sent?" Imogen asked.

"The Sul'toral sent us there."

She frowned and tilted her head to the side, looking off into the distance. A hint of silver flashed within her eyes again.

"What changed for you?" he asked.

"I will tell you, but only once we reach the Roasted Dragon," she said.

"You mentioned seeing something. Is that the same as the El'aras seers?"

She pursed her lips before shaking her head. "Not quite like that. What I can do now is tied to something different."

She motioned for them to keep moving, and the Leier who were spread out behind them marched forward. Gavin estimated nearly five hundred, but not all of them were dark-haired like Imogen. Some of them had brown hair, and some of them also didn't have swords.

"I thought all of your people were fighters," he said.

"Not all of these are my people, or they weren't at one time. They are now."

"And you brought them out of your homeland?"

"Very little of my homeland remains," Imogen said softly.

"What happened?"

"A great destruction. Which is why I'm here."

"The Sul'toral?" Gavin asked.

"Partly," she said. "But partly something else."

He waited for her to explain, but she didn't.

They crested a small rise, and in the distance, Gavin could finally see Yoran.

"I can get you back quickly," he told her.

"I know, but my people need to have me with them."

"What would happen if you weren't?"

"They would be fine," she said. She frowned as she did, though he wondered if that was true or not. "They have gone through too much change. First, they lost their understanding of the world. Then they lost their home, and now I'm asking something more of them."

"What?"

"To fight for someone else," she said.

"All of them?"

Imogen regarded him before shaking her head. "Not all of them. That is why I came. At least, why I thought I would come."

"Gaspar has been looking forward to seeing you."

She smiled tightly. "I'm sure."

"He's been going through a rough stretch," Gavin said. He figured he might as well get it out there so that Imogen knew. "He and Desarra decided they weren't the best fit any longer."

Imogen faltered a step. "No?"

"I'm not sure if it was his choice, her choice, or perhaps just circumstances, but I think it was hard on him." He explained what they had gone through, how Gaspar had been willing to help Gavin, fighting on his behalf, and everything they had dealt with. Imogen just stared at him for a moment before nodding.

"He still struggled with his purpose," she said.

"I wasn't expecting that from him."

"No, I don't think Gaspar expected that either."

She reached some of her people and then paused. He looked over to her, waiting for her to instruct them and guide them, but she merely nodded.

"What are you doing?" Gavin asked as many of them stopped walking and started to set up camp.

"We are not going to violate Yoran," she said. "We will set up camp out here."

"You would be welcome in the city, especially as there are enchantments attacking outside it."

"Do you think we fear enchantments?" Imogen asked.

He regarded her. "Well, I suppose not, but I don't know if you want to invite an attack if it's not necessary."

Imogen chuckled. "We aren't inviting anything. Consider this an offer of protection, at least while we are here."

"How long will you be here?"

"I have not yet seen."

She strode forward, and Gavin looked up to see the renral still circling. He couldn't tell much about the Leier riding them, but he could feel that others were there. Strangely, he realized that they were using magic, but as far as he knew, the Leier didn't use magic. Something had changed.

Imogen didn't say anything, though she walked with him. When they reached the edge of the city, he found a few constables but saw no sign of Davel Chan, who had likely gone back into the city to regroup and plan for the next attack. Gaspar, however, was there waiting.

As soon as he saw Imogen, he straightened. He ran his hands along his jacket, and he locked eyes with her. "You came back."

She smiled at him, and there was real warmth in her eyes. "I came back. It was needed."

"You have your own command," he said. When she looked at him, he shrugged. "I see how they follow you."

She took a step forward and clasped him on the shoulders. "It's good to see you, Gaspar."

Gaspar held her gaze for a long moment, seeming to be at a loss for what to say.

Gavin stepped forward. "She wanted a drink."

"The Dragon?"

"I think it would be nice," Imogen said.

They made their way through the streets, and Gavin realized that several other Leier had come into the city, moving discreetly and flanking them.

"Do you have your people watching to make sure you're safe?" Gavin asked.

Imogen glanced over and shrugged. "They feel the need to protect me, even though they have no need to."

Gavin snorted. "That's an understatement."

They strode past the El'aras section of the city. The stone around here was a dull white, and increasingly, Gavin began to feel energy from within the stone, which seemed to wash out and radiate toward him. The buildings had begun to evolve, some of the stone taking on more and more ornate characteristics. Somehow, it was even cleaner than it had been before, less of a gray tone to it and now more of a pure, almost pristine white. Imogen paused for a moment and looked around. Her brow furrowed, and Gavin caught a flash of silver in her eyes again before she turned away.

"The El'aras moved here after they experienced an attack."

"So I've seen," Imogen said.

"The city isn't quite sure what to make of them," Gaspar explained. "Most of the enchanters don't see a problem with it, but the constables are worried about their presence and what sort of danger they will bring the city."

"It is not the El'aras who bring danger here," she said.

"No," Gavin said. "Apparently, it's me."

As they passed the El'aras part of the city, Gavin thought he saw Anna watching from a nearby building, but when he turned to look, he saw no sign of her.

Instead, he followed Imogen until they reached the Dragon, where she paused and stared at the door.

"I missed this place," she said softly.

"Jessica will be pleased to hear that," Gaspar said, then nodded at Gavin. "Probably happier to see you than she was to see him."

Imogen smiled. "I was not surprised that you would end up back here again, but perhaps a little earlier than I anticipated."

"Why did you think I was going to come back?" Gavin asked.

She looked at him, and for a moment, it seemed as if there was a flash of silver in her eyes again, but then it faded. "We all come back."

She stepped inside. It was late in the day, and the Dragon was relatively quiet. There were only a few people inside, but one of them was Wrenlow. He jumped to his feet and hurried over, his eyes going wide when he saw Imogen.

"We're all back together," he said, clapping his hands together. "I'm so glad, especially with what's been going on. Have they told you about what's happened?"

Imogen took a seat in the old booth. Wrenlow frowned, grabbed his stuff off the table he'd been occupying, and slipped into the booth with Imogen, taking up his old position back when they had worked in the Dragon. Gaspar took a seat next her.

Jessica walked out of the kitchen and came over to them. "What are you—Imogen?" She almost dropped the tray she was holding. "You're back! And… you're different. Something happened."

Imogen bowed her head slightly. "Many things have happened."

"Well, I'm sure they want to hear all about it."

"I'm sure."

Jessica flashed a broad smile, and she tucked a strand of her chestnut hair back before setting the tray on the table. She wiped her hands on her apron and began to set mugs of ale in front of them. She didn't have enough for all four of them, so Gavin pushed his over to Imogen.

"I can wait," he said.

"I'm not going to have any," Wrenlow said. "I'm still trying to piece through some of the puzzle of what I've been finding beneath the city. You go ahead."

Gavin shrugged and took a long draw from Wrenlow's mug.

Jessica pulled a chair up to the table. "You mind if I stay?"

"Of course not," Imogen said.

Gavin had so many questions, but he also believed she had questions for them. Rather than probing, he waited. He didn't know her as well as Gaspar did, but he certainly understood that she preferred the quiet.

"Are we just going to sit here in silence?" Wrenlow asked. "I mean, we haven't seen Imogen in the better part of a year. She comes back here, and it sounds like she took on five Sul'toral all by herself, so there has to be a story to it. Can you tell?"

Imogen fidgeted, and she looked across to Wrenlow

before giving a tight smile. "There is a story. There's always a story." She took a long drink of ale and then set it down. "I went with my brother. He needed help." She glanced over to Gaspar before turning back to Wrenlow. "You remember Timo."

Wrenlow nodded. "Oh, I think we all remember. He was getting uptight before you left."

Imogen's smile faded. "I thought I could help him. I was wrong."

"What happened?" Gaspar asked, his voice low.

"He betrayed me. He'd been going after power. I don't know how long, and I've still been trying to understand where that pursuit of power has guided him, but he went after the Sul'toral thinking he could gain power like them."

"He wanted to *become* one of the Sul'toral?" Gavin asked.

"Timo first became a Toral, serving a Sul'toral, and he attempted to steal power from a Porapeth. Then he tried stealing power from creatures known as the branox, terrible and evil beasts, and has made many attempts since then. Somehow and somewhere, he has come across the power that he seeks. It also seems as if he is working with another. It is Timo and his search that brought me here."

"Well, we're glad you're here," Gaspar said.

Imogen nodded. "I had hoped to find peace, as my people want a place they can call their own, but now that I'm here, I can't help but feel as if I have a different path." She looked down, gripping her mug before taking a long drink.

"I can tell you what I found underneath the city," Wrenlow said. "There's a whole maze of El'aras tunnels, mostly because this place was once tied to them, but we think it was something older. Gavin had to come back and stop a strange attack where they were calling on a power called nihilar. Then he decided to stay, mostly because there wasn't any other place for him to go, and then the El'aras moved here during an attack while he was gone."

"I thought you could piece a puzzle together better than that," Gaspar said.

"What's wrong with the way I said it?" Wrenlow asked.

"It just sounds like... a bit much."

Wrenlow scoffed. "It's not much. That's what happened, isn't it?" He looked at Gavin and then Gaspar. "Well, I didn't even tell her about the strange prison world where you had to fight your way back after freeing monsters..." He shook his head. "Gods, I don't even know what you freed exactly."

"You freed monsters?" Imogen asked.

"They were not freed," Gavin said. "They prevented us from returning. We were dealing with some strange, unusual power. Trapped power, I suppose. In that regard, maybe it was not all that dissimilar to what you've described of Sarenoth. In this case, it was the Ashara ancient. There were other Ashara there trying to free the ancient, and when we succeeded, we were sent back here. The only concern is that we might not have been the only ones sent back."

"You think there were other creatures trapped there," Imogen said.

"Oh, there were," Gaspar muttered, and he drank a long sip from his mug of ale. "Stone monsters. Renral that try to poison you with their saliva. Unnameable creatures that hide in the darkness. It was all too much. Gods, and without enchantments, we weren't able to do a whole lot. We were lucky to survive."

Gavin frowned at him. He had a sense from Gaspar that he was more upset about the loss of his enchantments.

"But you did survive," Imogen said.

"We made it back," Gaspar said, waving his hand. "We've been trying to understand what happened ever since."

"It's good that you're here," Gavin told her, "and I'd like to talk to you a bit more about other things."

Imogen offered him a slight nod.

He hesitated a moment. "But not just yet. We have time." He hoped that was the case, at least. He tapped Wrenlow on the shoulder. "Why don't we let Gaspar and Imogen catch up, and you can share with me what you uncovered?" Gavin tipped his head to Imogen. "You and I can talk later."

"Indeed."

He got up, made his way from the table, and sat in a booth near the door to the Dragon. From here, Gavin could look out and see the surrounding city more easily, but he could also keep an eye on the inside of the tavern, something he still felt an obligation to do, even though he knew it was not his responsibility.

Wrenlow set his stack of books on the table and sat

across from Gavin. "What was that about? Why do we need to leave them alone?"

Jessica had also joined them. She leaned over the table, glancing from Gaspar to Imogen. "You've gained a little insight over the last year, Gavin."

"I just got to know him better," he said.

She snorted. "Perhaps, or maybe you're just becoming a bit more intuitive. Either way, you did well."

Wrenlow looked at both of them. "What did you do well? He did… Oh. Gaspar and Imogen?" he asked, in a voice that was a little too loud.

"Keep it down," Gavin said.

"He's got to be twenty years older than her."

Jessica cuffed Wrenlow on the side of the head. "He's probably no more than ten years her senior, if that. Imogen just looks young. And it's not as if age matters. How much older is Olivia than you?"

"Oh."

Gavin snickered. "He's still an old man."

"And he's going to call you 'boy' as long as you call him that," Jessica said, and then she headed to the kitchen.

"What did you find?" Gavin asked Wrenlow.

"I've been down in the tunnels, but I haven't really figured out what's down there. I keep thinking there has to be something tied to the El'aras prophecies there that we need to understand. There is information in that place, but I haven't been able to figure it out." Wrenlow let out a heavy sigh. "I just don't know. There's something to it, I'm sure."

Gavin had known Wrenlow long enough to trust that

if he believed there was something to it, then there probably was. That meant he needed to investigate it. But when? He had no idea how they would have enough time to do all the things he thought they needed to.

Imogen stared down into her mug, though there was a hint of a smile on her face as she spoke to Gaspar. Every so often, she would look up and lock eyes with him. They would come with a flash of silver—something Gavin increasingly felt was significant—before that faded. And then her smile would fade too.

Imogen had come for a reason. But, Gavin suspected, once she resolved that, he doubted she would be able to stay. How would Gaspar react to that?

CHAPTER TWELVE

Gavin followed Imogen and Gaspar out of the tavern and into the street. They had sat and talked for a little while before they stood up together, looking like they were going off to explore the way they once had, as though no time had passed. Gavin approached Imogen, who waited for him, as if knowing he wanted to come speak with her. She probably did. If he was right about what was going on, he suspected that she had *seen* him coming.

"Go on. Say it."

"How did you learn to fight like that?" Gavin asked.

"Don't push it, boy," Gaspar said.

"It's fine. And it's such a simple question with such a complicated answer," she said, motioning for him to follow.

"You don't have to share if you don't want to," Gaspar said.

She tipped her head toward his hand. "You no longer need the ring."

Gavin held out his hand. "You noticed?"

"Before I left, you couldn't take it off. I assume you have connected to the power more thoroughly?"

His eyes widened. "You knew?"

"Not at the time," she said. "Even now, I'm not exactly sure." She frowned. "I can see things. Some possibilities."

"How?"

"I told you what happened. When Timo left, I went with him, and he tried to steal the power of the Porapeth."

Gavin knew stories of the Porapeth, though he never anticipated meeting anyone who had real interaction with them. He had never come across them himself. They had magic and were said to be incredibly powerful.

"Are they dangerous?" Gaspar asked.

She gave a small chuckle. "In some ways."

She paused at an intersection. Up ahead was a loud, bustling market, but in another direction was the Captain's fortress, where the enchanters lived. Imogen stared in that direction, as if she was looking for answers. Maybe she had come here for that reason.

"Timo was searching for the power of the Porapeth, thinking he could attack them, steal their power, and become a Sul'toral—or something along those lines," she said, her voice quiet. "But he did not succeed."

"You did," Gavin said.

She shook her head. "I didn't steal the power of the Porapeth."

"When I saw you fighting, I realized there was something different about it. You and I were always evenly matched."

Gaspar snorted.

She looked over and smiled at him, another flash of silver evident in her eyes. It faded quickly, as though it had not been there at all.

"I think you flatter me too much," Imogen said. "We were never evenly matched. I was always inferior to you, especially when you draw on your core reserves."

"My El'aras magic," Gavin said.

"Call it what you want."

"But some part of you has changed."

Imogen pulled her blade out of its sheath and held it up. It was different than what she carried before. She had always prized her sword, and seeing her carrying a different one felt strange.

"When I was here before, I had taken on the title of First of the Blade, but now I'm something else. I've come to understand the patterns differently." She regarded Gavin. "Though I suspect you would have learned them faster than I did, especially as you seemed to master them in a single session." She slipped the sword back into its sheath. "I proved myself against a master of the sacred sword patterns and was given this."

"And the power that you now have?"

She smiled. "My people feared sorcery. We hated it. At least, that was what I was taught. You knew that," she said, looking over to Gaspar. "Which is why I was sent off on my bond quest, why Timo took his bond quest, and why I hesitated to return." She stared down at the ground for a moment, and when she looked up, there was once again a flash of silver in her eyes. "Such a mistake. Such a waste. Sorcery is not entirely dangerous, but there are parts of it that are. It wasn't that, though. It was then that I came to realize that my people did not fear sorcery the way we claimed. There were many among my people who used sorcery, yet they didn't know that's what it was." She gave another small smile. "The sacred patterns. They are a type of sorcery. They are a type of power." She took a deep breath, then let it out. "When I began to understand the truth of it, I began to understand a part of myself that I had not known before. And now I understand it."

"That's not all that happened," Gavin said, ignoring Gaspar's warning glance.

Imogen shook her head. "That is not all. We traveled with the Porapeth for a while, one named Benji the Elder. He was near the end of his life. Or perhaps he wasn't, but he wanted me to think that way." She frowned and shook her head again. "When it came to Benji, I never really knew the truth. He was able to hide things from me in ways that I still am not even entirely certain of. Either way, Benji gifted me a fragment of his power." There was a measure of amusement in Imogen's voice as she spoke of him.

"Fragment?"

"Magical entities can leave behind a fragment when they depart this world," she explained. "I don't fully understand it, as I'm trying to get a better idea of it myself, but they do have a way of connecting. It doesn't always make sense, especially if you are one who has the particular view of the afterlife that my people did."

"Which was?"

"It's complicated," she said softly.

When she fell silent, Gavin decided to take a different tack. "And that power allows you to see things?" he asked.

"I see possibilities, and that has opened up a new world for me."

That might explain how she could fight the way she did. If she could see possibilities, then she could anticipate where a fighter might move and react and then have a counterattack in place before they had a chance to even move into position. She had disarmed the Sul'toral in moments.

"Why didn't you kill the Sul'toral when you had the chance?" he asked.

"Killing one Sul'toral strengthens another. They are— or were, as I'm not sure if they still are—drawing on an ancient power called Sarenoth."

Gavin nodded. "I know this, Imogen."

"What you may not know, however, is that Sarenoth was a Porapeth who was imprisoned by his followers to steal his power. They succeeded, but in doing so, they shared that power. Over time, some learned that they could strengthen themselves by stealing from others, so they did. I no longer know how many of the original twelve survive. I think they have all died, but new ones may have taken their place—and their power."

"So what does that mean?" he asked.

"It means that we must destroy them all at once. Then that power can be freed."

"For you to use?" Gaspar asked.

Gavin appreciated that he was interested enough to ask.

Imogen held his gaze. "I would not use that fragment of power. I would see it restored to Sarenoth. Unfortunately, one among them is now my brother. I have a feeling that he remained nearby, but I cannot see him as I should. Aspects of his power remain opaque, and the visions are difficult to understand."

Visions. It was so similar to what Anna had described, and so strange to hear Imogen talking about that, but this was a different person than the one he had last seen. He knew nothing about this version of Imogen, and he increasingly felt like he needed to get to know her so he could understand just what she could do to help them.

"What can you see about me?" he asked.

He thought about what Tristan had said to him, about finding himself and trying to understand who he was and what he had come from. With his injury, Tristan hadn't been able to tell Gavin anything, which still irritated him.

He needed to check on him, but not yet.

"As I told you, Gavin, I see power starting to converge around you," Imogen said. "I'm not exactly sure what it means, only that there is a distinct sense of it. It continues to swirl around you, as if you are gathering it to you or attracting it. That is all I see, but not only that. There will be another attack. It is why I'm here. Power is drawn to you. I see flashes of brightness before that goes dark. I don't understand what it means, nor do I understand how to explain it, but I felt as if I needed to be here, mostly so I could anticipate what else might come." She frowned at him. "Does that make any sense to you?"

Flashes of brightness. Gavin closed his eyes, and he could practically see the power coming from the bralinath trees, the way flashes of brightness obscured his vision of the ancient city.

"It makes a bit of sense," he admitted as he opened his eyes. "Now that I'm connected to the power of the El'aras, I am somehow bound to their history. I'm not sure what to make of it, only that I can channel some ancient power of the El'aras and use that to guide me. I can see things that once would have been obscured from me."

"You can look into the past," she said.

"I can."

"I imagine that is useful."

Gavin shrugged. "Perhaps not as useful as what you can do."

Imogen clenched her jaw. In that moment, she looked like the woman he remembered from before, not this powerful person who had returned to Yoran. "I wish I could look back and understand my people, the reason we settled in the mountains, why our sacred temples were necessary, and why the sacred sword masters hid the truth from my people. But so much has been destroyed."

"Your brother," Gaspar suggested.

"Not only my brother. He was working with a Sul'toral

who was involved. I was not there in time, and Timo and the others were too powerful for me."

"And the sword masters can fight like you?"

She looked as if she wanted to answer immediately, and he could see her practically forming the word *yes*, but then she hesitated and shook her head. "I once thought they were the most skilled sword masters that could ever be imagined, but I no longer do. They knew the sacred patterns in ways that others could not, but they do not see the way I do."

She fell silent, and then she looked behind her toward the Captain's fortress like she was looking for something there.

"There is much I still don't understand," Imogen said. "Much I still can't see. But I am not locked into the same restrictions that the Porapeth are. Or that most Porapeth are."

"What are those restrictions?" Gavin asked.

"They avoid favoring one path over another."

"How many paths can you see?"

"There are many," she said, "but seeing far along them is a skill that I'm still working on."

"And you can't see any reason why power has gathered around me?"

Imogen regarded him, a flash of silver coming to her eyes before fading. "It's there, but I don't see it."

"And you are not restricted the way the Porapeth once were?"

"No. I think that's why Benji chose me," she answered, then smiled to herself. "To be honest, though, I don't really know if that's the entire reason he chose me, or if he was more concerned about Abigail."

Gavin thought through what he knew about the Porapeth, which, admittedly, was not as much as he thought he should know, especially if he was now dealing with somebody with those powers. It would be smart for him to learn more about the Porapeth and what they were capable of doing, given how he was going to be interacting with Imogen. If she had that ability, he didn't want to be surprised by what she could do, how she used her power, and what it might mean for him and those he worked with.

"So you came here because you intend to influence some path," Gavin said.

"I came here because I saw that I needed to. I don't know if it was because of you, my brother, or the Sul'toral. Regardless, the path is there before me, like a spider web that I'm trying to piece together to understand how I can crawl to the center of it."

As he looked at her, he couldn't help but wonder whether he could even withstand Imogen and what she could do, and that was with his connection to the bralinath trees and the nihilar.

"You can say it," Imogen said.

"Say what?"

"He's not always the brightest," Gaspar said to Imogen.

She smiled. "You want to spar with me."

Gavin couldn't help but grin. "That wasn't exactly what I was thinking, but it has been a while since I've sparred with anyone. There are other questions that I think we need answered."

"Such as why power continues to converge." She nodded to the north. "We've faced Toral and Sul'toral, both of them accumulating power, right around the same time you had begun to progress with your skill, though I thought it was a natural progression of who you were supposed to be. Now I question if there is something more to it." She frowned deeply. "Then there's me. I've been trying to figure out why me. What does it mean that I have this ability, and why have I suddenly started to grow the way I have?" She glanced back to Gavin. "I haven't come up with the answer, if that's what you are thinking."

"How far can you see?"

"Not as far as I would like."

"We've had stronger and stronger attacks on Yoran," Gavin said.

"I've heard. And I have seen some of them." She frowned again. "Not all of it, though. You talk about going to this prison realm, but I wasn't able to see that."

"Magic worked differently there, if at all."

"Maybe that's all it is. Or maybe it's just beyond the field of my vision." She shrugged and tipped her head to the side. "There's something I need to check on. I can talk with you later, Gavin."

"Or we could spar."

She smiled and shook her head. "Or we could spar."

He had a feeling that she would welcome that opportunity the same as he would. Maybe she was just as curious as he was as to whether she could handle him now. When he had sparred with Imogen before, she'd been dangerous, but now she would likely be deadly. How could you counter someone who could anticipate your attack?

He watched as Imogen marched with Gaspar away from him.

CHAPTER THIRTEEN

IMOGEN

I mogen walked alongside Gaspar, feeling a bit strange being in the city. It hadn't been that long since she'd been here, but so much had changed for her and so much had changed around her that it felt like a different place. Probably because she felt like a different person.

The day was quiet, and though there was a slight breeze that blew through, she was not uncomfortable. She had never been uncomfortable here, which she thought was strange, but perhaps it should not be. Yoran had been her home for a while, long enough that she had found a place of her own, become settled, and even begun to feel as if she could stay. It was only when Timo had returned that she had started to question if that had been a mistake.

"You've been quiet," Gaspar said.

They passed by a bakery, and Imogen glanced up. It was a place she had stopped at for bread from time to time, and she peered in the window, unsurprised by the

activity inside. Things seemed busier in Yoran, for whatever reason. Imogen wondered why that was the case.

"Should I not be?" she replied.

"I don't know. You seem different."

She chuckled. Gaspar had not been her first friend
outside the homeland, but he was the one who meant the
most to her. When she'd first met him, he had sort of a
grizzled appearance that made him look older than he
was. Now she saw some of the youthfulness starting to
creep into his eyes, and as she followed his possibilities,
she saw nothing but haze surrounding him. How many
enchantments did he have on him?

Maybe that wasn't even the key to the haziness she
observed. Some of that may have stemmed from the fact
that he was so closely aligned with Gavin that there was
no way to separate the two. And Gavin himself was a
bright, practically burning energy in her mind.

But she could see nothing from him. No real possibilities, though she had claimed that she could. Eventually,
she suspected she'd need to learn to look from a different
perspective in order to find a way to understand what was
happening and how she might be able to influence it, but
Imogen didn't know if there was any way for her to do
that.

"I suppose I *am* different. Chasing someone you care
about and realizing they cannot be saved does that to
you."

"I don't think this has anything to do with Timo."
Gaspar regarded her with that quiet intensity in his gaze

that she had come to know. "It has everything to do with who you have become, doesn't it?"

Imogen ignored him and looked down the street. A small market was not far from them, and given that they had no real destination, she was more than content to go along with Gaspar toward the market and see what might be there. Aspects of the city had changed in the year she'd been gone. It was more than just the number of people that now seemed crammed into the city, though that was part of it. It came from the power she felt here. Most of it was because of enchantments, but not all. Some came from sorcery, though from what Imogen could tell, there was no obvious sorcery used. At least not openly. She didn't think it was tied to the Koral, but perhaps it was.

"Do you want to hear the story, or do you not care?" she asked.

Gaspar snorted. "I've always been willing to hear the story. Sometimes you haven't been eager to share, and I never wanted to push."

"No. You never did."

"I figure a person has the right to tell their story when they want to."

"My story isn't quite complete," Imogen said.

They reached the outskirts of the market, and she paused for a moment, listening to the sound of the city around her. Even that felt familiar to her, and strangely more welcoming than she had felt even when she had returned to the Leier homeland. Returning to her home had left her with an unusual sense of unease, though Imogen wasn't sure if it was an uncertainty that stemmed from how much she had been doing since she'd left or from knowing that she did not mind magic the way that others in her homeland did.

"Everything feels more active," she said.

"Well, because of the boy, the city has been more active lately. El'aras have started to take up positions around the outskirts of the city, but—"

"This is not El'aras," Imogen said as she studied the crowd gathering in the market.

"It's not. I've tried getting word to the constables, but I don't think they want to hear from me."

Imogen glanced over and arched a brow at him. "I'm sure if you approach Davel Chan the right way he would be more than interested in hearing your perspective."

"Oh, I'm sure he would be," Gaspar said with more irritation than he probably felt. "It's just that I don't have the same relationship with him as—"

"As Gavin does?"

Gaspar nodded. "Right."

"Does that bother you?"

"The boy is the Chain Breaker. I don't need to be that person. Gods, I'm not sure I *could* be that person. I'm happy and content being just what I am."

"No, you aren't," Imogen said.

He looked over. "What's that supposed to mean?"

"You've never been content. Even when you tried to claim that you were. You are always looking for something."

"Well, when you were in Yoran, I was looking for ways I could help you." Gaspar gave a slight shrug.

"And you did."

"And I did," he said softly.

They entered the market, weaving through the crowd, with Imogen holding on to Tree Stands in the Forest every so often just to give them enough space. She didn't want to make it so obvious that others knew what she was doing, but she also didn't want anybody to squeeze in around her. She liked having some space.

"How long do you plan on being here?"

"My people need safety," Imogen said. "I thought we could have it in the homeland, and…" She shook her head. "And maybe I wouldn't have been content there."

As she looked around, she realized that the idea of a city like this—a place where she had come to feel at home—might be what she had been missing. But would her people want the same thing as her?

"Now you worry you're pushing your agenda on your people," Gaspar said.

"Somewhat," Imogen admitted. "I was less concerned with asking them to be here when we were looking for safety, and then when we confronted my brother and the Sul'toral. I thought it fit with what needed to be done. But once we stopped them"—and it was *once*, not *if*—"I became unsure of what will become of my people."

"You will go with them?"

"I am the general," she said.

"You always seemed like you were more than you permitted yourself to be."

They squeezed in between the people crowding around them and paused near a food stand. Gaspar looked over to her briefly, almost as if he wanted to say something more, but he didn't. Instead, he turned away and bought several pieces of jerky and two apples. While he purchased the food, Imogen focused on the possibilities she saw from him. They seemed to shift and slide, making it difficult for her to track what he might see and say, but she could see nothing. It seemed there was more to what Gaspar wanted to tell her, but he kept it from her.

He handed her some jerky, and she took a bite, savoring the smoked meat and the flavor. "I have to say that we don't eat quite so well on the road," she said. "Nothing at all like what's found at the Dragon."

Gaspar snorted. "I'm sure Jessica will be thrilled to hear that her cooking brought you back to the city."

Imogen smiled. She flicked her gaze up toward the sky, and off in the distance, she caught sight of the dark shapes of several renral circling. One of them, the largest, seemed to patrol the city more regularly. Zealar, as she called him, had a connection to her that she had formed through the sacred pattern that summoned the power of the renral. The bond allowed her to feel the electrical energy of the renral, and she could even bring that power through her.

She didn't, though. Not here, not now. She had found that she could draw only a little bit of that power through her, and while she could use it, she did not need to do so often.

"Imogen?"

"I'm sorry," she said.

"You look like you're planning a raid."

"Perhaps that's all it is. I have been trying to understand why Timo would come here." She looked over to Gaspar, and when others got too close, she gave them a little shove with Tree Stands in the Forest to create more of a barrier around them. "Why this city?"

"Well, the boy has been trying to find that answer for quite some time. It seems that this is some sort of a nexus for power, but he doesn't really know why. First, it was sorcerers versus enchanters. Then it was old El'aras power. And now..." Gaspar shrugged. "I don't know what to make of this nihilar power that he has, though I don't think he knows what to make of it either. It seems to bother him the same as it bothers me. Not knowing about the power makes it dangerous."

"What can you tell me about this power?"

"Not a whole lot," Gaspar said. "We had to chase it down and keep it from Chauvan. He and his followers were using it to attack the El'aras, but I don't understand it."

"What have you done to try to understand it?" Imogen asked.

"Nothing really," Gaspar said. "He just took it."

"What do you mean that he took it?"

"Exactly that. He took it," Gaspar said.

Imogen frowned. "There's the possibility that what he took is a fragment of some sort." She let out a sigh. "I wish there was something more I could see, but there is nothing to it. Perhaps if I was to meditate and speak to Benji..."

"This is your Porapeth?"

She nodded. "He is still a part of me."

Gaspar's brow furrowed. "It sounds so strange. I don't understand how that is even possible."

"I felt the same way once. Perhaps I still do. If I were to ask him, he would tell me that magic cannot die, it merely changes form. And given my experience with the Sul'toral and others like them, I would have to say that the idea is right. There are different aspects of power, what I call fragments, that are left behind when somebody with any real potential passes on."

Gaspar frowned. "Fragments?"

"Well, when my mentor died, he was shattered into three fragments. We were able to reunite him, and now..." She glanced up at the sky. She didn't know if Master Liu watched from above or if he had turned away from their people, but that was not her concern any longer. Since she had saved him and reunited his fragments, he was no longer even with them, which Imogen thought was best for him.

"And this Porapeth?"

"He fragmented himself," Imogen said. "In doing so, I think he made certain that he could not be used. The other Sul'toral were not quite so lucky. That is how Timo and this Chauvan have been able to acquire power that they should not have had access to."

"Strange," Gaspar said. "Perhaps unusual as well. I wonder what Gavin knows about this."

"I doubt he would know anything. He has his own natural magic, and it seems as if he has been drawing on more and more powers."

"Well, he has his El'aras ability, what he claims he was

gifted as the Champion, which turns out to be some connection to old El'aras magic, but it's this nihilar that bothers me. I haven't told him, but something about it just doesn't feel right. I can't quite explain it. This Chauvan wanted that power for himself. Gavin seems to believe it's some ancient power, much like that of the El'aras, but..."

"But what?"

"I don't know," Gaspar said.

Imogen frowned. "You're worried about him."

"I don't think we need to be worried about the boy."

Imogen gave a small nod. "Probably not, but that doesn't change that you are."

"He can be foolish. He lunges into situations he should not, and he is willing to take on dangers that he probably should not either." Gaspar shrugged. "He also doesn't really understand this power. That is what concerns me."

"I will meditate on it," she said.

Gaspar started laughing but trailed off as he watched her. "Oh. You're serious."

"Often, many answers can be found through meditation."

"I see. Well, then I hope you find some answers we might be able to use as you meditate. For now, how about we keep walking, eating, and eventually get back to the Dragon to get to drinking."

She smiled. "I would like that."

But as she followed Gaspar, her mind worked. She thought about what she had seen and experienced and the various powers that she knew were in the world. Much of the power that existed was tied to Porapeth magic, or at least that was what she had seen. What if this nihilar was somehow tied to it as well?

Imogen needed to better understand what it was and what it might do. If she did not, she wasn't sure that she could keep her people here.

CHAPTER FOURTEEN

Gavin made his patrol around the edge of the city as he often did these days. He preferred to go alone, since he didn't know whether he might find anything, but that was only part of it. Others had responsibilities, while he did not. At least, not necessarily.

At one point, he caught sight of Davel Chan making his way around the border as well. He was adding enchantments, Gavin suspected, but he never slowed to look toward him. Not that Gavin expected him to. Davel moved around steadily while Gavin stared at him. He waited for a moment, then chose to go a different direction. When he did, he found others working outside the city. Zella's people, who were not affiliated with the constables, had begun to place enchantments. Mekel was among them, and if nothing else, Gavin trusted his enchantments more than anybody else's. He watched them work for a little while but didn't think there was anything he could do to help.

Then there were the Leier. They were camped beyond the border and had set up neat and orderly lines, creating a different kind of defense. It was odd to see what was essentially another army camped just at the edge of the city, even though he knew they would not harm the people of Yoran. Still, there was something unsettling about their presence. From what Gavin had been able to tell, they were more than only the Leier as there were sorcerers of a sort among them, something Gavin knew the Leier had never before had. Somehow, Imogen had united disparate peoples into a whole.

Maybe they aren't even the Leier any longer.

Imogen had them well organized, though even that wasn't all her doing. She had entrusted others to keep her people in line. He still found himself marveling at her and how much she had changed in the time she had been away. There was something intriguing about it, but he didn't fully know what it was.

"I see you, Gavin," a soft voice said from a nearby bells tree.

He spun and started toward Alana. She was getting taller, and her hair was longer, now bound behind her head with a blue ribbon. She had an easygoing smile that she had never lost, despite the fact that she seemed to have lost so much.

"Are you following me?" he asked.

"I like to come out here and look. It's quieter. The city is different these days."

"Too many people for you?"

"Different kinds of people." She looked over to him, meeting his gaze. "I like different. I feel different sometimes."

"You know, sometimes I feel different as well," he said.

"Well, you *are* different. You're the Chain Breaker, after all."

He snorted. "You can just call me Gavin."

"I know, but I like to tease you. How are my ravens?" she asked.

"Useful as ever."

"I've folded some different things for you if you want them."

"You know that your enchantments are some of the best that I use." He patted his pocket where the paper dragon was nestled. He always kept one with him. The ravens also offered him things that many of the other enchantments did not. Learning what he had about connecting to these enchantments, adding some part of himself into it, made it so that he could use them much better than he once had been able to. "I'm still careful with them. I don't want anything to happen to you if something were to go wrong with the enchantments."

She wrinkled her brow. "I don't want that either. I don't like it when they get hurt."

"What does it feel like?"

"Sometimes a snap. Sometimes it's like something inside of me fades." She looked over. "Don't worry. It's not permanent. It's just something I am aware of."

"I've always wondered where you learned to fold them like this."

Her expression went dark for a moment as a hint of confusion crossed her brow. "Well, I feel like I have always known," Alana replied. "I don't know how to explain it. It's just been there with me."

"It's just been there?"

"Oh, I'm sure somebody taught me, but I don't remember my parents very well."

"You and me both," he said. "But I didn't realize that you don't remember them." It occurred to Gavin that he didn't actually know all that much about Alana's life before she ended up with Zella. She was a powerful enchanter, but that was all he knew. "What can you tell me about them?"

"I see flashes from time to time," she said. She reached into her pocket, pulled out a folded piece of paper, and began to fidget with it. "Sometimes I see them in dreams. It's like when I fold these, I feel like I can find something, but other times... Well, I don't know. Zella has been working with me to try to help me uncover anything, but it's difficult. And with everything we have been going through, there really hasn't been much time."

"I can talk to her for you, if you'd like."

"Oh, I appreciate that, but she does want to help. I also wonder if I had something terrible happen to me. Maybe that's why I don't remember." Alana lowered her voice almost conspiratorially. "She tells me that some people forget on purpose. I like that. If something had happened to me, I'm not sure I would want to remember. It might be better for me to have forgotten on purpose."

"I think that's something else you and I share," Gavin said.

She smiled. "What are you doing out here, anyway?"

"Clearing my head."

"I do that too. Have there been any more attacks?"

Gavin shook his head. "Not so much. We've been safe. We will be safe."

"I hope so. Especially with them out there," she said, nodding to where the Leier were camped. "I hear Gaspar is happy that his friend is back. Are you happy?"

"Very much so," he said.

"Oh, good."

"You shouldn't stay out here."

"I'm not going to stay for very long. Just a little bit. Just to clear my head," she said, grinning at him.

He snorted and patted her on the shoulder before heading off. He had other things to be doing. He needed to return to Nelar to check on Tristan, if only so he could learn more about what Tristan knew about him. He had to make sure that any enchantments out on the plains were…

But he didn't need to do that. With the Leier's presence, it was no longer a concern for him. They would be powerful enough—at least Imogen would be—to draw the enchantments to them. Besides, if they were camped out there, it was unlikely that any Sul'toral or Toral would risk coming all this way and facing them. The Leier offered a layer of protection that they hadn't had before.

Then it was a matter of him coming to terms with what else he needed to do. Understand himself. Learn about his abilities. Try to master what the bralinath trees were trying to show him. All of those seemed important.

His enchantment crackled, and he paused for a moment.

He heard Anna's voice in his ear.

"I can come and talk to you," he said.

He didn't have to go far. Anna must've already been coming to try to find him, and perhaps she had even been attempting to listen to his earlier conversation with Imogen. Her golden hair caught the light as it streamed down on her, and she was dressed in a white gown. Her hands were clasped in front of her as she walked. Several others marched with her, though they stayed in the shadows, much like Imogen had people who did the same.

He smiled to himself at the idea that he was surrounded by powerful women. Anna had been the first one he had interacted with, which was tied to the job he'd been hired for long ago. Then Jayna. He wasn't necessarily around her often, but he certainly had some experience with her. Eva too, but she wasn't alone in her power. There were other Ashara like her, but there was something about Eva that made her unique. And now Imogen.

Where did Gavin fit in with all of this?

Anna came up to him, and he nodded toward a pair of neighboring buildings, his gaze darting toward the rooftops.

"How many people do you have stationed up there?" he asked.

"I don't command them to follow," Anna said, though he had a feeling that she also didn't mind that they did.

"You might not command them, but they are there nonetheless."

She shrugged, then nodded. "They won't allow me to venture too deep into the city without accompanying me. I think Thomas would have had a better chance of distracting them, but…"

There was a note of sadness in her voice. Not as much as Gavin would've expected, especially given how long Thomas had served her and protected her. He thought she would've been far more bothered by Thomas's death, even though he had died in service to her.

"How much of my conversation with Imogen did you hear?" he asked.

There was no point in denying that he'd had the conversation, and he didn't want Anna to deny that she had been listening. He suspected that she had some way of controlling his enchantment from her end, and if that was the case, she probably could hear everything he said.

She frowned. "I paid some attention to it."

"Some?" Gavin asked, chuckling. "I think it was probably more than just some."

"What do you want me to say? That I want to know what you might be saying to her? She's a dangerous one, Gavin."

"You said the same about the Toral."

"Because she is also dangerous," she said.

"Is it because she's not El'aras?"

Gavin had never felt like Anna was an isolationist, but

increasingly, he started to question if that was the reason behind her hesitation. Did she fear having others around?

"There is something to be said about understanding the people," Anna said softly.

"Well, I'm not El'aras the way you are, so perhaps that's part of the issue."

She regarded him for a long moment, and there was a weight behind her eyes that lingered in her gaze. "You are not," she said.

"She took on five Sul'toral. By herself. I think she could have taken on more of them," Gavin said, still in shock about that.

"She has been touched by the Porapeth."

Gavin pursed his lips. "You knew."

"I could feel it coming."

"You could *feel* it?"

"The El'aras are not the only ones touched by the ancients," Anna said.

"So there is a Porapeth ancient?"

"When it comes to the Porapeth, I don't have the answers, unfortunately. They are rare and do not interact with the El'aras often. At least, they do not interact with us any longer."

Could there be some hidden Porapeth that needed to be freed, the same way there had been a hidden Ashara? If that was the case, then Gavin would have to ask Imogen if some part of her mission was designed to rescue this Porapeth. She wasn't Porapeth, but being granted some aspect of the ability might have turned her into something else.

"She came here for a reason," Gavin said.

Anna regarded him. "She came here because of you. I warned you, Gavin Lorren, that you are drawing on power and calling it to you. The more you continue to do this, the more that danger will persist around you, as well as around others who care for you."

It was a warning about Imogen, but that was a warning Gavin was not about to heed. He had spent some time with Anna training, learning, and generally coming to understand his El'aras abilities, but it was far different than the time he'd spent with Imogen. He and Imogen hadn't ever had deep conversations. There hadn't been the need. Gavin had a sense of her from her actions and the way she fought. In his mind, fighting alongside someone was far more meaningful than talking with them. He had a better feeling for who she was and what things meant for her.

It wasn't that he had not fought next to Anna, but for the most part, she had fought for her people, not for other causes. Imogen, on the other hand, had fought for causes that Gavin had come to believe in.

"What would you have me do?" he asked Anna.

"I need you to try to understand who you are and what you are meant to do."

He gave a slight smile. "I'm not sure I'm *meant* to do anything."

"I see it differently," she said, her voice soft.

"What do you see when you look at me?"

"I see surges of brightness," Anna said, then frowned at him. "And when I tried to peer into those surges of brightness, I failed to separate them out. That tells me something is coming. Something that obscures the ability to understand."

That was similar to what Imogen had said, which left Gavin wondering why that would be the case. "That reminds me of what I see when I look at the bralinath trees," Gavin said.

"That is not surprising. What is time but a loop? The past becomes present, which becomes the future. When you look into the past, you see brightness that would have taken hold before, much like I see it now."

"Then you think whatever we are dealing with now is something we might have dealt with in the past?"

"I don't know. I can't see it, and the elders are not speaking of it, so…"

She took a step toward him, and Gavin realized that the shadows around them—those of the El'aras warriors who were standing guard on the rooftops and in the streets—started to shift, as if suddenly tense at Anna's movement.

"I don't particularly care for you having your people surrounding me, Anna. I pose no threat to you. You know that."

"They will not act unless I tell them to," she said.

Gavin glanced around him for a moment before turning his gaze back on her. "I'm not so sure about that."

She frowned. "You asked what I would have you do. I would have you try to understand your purpose, your place, and what it means for you to be the Champion. I want you to truly connect to the power of the El'aras, along with that of those who came before you." She frowned again, and she regarded him for several long seconds. "That is what I want you to do."

"I'm not sure we have time."

"And I'm trying to tell you that time is merely what you make of it. Even you have to see that."

"What do you mean?" Gavin asked.

"When you were with me in the El'aras homeland, I'm sure you had seen—"

She tilted her head to the side, and Gavin noticed something at the same time. A surge of power outside the city.

Another attack.

She looked up at him. "We can continue this conversation another time. It seems that you are needed."

CHAPTER FIFTEEN

Gavin's energy was drained.

The fight had been waging for what felt like days, though he knew it was not that long. Every time he had a chance to rest, it felt as if another enchantment was triggered, warning him of another impending attack so that he had to protect the city once more.

He didn't fight alone, though.

Very few people from Yoran came to fight with him, though the Leier, several El'aras soldiers, and Gaspar did. They were all skilled, which mattered more than the numbers.

A strange enchantment made out of what looked like a tree swept razor-like branches at him, though they did not seem to have metal embedded in them as others had. Gavin had to duck beneath the branches and stab toward the trunk like he had when fighting the seeker trees.

A pair of Leier streaked toward the tree, dropping

underneath one of the branches swinging toward them and dancing upward with their blades a blur. They were skilled, but not nearly as skilled as Imogen.

Still, Gavin could tell that they had been fighting and training with her. He recognized the technique, even if he didn't know what the patterns were called. People who celebrated fighting the way the Leier did would have names for them. Probably something pompous. He had worked with enough people who had their own fighting styles over the years that he had come to know dozens of names for dozens of patterns. For the most part, that was all they were, though. Patterns.

That was what Gavin kept in mind as he fought.

He jumped, barely missing a branch sweeping at him. He carved his blade up, pushing power out through the end of the weapon and feeling resistance against him. As he did, he swept the blade back down again and hit a branch. There was a strange sound of splitting wood that mixed with something he would almost call a scream. That was different than the seeker trees. They had cried out when he had attacked them, but not in the same way.

Gavin tried to twist, but a branch struck him and sent him tumbling away. He rolled and bounded upward, only to see a Leier who had been riding on a renral dart forward. The man was a blur of movement, a sword master more skilled than Imogen had been before she left, though Gavin doubted that this man was her rival now. He flowed beneath one of the branches, swept up around another, and danced free again, entirely unscathed.

"What's your name?"

The man frowned at him. "Jorend."

"I'm Gavin Lorren."

"I know you, Chain Breaker. The general speaks highly of you."

Gavin smiled. *The general.* He'd have to get used to Imogen being referred to like that.

A tree moved toward them, speeding faster than Gavin would've expected. Two others marched next to it.

"We have an entire forest that moves?" Gavin muttered.

"This is not the first time we have faced something like this," Jorend said.

Gavin regarded him. "It's the first time I have. I dealt with trees that attacked me out west, but I think they were defending themselves."

"These have been corrupted. Can you feel it?"

The problem was that he couldn't feel it, even as he focused on it.

More of the metal vines attempted to snake around him. These were trees, so could he not treat them like the vines working up the bralinath trees? He focused on his El'aras core reserves and the bralinath connection that built, then pushed out magic with a burst. When it struck the tree, there came a shriek as heat began to build.

The power was absorbed, as if the tree swallowed it.

"Did you know it could do that?" Gavin asked.

Jorend ducked beneath one branch, sweeping his sharp, narrow blade at it and cleaving off one end of the branch with a soft hum. He glanced over to Gavin. "Do you think we haven't tried to burn them down before?"

"It was just a thought."

"I thought you were the Chain Breaker."

"Chain Breaker," Gavin said. "Not Tree Breaker."

Jorend wasn't the only Leier fighting alongside Gavin. A half dozen other soldiers darted forward, their movements just as precise as Jorend's as they battled with the tree branches. They dashed underneath the branches and carved their blades up. They needed axes, not swords.

But maybe there *was* something more he could do.

He had never attempted to hone the power he called, and he wondered if he might be able to use that like a blade to carve through the tree itself. As he focused on his core reserves and pushed the power out, he used it through his sword. The edge of the blade was sharp enough, but maybe with power coursing through it, he could make it even sharper.

He sliced toward one of the massive branches coming toward the Leier. There was resistance, as if the tree itself pushed back with magical power of its own, but Gavin sharpened his power even more.

The branch sheared free, and Gavin staggered back.

The enormous tree that was swinging its branches toward them suddenly froze in place.

Jorend glanced over at him and regarded Gavin for a long moment before he jumped forward with his blade outstretched and plunged it into the center of the tree. It pierced the trunk far more easily than Gavin would've expected, as though he using some magic along with it.

The tree shrieked again, then shuddered. All of its branches drooped.

They'd killed it?

Jorend leapt back and looked over to Gavin. "Maybe you *are* the Tree Breaker."

"It took more than I was expecting."

"We might need your help on these other two. The key is getting through the tree's defenses, and then you have to use Lightning Strikes to pierce the heart of the tree."

"Lightning Strikes?" Not as pompous as he'd expected, but then these *were* the Leier.

Jorend nodded. "It's a technique."

Gavin realized that what he had seen Jorend doing must've been that technique. If that was the case, then it was one Gavin thought he might be able to replicate.

"Give me a moment," he said.

"And then you will be the Tree Breaker again?"

"No. Then I will destroy the trees."

The power of the bralinath trees built within him, and Gavin focused on it. Those trees were a connection to the El'aras, but what about these ones?

Jorend had suggested that these trees were corrupted, though Gavin wondered if he would even know. Other creatures had been corrupted by dark purposes, typically by Sul'toral, so he could see that these trees might be something similar.

Gavin focused on the magic within him, and as he saw the next tree moving toward him, he focused on that power, followed the pattern he had seen Jorend use, and launched himself forward.

FAITH OF THE FALLEN | 187

The tree tried to bring its branches toward him, but Gavin had summoned the power of that pattern. As he shot through the air, he realized there was far more energy in that pattern than he had expected. He hadn't known there would actually be real power in it.

He struck, and the tree quaked as his blade went all the way through it. Gavin held the sword in place, and branches drooped around him.

A part of him felt the loss of the tree. But why should he care about it?

He withdrew his blade and spun, anticipating that another would be near him, but the tree that had been coming toward them started to retreat. The Leier pursued it, though not nearly fast enough. Somehow, the tree managed to outrun them.

Jorend regarded Gavin for several seconds. "She said you knew our techniques."

"I sparred with her," Gavin said, as if that was enough of an answer.

"I would like to see that."

"Me too."

He moved away from Jorend and the other Leier, then made his way across the plains.

More enchantments bubbled up around him. Each time they did, the Leier were there, or some of the El'aras, and even a few of the enchanters, though not nearly as many as Gavin wished there were. The enchantments shattered quickly, which reassured him.

He finally paused to stare out into the fading daylight. Using his core reserves and the power of the connection he shared with the bralinath trees, he opened himself so that he could feel power. Some part of it wasn't quite right.

"They still come to you," a voice said.

Imogen appeared next to Gavin.

"Is it me, or is it the power that's accumulating here?" he said.

Others had said the same thing. Gavin began to question whether it was him or something else. And if it was not him, then what was it about this place? Ever since he'd come to Yoran, he had wondered why it had been a target. He still did not have an answer. It had become a battlefield. They had managed to defend it, but how much longer would they be able to do so?

"Are they the same?" Imogen asked.

"Are they?"

Gavin might be the reason why power was coming here, at least in some regard, but it wasn't entirely about him. Distantly, he could feel the enchantments and those fighting them. He could feel everything that everyone was doing to take on those enchantments to ensure that the plains were safe again. How long would it be before another attack came?

"What would you have me do?" Gavin asked, glancing to Imogen.

She shook her head. "It's not that I would have you do anything."

He chuckled. "I suspect you have something in mind."

"I can't see it, Gavin." There was a measure of frustration her voice. "I wonder if there is fragmented power here. I've been chasing it, and I feel like it is tied to something. Perhaps this attack."

"Then what should I do?" he asked.

"My people are able to offer some protection around the city."

It was not only the Leier soldiers helping. The enchanters who had joined in the fray, including Mekel and others, had managed to put up defenses against the attacking enchantments. Even the El'aras had added their abilities to the fight and offered an additional layer of protection to Yoran. The combined powers were building enough that Gavin started to feel as if maybe there would be enough defenses here to keep the city safe.

"I feel like there is something else here," he said. "Something more."

As he looked over to Imogen, Gavin noticed a gleam of metal in the distance.

He raced toward it. Several Leier were there before him, but as they hacked at the metal, they weren't able to cleave through it. Gavin jumped in, and the metal immediately reacted to his presence. The vines constricted around him, threading up his legs, and then began to squeeze. He focused and called on the power of the El'aras trees, that power within him, and he pushed out.

It wasn't enough.

The vines constricted again in a way that was different than when he had faced them in the forest before. Now it felt like the vines had learned some new technique. Metallic barbs pressed into his flesh. Gavin ignored the pain as they squeezed him.

He was the Chain Breaker, and this was a chain. Nothing more than that.

He focused on the power inside him. This time, he concentrated on the core reserves deep within him, then pushed outward. It was the same technique he had used all those years ago, a technique Tristan had trained him on. As he sent it surging away from him, he could feel the metal starting to shear and bend.

He added another element to it, one he had used when the vines had constricted around Tristan. He concentrated the power within him and pushed out its heat. It was a new technique, advanced for Gavin but effective. The metal started to melt.

The metal changed tactics and began to saw at him.

Gavin needed more power from the bralinath trees.

Distantly, he was aware of them. Aware of the memories they had.

They flashed in his mind.

It was almost like he was standing among the bralinath trees and they were feeling the metal constrict around them, as if the vines were attacking them the same way they were attacking Gavin now. But what he saw in the back of his mind was something that happened in the past, not what was happening to Gavin now.

He didn't have to use only the bralinath trees, though. He had the magic of the nihilar too, which was always there. Gavin had started to forget that he had drawn that power into himself, but it was a part of him as well.

He focused on that combined power, both El'aras and nihilar. One that neutralized another, but he had not attempted to use nihilar against the metallic vines before. Gavin didn't even fully understand the nihilar power, though he knew he should try to. He had never mingled the El'aras power with the nihilar, but if he could somehow combine them, perhaps he could do more than what he had so far.

As he attempted to do so, the vines struggled against him. He tried to wrap his power around them until they stop squeezing. Then he pushed outward, flexing as he had long ago learned to do with his core reserves. There was an explosion, a screech of metal, and the vines shattered away from him.

Gavin blinked. Only then did he realize he was lying on the ground. Leier hovered around him, all of them having staggered back when the vines had exploded, but it became apparent that they had been trying to peel the metal away from him.

Imogen stood with them with her sword unsheathed. Sweat streamed down her brow. She regarded Gavin for a long moment, a question burning in her eyes.

"What?" Gavin asked, getting to his feet.

He looked down at the broken fragments of the vines. In the past, the vines had come back together, and he was worried that they would do the same thing now. He was prepared this time. With the vines no longer wrapped around him, he thought he might be able to draw on his core reserves and concentrate heat around the vines in a way that would help him avoid any further attack.

But he felt nothing. The vines lay motionless. He had stopped them. Nihilar had stopped them. When he had

freed Tristan, he had focused on using his El'aras side—
the connection to himself he knew. But he had never
given any thought to the fact that he had that nihilar
power building within him. Perhaps Gavin could have
done something differently when helping Tristan.

The other Leier backed away, letting Gavin stand up
across from Imogen. He examined the broken fragments
of the vine and tested them, but each one he touched
crumbled before him.

He suspected that was for the best. He made a point of
walking around and tapping on each of them, causing
them to disintegrate before him. Finally, he turned his
attention back to Imogen and breathed out. He still held
his sword unsheathed, not wanting to release the blade
but focusing on feeling the energy within it.

"How did you learn to do that?" Imogen asked, her
voice low and quiet.

"You can't see that?"

"There are many things about you that I cannot see."

Gavin frowned. Was it because of the nihilar? Or was
it the El'aras power?

"Chauvan attempted to open a gateway near here," he
told her. "They sort of fold and disappear. I don't understand it, and I can't replicate it, but—"

"You saw this?"

"I did. I can't repeat it. Well, I can sort of get trapped
by it, but the only way I was able to do anything similar
was when we escaped the prison realm."

"Perhaps it was Chauvan who taught Timo," Imogen

said, though it seemed mostly to herself. "I wonder how he would have learned such a thing."

"I think he was trained to be the very first Champion. He failed, or it seems that he failed," Gavin said. "He tried to come here to take the El'aras ring from me, and he tried to use that in some way to open up this gateway, but..." He shook his head. "Something happened. I don't really know all the details of it, or what it means for me to have connected to that nihilar power, but we stopped him and he disappeared."

But not entirely.

"He's another one who has been chasing power for the wrong reasons, much like my brother," she said.

"And what happens if he acquires it?"

Chauvan had been after power. When Gavin had faced him, he had known that Chauvan had been chasing a different sort of magic, and he had likely been successful despite everything Gavin attempted to do to slow him. Eventually, Gavin would have to stop him. Somehow.

"We have talked about dark magic," Imogen said.

"You and I haven't talked about that much."

She nodded. "Others have. Most of it has to do with the intent behind the dark magic. This Chauvan, along with others like him, want to use it. To call on power in ways that would damage others. To rule with it. I have felt the way Timo has been using this power, how he is using these fragments to try to corrupt and form this dark magic."

"Unlike the Society?"

"The Society was long ago influenced by this kind of

power, but they have never intended to use it in quite the same way. Chauvan, and perhaps even my brother, want to control it. I fear that if we don't stop them, we may ultimately face something far worse."

"What is worse than that?" Gavin asked.

"The fragments they leave behind," she murmured. "Or perhaps the fragments they chase in this life."

"I don't want anything to do with fragments of power. I want to stop Chauvan."

"You may not have much choice." She looked down at the ground, toward the shattered remains of the metallic vines. "It's possible that your El'aras power is what they seek, and if they can steal that, they will be unstoppable." She closed her eyes for a moment, and when she opened them, they were a bright, blazing silver. In that way, she reminded him a bit of the vines that had been wrapped around him. "I think I see what we must do," Imogen said.

"What is that?"

"We need to ensure that you are fully protected. And there is only one way I can see to do that."

He waited for her to explain what that was, but she strode away from him and marched toward Yoran.

CHAPTER SIXTEEN

Gavin sat back in the booth inside the Dragon. His mind wandered as he thought about fragments of power and, more than that, whether he could learn something through those fragments. He had been close to learning something about his parents from Tristan, but then his old mentor had gotten injured. Now he wasn't sure if he would get the answers he wanted and needed.

Gaspar took a seat across from him. A frown creased his brow, and his eyes were dark, with worry lines wrinkling the corners of them. "I hear you showed off a little of your ability," Gaspar said.

Gavin shook his head. "That wasn't really my intention. I was trying mostly to show…" He shrugged. "Gods, I don't even know what I wanted to show. I was trying to stop the damn vines from squeezing me." He took a drink of his ale and set the marker he was holding down on the table. "It was the same thing that nearly took Tristan."

"Nearly, but it didn't," Gaspar said.

Gavin looked up and held Gaspar's gaze. "I could've done something differently to help him. I was trying not to use nihilar. Or maybe I had forgotten about using it. Either way, something there made it so I didn't use it." He frowned as he looked back down at his ale. "I tried to burn off the vines. That was what had worked in the past, and I knew it was going to work, but I think my attempt to burn that power off actually harmed Tristan more than anything else."

"You saved him, though."

"Did I?" Gavin said, tapping on the marker resting on the table.

It had a symbol of interlocking triangles around the border, with swirling lines in the middle. It was a far more complicated enchantment than any he could ever try to make. Gavin had linked to it, pushing some part of himself through it and binding to it in a way that would allow him to connect to Char. This way he could know if Tristan came around. So far, there had been no response, which meant Tristan remained unconscious.

"I haven't heard any word. I keep thinking that I'll get a message saying he has woken up, but there has been none."

"He's a strong man," Gaspar said. "And he's tricky."

Gavin frowned at him. "Tricky?"

Gaspar shrugged. "It's been my experience that the tricky ones are the ones who tend to succeed where others don't. Then again, maybe this will be what takes him. How old did you say he was?"

"Centuries. I don't know how much beyond that, but..." He shook his head. "He was about to tell me something, though."

"That's what this is about, then."

"You don't think I would mourn Tristan?" Gavin asked.

"I've seen you lose people you fight alongside," Gaspar said. He set down the mug of ale that one of the servers brought over to him and flipped a silver coin to the young woman, who took it and stuffed it in her pocket. "I know how much he meant to you. He trained you, so it's hard not to expect him to mean something to you. But you and him had grown apart long ago, so mourning him..." He took a long drink before placing the mug back on the table. "That's not what I would expect from you. Not that you're heartless, boy. It's just that I don't see you missing the man you've never known how to feel about."

"He was still something of a father to me."

"You already mourned that man long ago," Gaspar said. "You lost him when you thought he was dead. This is different."

"It's more than that," Gavin agreed. He grabbed the marker, and he twisted it in his fingers again. It was cool to the touch, and he kept waiting for it to warm up, thinking that maybe the heat in the enchantment might signal that Char was trying to get a hold of him. Gavin had attempted to send a signal through the enchantment several times himself, but each time he had, there had been no response, so he didn't think there was any way for him to reach Char.

"See?" Gaspar said. "I can read you. I knew it was more than that."

"He was telling me something about where I came from."

"That's a different reason to be concerned, isn't it?" Gaspar set his hands on the table, leaned across, and stared at Gavin. "All men need to know where they come from. Me, I grew up on a farm outside the city, and we lost it in a dust storm. A drought." He smiled tightly. "When I became a constable, I went back there a few times, but it was nothing more than the rotted remains of the building. Although my memories still lived there."

"I didn't know."

"We came to the city. My parents made sure I got an education. My father worked for a local cartwright, and my mother found half a dozen different things to do over the years so they could provide for me and my brother."

"What happened to your brother?"

"He got married. They moved south. I don't hear from him anymore."

"You didn't go looking for him?"

Gaspar grunted. "What's there to do about it? He moved south because his bride's family was there and they had an opportunity for him. More opportunities in the far south than there were here in Yoran, especially with the war brewing." He shook his head. "At that point, I'd gotten tied into the constables, so I had a position, but he didn't."

"Did he have any magic?"

Gaspar said nothing for a few moments. "You keep assuming I have some magical talent."

"Actually, I haven't assumed it for a while."

"Well, you always make reference to it."

Gavin shrugged. "Because many of the constables do. I just suspected you might have."

"No ability. Might be easier if I did. I wouldn't have to go around begging for enchantments the way I do now."

"I don't think you necessarily have to beg for enchantments. You have Zella, you have Olivia, and—" Gavin cut himself off, as he'd almost said Desarra, but Gaspar let the comment slide. "Anyway, you don't have to go begging for enchantments regardless."

"I suppose I don't. But if I had the ability to make them myself, I would've done so by now." He took a drink of his ale, then looked up and locked eyes with Gavin. "None of this has anything to do with what you are looking for. You still need to know more about yourself, don't you?"

"It's becoming increasingly important, it seems," Gavin said. "Given that I know I'm El'aras—"

"At least half," Gaspar said.

Gavin frowned at him.

Gaspar shrugged. "Lately, you started to believe you're a full El'aras, but what if that's not the case? You have their ability, that much is sure, but we don't know. It's possible your parents aren't both El'aras."

"I doubt I'd be able to reach for the elders the way I can without being full El'aras."

"Are you so sure about that?"

Gavin snorted, and Gaspar nodded as if the question was decided.

"So you want to figure yourself out," Gaspar said.

"If Tristan comes around, I might be able to get some answers."

But even if Tristan woke up, Gavin wasn't sure his old mentor was the one who had the answers he needed now. Chauvan had moved on from Tristan, much like Gavin himself had.

The answers Gavin needed might be found in the past, but with the time he spent with Imogen, he started to wonder if perhaps there were answers that might be found in the future and in what she could see. Perhaps he should go to Anna and learn what she might be able to discern.

"We need to trust Imogen," Gavin said. "Does that bother you?"

"You think it bothers me that she is suddenly far more powerful than she was before?"

Gavin shrugged. "I don't know. That's what I'm asking. Does it bother you?"

"When she was here before, she always had something on her mind. She always had a purpose." Gaspar grabbed his mug, and he took a long sip. "I thought I could help her find it, you know? I don't know why I'm even telling you about this."

"Because we're friends."

Gaspar snorted. "Friends. Didn't always feel like that, did it?"

"She is different, but she's also the same," Gavin said. "That makes a difference too. I can feel it within her." When he hesitated, Gaspar looked up at him. Gavin let out a sigh. "You just have to get past what she's gone through and the fact that we can't really know what it's been like for her. In the last year, I think she's probably changed more than anybody I've ever met. Yet deep down, the core of Imogen is still there. She still wants to help, she still wants to serve, and she still wants to be…" Gavin wasn't entirely sure what she wanted.

"That's just it," Gaspar said. "She still wants, but none of us know what that is. I used to be able to help her."

"And it bugs you that you aren't able to help her the way you once did?"

Gaspar shook his head. "It's not about that. It's more…" He took another drink of his ale. "I suppose that's part of it. When she was looking for the hyadan, I thought there was something I could do. Find an enchantment. That seemed easy enough. We had experience with it, and I knew the city. Since she knew it was here, we thought the two of us could work together. When you showed up, you put a wrinkle in things, but we were still looking for the hyadan during that time. It's just that now that she's completed her quest, she doesn't need me."

Gavin chuckled, thinking about what Jessica had said to him. "Maybe it's just that she doesn't need you to help her find something. Maybe she just wants to have you."

Gaspar sat quietly, working his hand around his wrist as if trying to squeeze some pain out of it. "I doubt she sees me that way."

Imogen came over to the table, flanked by Jorend. She looked down at the two of them. "I think it's time."

"Time for what?" Gaspar said.

Imogen closed her eyes. When she opened them, there

was a flash of silver that burned in the back of her gaze. "I've been trying to make sense of everything here. Every so often, I catch glimpses. It was part of the reason I came to Yoran in the first place. I feel like Benji has guided me here, but even in that, I don't know if he knows why he guided me, nor do I know why he thought there was something here to follow. I just believe there was a purpose for it. Now I'm starting to see something else. Different glimpses. Different visions. And as I look to try to make sense of it, I still cannot tell if there is anything there I can use."

"Why would you need to use it?" Gaspar asked.

"Because the answers are there. Somehow. I can see them. At least, I could see them when I tried to look, but now they seem scattered. Before, those visions brought me here. Now I'm starting to think that whatever Timo and Chauvan are after will carry us elsewhere."

"Then we need to follow," Gavin said.

"It will take preparation," Gaspar said, glancing from her to Gavin. "Unless you want to just go running off."

"No. But I don't think we can wait too long."

Gavin watched her for a moment. "Then let me get started." He got out of the booth and pulled Jorend with him. The Leier resisted, but Gavin pulled harder. When he got Jorend away from the table, he nodded toward where Gaspar and Imogen were seated. "You're coming with me."

"I'm not leaving the general."

"She's fine with Gaspar."

"That's Gaspar?" Jorend asked.

Gavin nodded.

"He's different than what I was expecting. Younger."

Gavin snickered. "I think that might be the first time anybody has ever said Gaspar's younger than they expected."

They stepped out of the Dragon and into the street, where bright sunlight shone down. Only a few hints of clouds smeared the blue sky. The city seemed to crackle with energy in a strange way, though Gavin didn't know if that sense came from the protections that had been placed around the city or the threat of another attack.

"Why are you pulling me away from here?" Jorend asked.

"Because the two of them need to make their own preparations," Gavin said.

Jorend turned, glancing back at the Dragon. "Are you sure the general is safe?"

Gavin stopped and looked over at Jorend. He was probably the same age as him—at least, as old as Gavin thought he was—and there was a flicker in his eyes that suggested a maturity. But there was also something else. Fear?

Gavin couldn't quite tell.

"You've seen her fight?" he asked.

Jorend nodded. "I have seen her fight."

"Then you know she's not in any danger. And if she can see things the way she claims—"

"She can."

Gavin waited, hoping he might expand on that, but he didn't. "If that's the case, then you know she's in no danger from Gaspar," he eventually said. "In fact, I would say that

204 | D.K. HOLMBERG

Gaspar would go to incredible lengths to protect her, as he has in the time I've known him. And her."

They were a team.

Was it the team that Gaspar had missed, not just Imogen herself? As Gavin thought about the way Gaspar looked at her, he didn't think that was the case. It wasn't just the team. It was Imogen.

He motioned for Jorend to follow him.

"Where are we going?"

"There's a place I thought we could visit," Gavin said. "I don't know if you have any use for enchantments…" He watched Jorend for a moment. He had no idea how he might feel about them. Knowing what the Leier thought about magic, Gavin couldn't help but wonder if perhaps Jorend felt the same thing. If so, maybe it was a mistake to bring him along in his search for anything that might provide them with answers.

"I never cared much for them. I only needed my blade."

"Tell you what," Gavin said, patting his own sword. "There was a time when I thought the same thing. Well, at least about fighting in general. Never about a sword specifically. But when you get into a pinch and you have something that makes your reactions faster, your eyesight better, or even your skin harder, you come to realize that you don't need to be so dependent on your own abilities. Sometimes it's better just to recognize that there are others with skill and to embrace that, mostly so you don't end up defeated by your own stubbornness." He winked at Jorend. "Are you one who would let that happen?"

Jorend frowned at him. "I would not."

"Good. Then join me."

Gavin gestured for him to follow, and they made their way toward the fortress. A humanoid-looking stone golem marched up the street as they neared.

He raised his hand for Jorend to slow.

"What is this?" Jorend said. "Have they penetrated Yoran?"

"This would actually be the work of the enchanters in the city. A kind of protection they place," Gavin said. "This creation is from a man named Mekel, who has pretty good skill with enchantments. He's able to station these around the city and defend it from various attacks."

Gavin stepped up to the enchantment and waited for it to react to him, but it did nothing. Did it recognize his presence? He followed it for a little while, detecting the energy within it.

"He has others that are even more impressive," he said, patting his pouch. "I have a wolf I like to ride."

"You ride a wolf?"

"Not a real wolf. A stone one, though these days, I prefer a dragon."

Jorend snorted. "That was an interesting creature."

"It was paper," Gavin said, pulling it out of his pocket.

Jorend took the enchantment, turned it over, and tapped it a few times before handing it back to Gavin. "I prefer to use the renral."

Gavin chuckled and shook his head. "How did you manage to tame the renral in the first place?"

"It's complicated. They hunted us for a time, and we killed several of them, though we lost many..." His voice trailed off, and he went quiet for a moment. "But then the general found their eggs and protected them. That bonded the renral to us. Or to her, I suppose. Over time, she's learned how to connect to the renral, and the rest of us have learned from her. They have proven to be skillful hunters for us."

"I know some places where they use falcons like that."

"Falcons can't feed a dozen people with their kill," Jorend said.

Thinking of the size of the renral, Gavin shivered. "I suspect there are quite a few stories about what you went through with Imogen."

Jorend stared off into the distance. "The stories of the general can be difficult to believe," he said, as if picking his words carefully. "But if you would like to know more about her, I'm sure any Leier would love to tell you about her. Get them a mug of ale, a warm fire, and a quiet night, and they would be happy to share with you."

They rounded a corner, and in the distance, Gavin saw a crowd gathering. He slowed and raised a hand for Jorend to stop again. The crowd was unusual, though he didn't have a sense of anything dangerous within it. There wasn't a market in this part of town, so why would there be a crowd here now?

"Enchantments," a voice said from behind him.

He turned to see Mekel striding toward him with another stone golem marching behind him, though this one was slender and looked almost like a tree that had attacked Gavin before. He was reminded of the fact that many of the stone golems had real manifestations in the world and that Mekel had taken to creating them in the image of actual things. Gavin wondered if some part of the enchantment needed to be anchored in the real world in order for it to work.

"Enchantments?" Gavin asked Mekel.

"They've set up a market." He shrugged and nodded to the crowd. "Actually, that's where I was going. I have a few I thought I might sell." He looked back at the tree enchantment. "These aren't as effective for defending the city. Too small, you see, and not ferocious enough. But they would be good for defending a home, and they can be used for other things. At least, I think they can. I can't talk to them quite as well as I can the others."

"You can talk to them?" Jorend asked.

Mekel turned to him, frowning. "Do I know you? You look familiar."

"He came with Imogen," Gavin explained.

"That's right. The soldiers on the battleground."

"Battleground?" Gavin asked, arching a brow.

"I don't know. What else would you call it? It sure looks like a battleground now. There are enchantments littered everywhere. Ours, theirs, and even a few people who have fallen…" he said, his voice drifting off at the end. "I would much rather lose enchantments, regardless of how much it hurts when I do."

Jorend's brow furrowed, but he stayed silent.

"I wasn't expecting the enchanters to start selling their creations openly," Gavin said.

"I've never seen anything like it," Mekel said. "Even from before."

It was easy to forget that Mekel was older than he looked. From his appearance, he could be a man who was no older than his late teens or early twenties, with dark brown hair and a slender build. But his appearance had been stunted by the curse placed by drawing power through the jade egg in order to stop the Fates, much like all of the enchanters who had used magic at that time. It had half frozen him in time so that he aged slowly.

"You're now openly selling what you make," Gavin said.

"We are. Some don't care for it still."

"Davel?"

Mekel frowned. "He's not as concerned as I would've expected. I thought he might be bothered by the enchantments moving around the city, but he has been working with the most powerful enchanters and made sure that he has control of the most powerful enchantments. People still make other enchantments, and the substrate they use modifies the way the enchantment forms, but it still doesn't take away any of an enchantment's power."

"They have something like this in Nelar," Gavin said, motioning to the market.

Mekel nodded. "I think that's where Davel got the idea."

Gavin blinked. "This is *Davel's* idea?"

"He wants enchanters to be able to fend for themselves and to be able to afford living here."

It was a far cry from the way the city had been before. Having the head of the constables be the one in charge of setting up a market the enchanters could use to sell their wares seemed impossible to believe. Yoran had come so far from where they had been in the past.

"How about it?" Gavin asked, looking over to Jorend. "Any interest in checking out an enchantment market? I doubt you would have to pay for that many." He glanced over to Mekel. "I generally just get them for free."

Mekel snorted. "Considering what we owe you, it's a small price to pay."

"That sounds like a story I would like to hear," Jorend said.

They followed Mekel until they reached the market, and Gavin nodded to a few familiar enchanters. For a little while, he thought he could forget about the dangers around them, forget about what Imogen had claimed they needed to do, forget about what threats were out there.

For a little while.

But as he picked his way through the crowded market, he saw how each of these enchantments was designed for protection and defense. And he realized that all of this was needed because of the danger out on the battle-ground. All of this was tied to him.

Even as he was making his way through the market and trying to examine what they sold, he realized that he wasn't going to be able to ignore his presence in the city, nor would he be able to ignore what role he had in any of this. He was a part of it.

And it was because of him that the people of Yoran felt like they needed to have enchantments to protect themselves. Worse, they weren't wrong.

He was quiet while they walked around, and they

reached a large booth at the back. He recognized Zella and nodded to her as he approached slowly. Mekel started setting up at the end of one of the tables near her, bringing his stone golem alongside it. Jorend stopped at another table and spoke to one of the men as he looked at a set of rings.

Gavin wondered if he should equip the Leier with enchantments. Given that they had shown a willingness to defend the city, it seemed that they might need those enchantments so that they could defend themselves, especially against what threats were going to come.

"I didn't expect to see you here," Zella said.

"I was just showing one of the Leier around."

She gave him a tight-lipped smile, and she immediately glanced toward Jorend. "One of the defenders."

"Is that what you're calling them?" Gavin asked.

"We've seen what they are able to do. They carved through enchantments with little more than their blades, and they had no enchantments of their own."

"They are skilled," Gavin agreed.

"They have others with them who have innate magic."

Gavin frowned. "They do?"

Zella scoffed. "They call them shamans, but they have power that rivals that of sorcerers." She let out an exasperated laugh. "You didn't know?"

"I've been a little preoccupied with other things."

"You have to look at the bigger picture, Gavin. Sometimes you get so focused on the details that you forget to look on a grander scale."

"Well, when the details involve my survival, I think it's hard to look at anything else."

"You might be right," she said, shaking her head and laughing again. "What can I get for you?"

"The usual?"

"Oh, I think I can do better than just the usual." She nodded to a man who raced over to the booth. She leaned toward him and whispered something, then the man scurried away. "Now," Zella went on, "why do you need the usual?"

"I'm going to be chasing down dangers. Sort of like every other time."

Zella watched him, and there was a sense of darkness in her eyes, but it was also mixed with an edge of worry.

Gavin forced a smile. She was doing her part, wanting to protect and defend the city. He had to do his part as well, which meant he would have to do whatever he needed to help.

Only, he wasn't sure what that would entail. And he hated that.

CHAPTER SEVENTEEN

IMOGEN

Imogen often used sparring as her way of meditating and getting herself in the right mental state of what she was going to have to do, but she had not taken that same opportunity since she had come to Yoran. She felt as if she needed to spend more time sparring than she had, if only so she could get her mind right and possibly figure out what else she might need to do.

Yoran loomed in the distance, and Imogen found herself distracted by the presence of the city where she had once spent so much time but had not been in for quite a while. She was preoccupied simply because of everything she had known of the city, everything she had once believed about herself, and everything she now found to be quite different. When she had been here before, she had not known who and what she was, and she had not known who and what she could become. Now Imogen understood that she was the First of the Blade, but she

FAITH OF THE FALLEN | 213

was also beyond just being that. She was one of the Leier, and she was connected to the Porapeth. That meant she was something more than she had ever been. It meant she could be more than she had ever been.

Now she found herself connected to power that she never had imagined.

She focused on using Tree Stands in the Forest, holding on to that sacred pattern as much as she could. She found that she did not maintain it nearly as potently as she had intended, at least not at first. The longer she held it, the more Imogen began to question if there was some part of her that had been diminished because of that connection and because some part of her had changed.

"I've never seen you this distracted," Jorend said, looking over to her.

He was going through the patterns with her but not sparring. In this case, it was merely a matter of meditating and getting her ready for what they might face, as well as what she might need to do.

"It's this place," she said.

"But it's more than just this place, isn't it?" he asked. "It's everything you have been feeling here."

She smiled at him. "You know me quite well now, don't you?"

"I'd like to think that the last year we have spent traveling together has revealed you to me."

"I keep thinking of the fragments we found of Master Liu."

"Have you sensed him again?" Jorend asked.

A sharp shriek caught Imogen's attention, and she

glanced up to the renral that were circling overhead. They were powerful creatures that had provided a level of protection to her people ever since they had started following them. Protection from magic—something her people had always wanted—but a different kind of protection as well. Imogen could not take them for granted.

"I haven't seen Master Liu again, as I do think that he has gone off to find his own path. But what I have seen is something different," she said.

"We've seen evidence of these dark creatures on this entire journey here. Your brother has been using them against us."

Imogen nodded. "Unfortunately, Timo continues to think he can acquire power through nefarious means."

"Do you think he's holding any of it for himself?" Jorend asked.

"I suppose it depends on the fragments, doesn't it? Given what I know of Timo and everything he is willing to do, it is possible that he would try to draw fragmented power into himself. If he does, then it's also possible that he would try to use that fragmented power to grow even stronger."

That was her main concern, especially after having faced him however briefly outside of the valley.

"If there's anything we can help with, First," Jorend said, tipping his head in a nod.

"I know. There may come a time where I need that from you," Imogen admitted. "For now, I think we need to stay focused on defending the city."

"I had believed it would be more peaceful here." Jorend offered a hint of a smile.

"As had I."

"Do you regret returning?"

"It's not so much that I regret returning," Imogen said. "It's that I had hoped that my return would be one where I could relax. Where our people could find peace. I had hoped that we wouldn't have to keep fighting."

"Our people don't fear a fight."

"I know we don't, but there comes a time when all people need to find rest, if only so we can reach our potential."

It was something she had been giving thought to. She did not fully know if she had contemplated it as well as she should have, but it was something she believed she could know.

"Eventually, I feel like we will find peace. Perhaps here," Imogen said, and then she frowned. "Perhaps somewhere else. If it is somewhere else, then I do wonder what we will discover."

"We will discover ourselves," Jorend replied.

He turned and whipped his blade in a tight crack. Imogen didn't even move. She held on to Tree Stands in the Forest, blocking him, yet Jorend had managed to get a little closer than he had in the past. Maybe a hair deeper into her protection.

"Eventually, I will find my way through," he said.

"At that point, you become the master."

He sniffed. "I'm not sure I'm ready for that." He flourished his blade and slid it back into its sheath. "I will go and work with the others. If there's anything I can do to help you find your focus, please let me know."

He bowed to her. Imogen returned it, though not quite as deeply.

She turned her attention back to the city. Even from here, she could feel the protections that had been placed around it, various magic from the enchanters and now some of El'aras origin. At Gavin's request, the shamans had been adding other aspects to the defenses, though Imogen had been a bit reluctant to have them work too fast and vigorously on that, as they needed their own defenses. Still, with as many shamans as they had and the level of protection that they now had, it did not seem like she had to be concerned about a lack of resources.

She closed her eyes and began to focus, letting the meditation come to her. She had long done this, though usually she had held her blade while she was meditating so she could slide into the patterns. Lately, Imogen had found that even the blade was no longer necessary, and in her mind, she moved from sacred pattern to sacred pattern. When she completed those, she began to work on the traditional patterns, those she had learned before going off to the sacred temple, but ones that still had their own potential.

"What can you see?" Imogen asked, letting the question carry to the fragment of Benji within her. "It has to be tied to this, and to Timo."

Imogen didn't expect Benji to answer, but there were times when he came to her, manifesting in his fragmented form in the back of her mind.

"What are you hoping to find, First?"

She paused in her patterns and focused once again on Tree Stands in the Forest. "I don't know that I'm hoping to find anything," she said. "I merely want to learn if there is anything here I might uncover."

He snorted, which seemed surprising given that Benji had no physical form any longer, but there were times when he still acted much like he had when he'd been alive. Too often, Benji would swear, or else Imogen found herself swearing and taking on that aspect of Benji, which she found amusing. Other times, she felt him laughing as much as she heard it. Every so often, there was a connection to the other Porapeth who had lent her a bit of their fragments, though Abigail was generally quiet. Eventually, she wondered if she would ever feel the depths of that fragment and begin to understand just what it was that existed.

"You keep looking for answers, but you have them. At least for this."

Imogen held on to the connection and stayed focused with her eyes closed. "At least in this? You imply that there will be something else."

"There's always something else," Benji said. "Once you uncover that truth, then it opens up things for you. In my time, I dealt with far more dangerous threats than you could ever imagine."

Imogen found herself smiling. She had no idea how long Benji had lived, though she guessed that it had been countless centuries. The Porapeth had believed themselves immortal, but that immortality had only been for their magic and not for their physical form. Though Benji's physical form had passed on, his power had not, nor had the aspect that was Benji—what her people would call a soul.

"What other dangers will there be?" Imogen asked.

"You want to leap into battle after this one? Maybe you should focus on one at a time, First."

"I suppose I was hoping that we would find peace."

There was a moment of silence, and within that, she felt the various possibilities Benji had demonstrated to her all forming in her mind. Silvery lines seemed to shimmer and take on different forms until they settled.

"I believe your people will find peace," Benji said.

"Just my people?"

"I believe you will be needed."

Imogen nodded in understanding. "And if I don't respond?"

"Why wouldn't you? You are the First." He laughed, as if that was some grand joke.

Imogen smiled once more. "Is Timo after more power?" she asked.

"That boy has been chasing nothing but power from the first moment I met him. I thought I could stop him. I couldn't see what I couldn't see, and I couldn't see that I couldn't do it. You have to be the one."

"I'm not sure I'm going to be able to do it, though."

"Well, if you can't, then you intend to let somebody else take on your responsibility? That's not the First I know."

"I wonder if I'm strong enough," she said.

"Strong enough to stop him? That fucker has nothing on you."

"I don't know what different powers he might have co-opted for himself."

"And what about what you have co-opted?" he said, laughing again. "I suppose I'm nothing, am I?"

Imogen shook her head. "I didn't say that. But your lessons aren't always the easiest to follow."

"They'd be easier to follow if I had a good student. Instead, I have you."

"What can you see?" she asked, ignoring his insult.

"I see the same as you, First. Anything that exists for you exists for me. We are the same now."

It reminded her of when she had been helping Master Liu and he had referred to her as the Elder. Imogen hadn't felt as if she was the Elder, but having the fragment of Benji within her meant that perhaps she was.

"If it's fragmented power, I have to find a way of purging it from him," she said.

"Only if you think to save him."

"You don't think I should?"

"I get it. He's your brother. Or he was. What is he now?" Benji asked.

"I don't know."

"Each time you go after him, you tell yourself that you're going to do what is necessary. But each time you go after him, you hold some part of yourself back. That's why you haven't stopped him before."

Imogen wanted to argue, but even as she prepared to

do so, she wasn't sure there was anything to argue with. Maybe he was right.

"I haven't intended to hold anything back," she said.

"Well, intentions are about as useful as a body to me now. They mean nothing. It's what you do that matters."

"Thank you for your wise advice, Benji."

"Sometimes you need it. Sometimes you don't. These days, you've finally found your past, so I don't have to nudge you as much as I did before. I do feel like in this case, I need to give you a little kick in the pants. It might convince you to do what you need to do."

"And that is?" she asked.

"Taking care of this so you can move on to the next."

"That's now the second time you mentioned 'the next.' Why?"

"Because something else is coming," Benji said. "I can't see it because you can't, but I can feel it. Does that make any sense?"

Imogen shook her head. "Not really, but I will be ready."

"Finish this first, First." He laughed at his own joke. "But be ready to do what you must. From what I can tell, you might be the only one who can."

"Not the Chain Breaker?"

There was a moment of quiet, and she had a sense that Benji was thinking and preparing to answer, but there was also something else to the silence.

"Not that one," he said. "He's useful, but I feel something unusual there."

"This nihilar?" Imogen didn't know what to make of it, and she worried about what it meant.

"Maybe that's all it is. Or maybe he's just tied to somebody else's plan. I can't see that either, so don't you go asking me."

"There aren't any more Porapeth," Imogen said.

"Do you think we were the only ones with real magic?"

She waited for him to explain more, but then she had the distinct sense that Benji had retreated, as he often did after making grand proclamations like that. With his sudden absence, she had no way of pushing for answers. Benji had given her something to think about, but he had also reminded her that she needed to focus on the task at hand, not look ahead any longer.

She opened her eyes and continued to concentrate on Tree Stands in the Forest. She pushed downward as she did and began to feel something deep beneath her, a pressure that was squeezing upward as if there was some power that tried to push against her.

Enchantments.

Imogen shot upward. Lightning Strikes carried her up into the sky, and then she shifted into Petals on the Wind. She turned her focus outward, looking to see what had drawn her attention. As she did that, she began to realize that what she saw and felt was not at all what she had expected.

A line of enchantments marched in the distance, but it was what she felt from them that called her attention.

She focused and felt for the connection to Zealar. The renral flew over to her, and she dropped onto his back.

222 | D.K. HOLMBERG

She patted his oily wings, then began to feel the energy crackling through the renral. "Let's go and hunt," she told him.

As they took off and shot forward, she pulled her communication enchantment from her pocket and whispered into it, alerting the other Leier, as well as Lilah and the Koral shamans.

Imogen hurried toward the line of enchantments.

They were here. They would fight. They would protect the city.

At least for now.

Eventually, Imogen was determined to give her people an opportunity to rest and be at peace. What did it matter if she did not find the same for herself?

CHAPTER EIGHTEEN

"I hear you're getting ready to go somewhere," Brandon said.

Gavin turned, realizing that the El'aras man had been following him.

Brandon was alone on the street, near the edge of the current El'aras section, and he'd slung a satchel over one shoulder. He had a smile on his face as he often did, regarding Gavin with something that resembled amusement.

"We aren't sure quite yet," Gavin said. "Why?"

"I just wanted to offer my help."

"I'm sure you would."

Gavin strode down the street.

"You haven't wanted any extra help lately, have you?" Brandon said.

"Not so much. I don't know what's going on, and until

I have a better sense of what our plan is, I just don't know what I need to be doing."

Brandon chuckled and hurried after him. "You've been gathering enchantments, though."

Gavin finally stopped and spun toward him. "Are you following me?"

"Consider it a curiosity, nothing else. I was a part of what you were doing before."

"I'm not saying you can't be part of it," Gavin said.

"Right, but you aren't saying that I can be, either."

Gavin flicked his gaze toward the darkness near the edge of the city. When he turned back, Brandon was still watching him.

"It's because I'm El'aras and you don't know what you are, isn't it?" Brandon said.

"I'm El'aras," Gavin said.

Brandon laughed. "It might've been easier for you to believe that back when the families weren't so isolated. Well, not even isolated anymore. I suppose we are consolidated more than anything. But back when each family had their own space, you might've had an easier time."

"And how easy of a time are you having?"

Brandon shrugged. "It gets easier." He glanced back at the El'aras section. "At least here there is something that feels a little familiar to me. When I was living in the forest, it didn't strike me as home." His tone had turned more serious. "I suppose you don't know what that's like."

"I never really had a home," Gavin said. "I had to move around quite a bit during my training, and I was never really given the sense that I had a place of my own."

"That's too bad. And it's too bad that you never had an opportunity to see the mountains," Brandon said, turning and gazing to the north. "Far enough away that you can almost forget what it was like. And long enough ago…"

The comment raised a question for Gavin that he hadn't considered before.

"Did your people have bralinath trees?" Gavin asked.

Brandon gave a small laugh. "Of course we did."

"You did?"

"Well, of course, I said. We are not so dissimilar to our cousins. It's just that the way we go about things is a little different."

"So your elders stored some part of themselves as well?" Gavin hadn't considered that, though perhaps it made sense. More than that, he wondered if he should have asked that question before. The El'aras and the bralinath trees he had connected to were all of a single type, as far as he could tell, and all connected to Anna's family. Given the fact that Gavin had the ability to connect to them, that suggested he was also connected to that family. He hadn't considered that much, but it seemed to fit.

"The trees are a little different, but still bralinath," Brandon said. "They are the only part of the forest I actually didn't mind. I could take you to see them sometime, but I imagine you are too busy for such frivolity." He looked over and grinned.

"You'd be surprised by what sort of frivolity I'm interested in," Gavin said.

Brandon smirked. "So where are you off to? I thought you were making preparations to leave, but then I saw you coming out here, so maybe you aren't going as quickly as I thought. You're probably waiting on that other one to finish what she's been doing, aren't you?"

"Imogen," Gavin said.

"She's got the Shard all flustered. I think she isn't quite sure what to make of her."

That brought a smile to Gavin's face. "Well, I suppose that is something we share. She is quite different than the way she was when she was here before."

"I saw her in battle. I'd be curious to see you and her fight."

"You and me both." He nodded to Brandon. "If you don't mind, I do have a place I need to be."

"I'll come with you."

Gavin really didn't want the company, but he decided it might be easier to keep Brandon engaged rather than upset him. And it might be better for them, anyway, as he couldn't help but think that Brandon knew things that he did not.

"That would be fine."

"You don't have to sound so overwhelmed with excitement." Brandon laughed again. "Where are you going, anyway?"

"The tunnels."

Gavin strode forward, and Brandon caught up to him in a hurry.

"Tunnels, as in—"

"As in the tunnels beneath the city."

"But you don't need to leave the city to get to them."

"No, but it's generally easier to do it this way, and it usually draws a little less attention."

Brandon gave a small chuckle. "Well, I'm sorry I'm drawing attention to you."

"It's fine."

When they reached the boundary around Yoran, Gavin felt the same tingling sensation wash over him that he always felt ever since the constables had placed the barrier around the city. He paused for a moment. If things went wrong, this protection might be all that they had to defend themselves against the kind of magic that Chauvan and Timo used against them. So far, the defenses had not been fully needed, as people had taken a stand and helped protect the city, but there may come a time when they would need to do more than that.

"This is where we first dealt with the nihilar," Brandon said, his voice dropping to a whisper.

Gavin nodded at the entrance to the tunnel. It was late in the day, and the sunlight was fading, creating a hint of a shadow that hung over everything. The air had a stench to it, something musty but mixed with a bit of rot he couldn't quite place. He suspected that it came from the battles that had been waged here, though he didn't know for certain.

"That's why we're coming," Gavin said.

"The nihilar?"

"Well, I need to better understand it."

Brandon frowned. "I thought you already did."

"I understand that I have a connection to it, but I'm

still struggling to understand the nature of that connection and what it means. I have not used that power much, or with any real control, since I obtained it."

And it was more than just that. Gavin increasingly felt as if he had to understand it. It was a power that had been used against the El'aras. There had to be something within it for him to better understand so he could keep Chauvan from whatever he hoped to accomplish.

He had just started down the tunnel when Wrenlow's voice chirped in his ear. "Are you about here?"

"Very nearly," Gavin said.

Brandon looked over and arched a brow, but then he nodded at the enchantment in Gavin's ear and grinned.

"We've been waiting for you," Wrenlow said. "The others are already here."

"I didn't realize that others were coming."

"Well, Imogen wanted to see it, so Gaspar brought her down. That was about the same time I figured I needed to show it to you. We have to understand more about this."

Gavin didn't think that the tunnels and the ancient prophecy tied to the Sul'toral were really all that important for him to learn more about. But he was willing to do what his friend asked because Wrenlow would often find information that ended up becoming useful.

"I'm almost there."

He tapped on the enchantment, silencing it again.

"That one looks to be pretty well made. Did you create it?" Brandon asked, gesturing to the enchantment.

"Not me," Gavin said. "Anna helped with this one."

"Did she? That's interesting. I wouldn't have figured her for somebody to make a communication enchantment. That's what it is, isn't it?"

Gavin nodded.

"I can tell that something about it is different. Maybe better connected?" Brandon frowned and then shook his head. "Well, maybe not better connected. I don't really know what to call it. Just different."

"When I began to learn how to add aspects to enchantments, I tested it on this." Gavin traced his finger along the narrow chain that stretched from the enchantment down to the primary piece that was attached to him. A strange energy was present within it. He could feel the power of the enchantments, but he could not recreate it on his own. He had learned to augment it, which was relatively useful, and he felt as if he didn't need to do anything more for it.

"If you want, I could help you learn how to make one yourself," Brandon said.

"You know how to make something like this?"

"Well, my people were artificers, so we have a bit of experience with it. Maybe not this particular design, though. There's something about it that I am not fully familiar with, but I could help you learn how to create something similar. That is, if you're interested."

"I would be," Gavin said. Having the ability to make enchantments like this would be an incredibly useful skill. Then he wouldn't be dependent on Anna for the El'aras-based enchantments. More than that, he wouldn't have to talk to the other enchanters to find ways of adding power. He preferred to be self-reliant, at least as much as possible.

"It's a skill that takes a little while to develop, but I suspect you would have the knack for it. You are the Chain Breaker, after all," Brandon said, and he flashed a smile.

"What do you mean it takes a little while to develop?"

"Well, time," he said.

"How much?" Gavin asked.

"Oh, I could have you serviceable in about a decade."

Gavin stopped on the stairs leading down into the tunnel, having augmented his eyesight with his own connection to his core reserves rather than needing an enchantment for that. He blinked several times at Brandon. "A decade?"

"Well, that would be on the fast side of things for a true artificer ability, but I think you've shown other potential, so I suspect that you would be able to do this pretty well."

Gavin started walking again. "Well, unfortunately, I don't know that I have a decade to learn."

"Just like all the young," Brandon said, shaking his head. "Never wanting to take the time needed to truly master necessary skills."

"You can't be much older than me."

"I can't? I'm nearly a hundred and fifty summers old."

Gavin peered over at Brandon with a renewed curiosity. "A hundred and fifty?"

"I probably don't look a day over a hundred."

"I would've said you didn't look a day over thirty," Gavin said.

"Not all of us have lived the same hard life you have, Chain Breaker." Brandon winked at him.

They reached the bottom of the stairs, and they headed into the temple. He could hear Wrenlow's voice, not even needing the enchantment to do so, and listened to the echoes while making his way with Brandon. When he reached the others, he slowed.

"It was not that long ago that we were here, was it?" Brandon said.

"Not that long ago, but it feels like an eternity sometimes," Gavin said.

"Well, that's because you are so young."

Gavin snorted and continued to follow the sound of the voices. Inside, Wrenlow was talking to Imogen and pointing to a section of the temple.

"This was where we were before," Wrenlow said as he motioned to a wall. "It was down there that Gavin took on Chauvan the first time."

Imogen looked over as Gavin approached, tilted her head in a slight nod, and turned back to Wrenlow. "There is the sense of something here," she said. "I can feel it. I'm not sure why, though."

"What do you feel?" Gavin asked.

"I feel…" She closed her eyes for a moment, and when she opened them, they flashed with a bit of silver. "There is power here. Ancient, connected power."

"Well, that's probably tied to the crypts," Brandon said.

Gavin paused and looked over to him. "The what?"

"Well, this is a temple, after all. So it's probably tied to the crypts."

"I didn't realize there were crypts here."

"Oh, certainly," Brandon said, and he waved a hand toward a section of the wall. "Behind here are some of the greatest of our people."

Gavin frowned, and he stepped over to the wall. The stone had a bit of energy to it that he had never paid much mind to, but given what Brandon had said about this being a crypt, he thought he needed to focus on it more than he had before. Maybe there was something to it. He traced his hand along the stone but did not feel anything.

"It's usually pretty deep," Brandon said. "If you'd like to see the access point, you probably have to talk to one of the priests. It's only accessible to them."

Gavin stared for a moment, trying to make sense of it.

Gaspar joined him in looking at the wall. "What is it, boy?"

"I'm not sure. I didn't know this was a crypt. Maybe I should have, or maybe Anna should have told me, but it seems to me that this fact is significant."

"I'm sure it is," Imogen said as she approached. "This is where you encountered that strange power?"

"Yes. Nihilar power. This is where I accessed it. It seemed as if there was a way of containing it."

"An enchantment?" she asked.

Gavin pursed his lips in thought. "Well, I suppose that anything that connects and collects power is an enchantment, isn't it? That's pretty much what we have experienced consistently."

"This would be different," she said, her voice careful. "I suppose not so dissimilar to your sword. Or perhaps even the ring."

"The ring?"

"The one you wore. It was an item of power, was it not?"

Gavin nodded.

"I never understood the Toral ring, nor did I understand the power the Sul'toral harnessed until recently," Imogen said. "They used a connection to ancient power. To Sarenoth. Not in servitude, but more like a theft of power."

She looked around the room. Her gaze drifted up toward the ceiling before slowly and steadily turning back to Gavin and then the others. He wondered if she was thinking about when she had been here with her brother. Back then, Timo had still been… maybe nothing. Maybe Timo had always been chasing power at that point.

"The ring is an enchantment," Imogen explained. "They use it to bind the power of a fragment. That's why the Toral rings are valuable. That fragment can be transferred. Others can claim it and begin to harness it and use it. But it is an enchantment, nonetheless."

Gavin thought about what Chauvan had been after when he had been here.

"You think this nihilar power and what I connected to are somehow a fragment of power much like that?" he asked.

"I don't know, but I would not be surprised. When we are dealing with this kind of old, often overwhelming power, it is probably all fragments in one way or another. As Benji has told me, magic does not die. It merely transfers."

"We've not seen that with sorcerers," Gavin said.

"The power they tap into is so slight that you probably would not. Well, most sorcerers," she said. "I have one among my people who might be able to create a fragment, as she is quite impressive, but for the most part, the sorcerers do not. Only those with great natural power do."

Great natural power. The El'aras had great natural power, and they left aspects of it behind in the bralinath trees, so it could be possible that something similar had happened with the nihilar. It might even make sense that Chauvan would chase that kind of power. But why here?

It simply did not make sense.

"Can you see anything?" Gavin asked.

Imogen held his gaze. "I have looked for that answer from the moment we came, and unfortunately, there is nothing here I can see. It is bright, and I don't know if that's because of our presence or something else."

"And the others?"

"There are powers shifting," Imogen said. "We have to find it before it fades. We have to stop it before they succeed."

Distantly, the sound of thunder came.

Gavin tensed, and once he focused, he realized the source.

"I would love to talk about this longer, but unfortunately, we have another battle coming. I think we should go and help."

"We must find what they search for," Imogen said. "Before the attacks become too much."

CHAPTER NINETEEN

The edge of the city was quiet, with no evidence of the attacks that had been coming with regularity. The enchantments had stopped their assault, at least for a little while. Gavin didn't know how long they would hold off, but the Leier and their defense had made a difference so far. He had to hope that they could continue to offer a measure of protection for Yoran.

"Are your people willing to stay here?" Gavin asked Imogen.

She stood next to him, dressed in all black, her sword sheathed at her side. Strangely, a feeling of power emanated from her. "My people have lost our home, Gavin Lorren. We came here because I thought we might find a new place, but now I wonder if we were needed. Perhaps it was something else that I didn't see."

Gaspar stood a step behind Imogen and listened. He hadn't said much. That was unusual.

Gavin held out the paper dragon, then tapped on it. It unfolded quickly and started to take on its larger shape, and once he set it on the ground, it began to elongate. He pushed some of his core reserves into the dragon, forming a connection between the two of them. He felt that power settle inside of it.

He rested his hand on the creature, feeling his power shifting within it. An energy radiated inside the enchantment. Gavin no longer knew how much of that came from Alana and what she had done to create it—a technique that was considerably different than that of any other enchanter he had worked with—and how much of it came from him.

He climbed onto the dragon's back. Imogen and Gaspar approached as he settled and leaned down, with Gaspar hurriedly joining atop the enchantment. She regarded the paper dragon for a long moment, before pulling herself onto it and sitting behind him.

They took to the air and flew quickly. After a while, Imogen patted the dragon's side, and Gavin detected power that came from her and flowed into the dragon. When it did, the dragon changed course.

"Are you speaking to the dragon?" he asked.

"Not exactly."

"I felt something. The enchantment is not just Alana's any longer. Now it's somewhat tied to me."

"You've learned to make enchantments?"

"Not make them, but modify them," Gavin said.

She frowned at him for a long moment, regarding him with those strange eyes that flashed with silver every so

238 | D.K. HOLMBERG

often. Then she leaned down and touched the dragon
again. Her eyes seemed to darken, perhaps the color in
them changing and becoming silver, but only a little bit. "I
haven't modified the enchantment," she said. "I'm now
trying to speak to it."

As they headed to the south, Gavin looked into the
distance, trying to make sense of what might have brought
them this way. "What is here?"

"I can't see it," Imogen said. "I can only see where we
need to go." She smiled tightly. "Sometimes it's like that.
Too often, unfortunately."

"What do you see?"

"I described it as a spiderweb to you," she said, and
Gavin nodded. "It's something like that. I can see strands
of possibility. The one who granted me this ability spoke
about learning how to stretch those out, gather information, and dig into the possibilities, but I'm just too inexperienced with it."

"It didn't seem like you were inexperienced when
fighting the Sul'toral," he said.

"That was different." Imogen leaned forward, and the
wind whipped her long black hair around. Her cloak fluttered behind her, and she kept one hand near the hilt of
her sword. "When I fight against someone, the immediate
future is blazing with possibilities. But generally, there are
only a few that make any sense. Most people only know a
handful of techniques." She looked over to Gavin, holding
his gaze. "It's part of the reason I wonder how I might fare
if I sparred with you. You know more techniques than
most, and you can modify them in the middle of a fight in

a way that is different than what others can do. It's why I had a hard time with you when I faced you before." She turned her attention to the south, looking out over the dragon. "It's why the Sul'toral pose less of a danger than before. They've used the same techniques over centuries, which makes them predictable. All up until recently."

"Because of your brother?" Gavin asked.

She sighed heavily. "Timo is involved in this. He's been involved from the very beginning. That's the other reason I came here. I intend to stop him."

She fell silent as the dragon continued flying south, and the landscape shifted beneath them. In the distance, Gavin saw the city of Hester, and for a moment he thought that was where they were going. But they flew over it and headed across a vast blue ocean.

Enchantments had limitations. Power was not unlimited within them, though Gavin could add his own connection to augment what went into the enchantment, but if the enchantment failed, or if he did, they would plummet down into the water. For all of Imogen's talents, Gavin doubted she would be able to do anything if that happened.

Then again, it was possible that she might. He simply didn't know all of what she was capable of.

Gavin caught sight of an island up ahead, which seemed to be where Imogen was guiding them. The entire island was a vibrant green, with a mountain at the center. Smaller islands surrounded the larger one.

"What is that place?" he asked.

"Someplace ancient."

"I don't see any people there."

She shook her head. "It's too hard to reach."

"How do you know?"

She tapped on her eyes. "I can see boats trying but crashing against buried rocks. They sink."

"There could be people who already live in these lands," Gavin said.

He couldn't be the only one who had an enchantment to use. Imogen also had her renral. They could fly. There had to be some other way to reach an island like this.

They circled above the island. It was large enough that it would take him several hours to travel by foot, and that was even with enchantments. The trees that grew on it were dense, but Gavin didn't see anything below to suggest that anybody lived there. He didn't see signs of anyone.

As he drew on his El'aras connection, he realized he could sense bralinath trees nearby. Did Imogen know?

They started to descend, but the paper dragon didn't have any place to land easily, so they had to touch down near the rocky shore. Once they climbed off, Gavin tapped on the paper dragon to fold it quickly, and he put it in his pocket.

"Why here?" Gaspar asked.

"Bralinath trees," Gavin said, looking over to Imogen. "Did you know they were here?"

"I saw something. Flashes of brightness. I'm not entirely sure what it is."

Most of the trees on the island were different than what he had seen in the El'aras forest. They had broad leaves, and there were some with thick vines dangling from their branches, which initially caused Gavin to pause. He made sure there was no sign of metallic vines within them, and when he was convinced there was nothing, he moved on. He could feel a bralinath tree in the distance. Generally, they were enormous, but for whatever reason, the ones on this island were not. He started to slow as they neared one.

Gavin felt for his core reserves, but they felt faint in a way they normally did not. It was almost as if the distance from Yoran had weakened him in some way.

"Whatever I saw drew us out here," Imogen said. "It's bright, but I don't know why."

Brightness was the same thing Anna had suggested that she saw. It was also the same experience he had when it came to the bralinath trees. There were times when the trees showed him part of the past, but there were other times when it was so bright and blurry that it made it difficult for him.

That was what he had to try to understand. As he approached the tree, he heard something. At first, Gavin thought it came from the tree itself. Then he realized that wasn't the case.

"We aren't the only ones here," Gaspar said.

"We need to be careful," Gavin said. "If there are others here, I would not be surprised if they have some way of connecting to power, especially with these bralinath trees…"

He took another step toward the tree.

There was a soft swishing sound to the undergrowth.

And then a creature out of a nightmare leapt at him.

Its fur was dark, sleek, and almost oily, with a body nearly the size of a large horse. Steaming spittle dripped from a massive jaw filled with rows of teeth. A deep growl rumbled from the creature.

Gavin dove off to the side. He reached for his sword and felt a strange pressure from deep within him. The bralinath tree was warning him. He couldn't kill this creature. That was strange for him to be aware of, but worse, it posed a dangerous challenge.

"We can't kill them!" Gavin shouted.

He lost track of where Gaspar was, though he could feel Imogen somehow.

"You think you can do anything?" he asked Imogen as he moved closer to her.

She had not pulled her sword out either. Had she known? Or had she hesitated after Gavin had said something?

"It's too bright," she said.

"So you have to rely on your patterns."

"It is not such a difficulty doing so."

Gavin wondered about that. She was skilled, but without the ability to anticipate her opponent's next move, how skilled would she be? Probably still skilled enough.

He dropped beneath the creature as it jumped toward him, and he hurriedly lunged and pushed off the ground. His connection to the bralinath trees surged suddenly, and it gave him far higher of a leap than he was expecting. He bounded into the air, landing on top of the creature, and he immediately wrapped his arms around its back. The fur was thick, coarse, and damp.

The creature bucked and jumped, flying higher than Gavin had. That had to take incredible power.

He drove his elbow down onto its back, trying to neutralize it—maybe not kill it, but at least incapacitate it. There were other ways he could slow it, but there was also a distant part of his mind that wondered why he couldn't kill.

What would happen if I did? Would it be so bad?

Gavin pushed past that.

When he did, he felt something reverberating within him. It was almost as if the bralinath tree near him echoed that thought, telling him he was right to ignore it. That meant he was listening to something else when he was hearing that he should just ignore the dangers.

Gavin focused on the power around him. As he did, he could feel the energy coming from him. He jumped again and felt that energy continue to build, which caused him to shift his direction.

He twisted his body as he held on to the creature. It continued to thrash, and as it did, Gavin started to feel an odd connection to the bralinath tree, as if it had bonded to the tree itself. A line of power flowed from the tree into the creature.

He strained while squeezing his arms around the creature, connecting to his core reserves and then beyond, using the connection he now had to the bralinath trees. As much as he pushed, he felt something push back against him, making it difficult for him to fight.

Then a burst of energy sent him tumbling free. The creature yelped, and then it galloped away.

He found Imogen standing with her hands held out, silver eyes flashing. Gaspar was gripping a pair of daggers, facing her.

Gaspar grunted. "What was that?"

Gavin turned, sweeping his gaze around him. "I don't know. Some sort of a jungle cat, or maybe it's connected to the bralinath tree. It could be why the tree didn't want me to fight it."

Gaspar took a deep breath and sheathed his daggers, then stepped forward and looked over to Gavin. "You realize how strange that sounds?"

"Oh, I most assuredly do," Gavin said. "The problem is that I don't know what to do about it."

"I suppose we have to do what it wants us to, then."

"I'm not certain that was a bralinath tree. Or *is* a bralinath tree," Imogen said.

Gavin frowned. "Then what is it?"

"A fragment. The residual energy of some great entity that has left its mark on the world even though it has departed. And it has connected to the creature."

"Like some sort of dark sorcery?" Gavin asked. He remembered what Jayna had said about how dark sorcery was used, but he hadn't gotten that sense from the creature.

"Not the same. What do you know of your connection to the El'aras power?"

Gavin stepped toward the tree. It looked so much like

a bralinath. "The trees are sacred," he whispered. "They are tied to the El'aras elders."

If this was a bralinath tree, it would have been an impossibly old El'aras elder.

If it was a different fragment...

Was that the reason he needed to come here? He took a deep breath, closed his eyes, and focused. Then he pushed downward.

It was the same technique he had used in the magical prison realm. He pushed that connection downward, but it seemed right. It helped him connect, helped bind him to the power of the bralinath tree, guided him to it.

As he focused, Gavin realized that he could connect to it, but not the same way he could connect to the bralinath trees. Images came to him, though they were faint. He strained to understand what he saw, struggling with it. A few images seemed distant, but as Gavin held on to them, he started to connect to those images and recognize that they were tied to him and the power here. He could use that.

Then he saw it.

At first, it was a vague outline of the forest around him. Gradually, that outline began to fade, growing ever more distant. The forest faded with it. Then it was no more.

There were no trees. Just emptiness.

Through it all, he felt something. An ancient, powerful presence.

Could this be the fragment Imogen suggested was here?

When he opened his eyes, he looked over to her. "Why did you see this?"

"I don't know. Are you somehow connected to this power?"

"Not that I can tell. It's potent, but it doesn't feel the same as the bralinath trees do. I'm not quite sure what this is. Regardless, I don't know if this is where we were supposed to be." He had a hard time thinking Chauvan and Timo would be able to travel to this island easily. Not with the power that was here. They might be able to use their ability to fold themselves and travel, but doing so would take considerable power. Maybe more than they possessed.

"Perhaps we must follow the past in order to find our future," Imogen said.

"I don't understand."

She gave a tight-lipped smile. "I think it's time that we begin to chase this same power so we can understand what kind of fragmented power they're after."

They made their way back through the forest to the surrounding water. Waves crashed along it, and a powerful sense of energy spilled up over the shore, slamming down on the rocks. Gavin looked out, and he couldn't even see the distant shore.

This had all been part of the mainland at one point? He looked behind him. *How many others were like this?*

That was something the tree hadn't been able to show him, though maybe it could if he were to focus more deeply again and try to track that energy. As he tapped on the paper dragon, causing it to unfold again, a different question came to him about the power that was here.

As they took to the air, Gavin looked down and saw the creature that was bonded to the tree—probably not a bralinath tree, but similar enough that Gavin recognized it and felt the power that was there. Perhaps that was what he was supposed to find: the power.

But why?

Other creatures were scattered throughout the forest, and there were more trees like this one.

Was this place older than the bralinath trees? If so, what were we supposed to learn from it?

Gavin couldn't see it, but maybe there was nothing for him to see.

He drew on the energy of the distant bralinath trees, wanting to connect to that power and understand those creatures, but he didn't know if that would be possible. As Imogen guided them away, Gavin wondered what she saw next and what more they would need to do.

CHAPTER TWENTY

As they reached the volcano outside of Hester, the dragon started to descend. It seemed to know where Gavin was going, and given the connection they shared, it was possible that it did. So much had changed with the dragon since Gavin had begun using it, though he wasn't sure how or why.

Imogen leaned over with a frown, her eyes going distant—and silver.

"They have been through here," she said once they'd landed. "I can't see what it is, only that there's a fading sense here. I don't know what that means."

"I wish there were bralinath trees here that I could use to help me see," Gavin said. Gaspar looked over at him, and Gavin shrugged. "That's sort of how they work. I can look back into the past, and I can use them to guide me in the future. With that connection, I should be able to know what they are doing."

"Unless they are choosing places where you can't see," Gaspar said.

"Maybe."

"Perhaps it is not quite so simple," Imogen said. "It's possible that all they are after is collecting power."

The landscape was bleak around the volcano, though that was because they were on the northern side. The air suffocated him with heat, and Gavin could almost imagine the volcano erupting and spilling lava down it. Steam erupted in several sections, leaving everything swirling with a billowing cloud of steam that created a haze around them.

"What did it want me to know?" he asked, his voice a low whisper. He felt as if there had to be some answer here, and it was just a matter of finding it. "If this is anything like the last place, there should be a tree. Some sort of fragment at least. Unless the volcano burned it up." He looked over to Imogen.

She crouched down and stared off into the distance, her eyes flashing with the faint silver light. They didn't stay that color but often flashed that way, likely when she used her Porapeth connection.

Imogen got to her feet. "This is all wrong," she said.

Gavin nodded. "I see that."

"No. You don't see it." She frowned, glancing around before she turned her attention to Gavin. "Can you feel it?"

"What should I feel?"

"This place. Everything here. Can you feel anything about it? There is twisted power here. I can sense it." She stood in place, and Gavin recognized that she was holding on to her tree pattern, though he didn't know what she was doing with it. Some energy was pushing downward from her, as if she was using her magic in a way that only she understood. "There was something here. It's gone."

"What was it?" he asked.

Imogen moved, and Gavin was aware of her releasing whatever power she had been using. "I don't know what it was, only that it was significant. We should keep moving."

They climbed back onto the dragon, and she guided them to a desert. She used the same pattern as before, though she lingered even longer before finally motioning for them to keep going. Each time they paused, Imogen stared off, saying nothing, until she told them it was time for them to go once more. She never explained what it was that she detected, but Gavin wasn't sure she needed to. They were chasing power.

"They came through here, didn't they?" Gavin asked.

"Who?" Gaspar said.

"These have to be places where Chauvan and her brother came. If they had power like the bralinath trees, or what was on that island, then…"

"Fragments," Imogen said.

Was that what Gavin had with his connection to the bralinath trees? Were they fragments of power?

"Are they as powerful as what I connect to?" he asked her.

"I don't know. I can't see it. If we could find even some residual fragment, you might be able to know more, but unfortunately, it is too difficult for me to see anything."

Gavin needed to find a bralinath tree someplace so he could connect to it. Then he might be able to find something more and look back into the past the way Imogen attempted to look into the future. She might be limited with the brightness she saw around her, but that didn't necessarily mean he would be.

They flew farther east, and the land shifted. For a moment, it was rocky and barren, and Gavin thought that maybe they would find another tree, but then the terrain changed again. The sweeping grassland had greenery even taller than what was on the plains outside Yoran. A city loomed in the distance with a forest next to it, which reminded him of Yoran.

"This looks promising," Gavin said.

The dragon circled above the forest, then began to descend. Power pushed up at Gavin in a way that reminded him of the Leier patterns. He started to say something when Imogen gave a low snarl.

"Timo," she said.

Imogen jumped with her sword unsheathed and floated to the ground.

"She has to stop doing that," Gavin muttered.

"You've seen her do that before?" Gaspar said.

"When she attacked the Sul'toral. But I don't really know how she did it. It's part of one of her patterns, and —" He looked over to Gaspar. "You stay on the dragon. I'm going after her."

"I can help."

"I know. And you will. But you're going to help by keeping the dragon from getting taken over."

Gavin used his connection to the paper dragon, linked it to Gaspar, and jumped. He modeled his pattern after what he saw Imogen use, which allowed him to float to the ground faster than he anticipated. By the time he landed, Imogen had already raced into the trees.

Maybe there would be a bralinath tree here, or something similar that still retained a fragment.

He darted after Imogen, holding his core reserves open as he searched for her. He found her paused in front of a heap of bramble trees.

No, not brambles. Metallic enchantments. And they were snaking toward her.

Gavin focused on his nihilar connection. When that power touched the nearest bush, Imogen shouted a warning at him.

The nihilar power surged through the brambles and then crumpled.

Imogen carved her blade through the next one, sweeping it in a rapid pattern that shattered the bush and left it crumbling around her.

"You don't need to use that magic," she said, turning to him. "Everything I can see tells me that if you do that, you will draw the wrong kind of power to us."

"I need to stop them," Gavin said.

"And I need to stop my brother."

"What if it's not him?"

Another bramble bush came toward him. It didn't appear quite as fast or dangerous as the metallic vines that snaked around him, but he had little doubt that if he were to get ensnared by these bushes, he would get tangled up and likely shredded.

"It is him," Imogen said. "I can see that."

"It could be Chauvan."

Her brow furrowed more deeply. She had some experience with Chauvan as well, though Gavin didn't know what it was, as she had not elaborated on that. There was much about Imogen's experiences that he didn't know.

Another bramble bush came toward them. Gavin brought his blade around in a sharp arc, carving toward it, and he pushed out with his El'aras abilities without meaning to. As soon as he did, he could feel something feeding on his magic, as if it was drawing on the bralinath tree and stealing that power.

He carved through the bush, but it immediately came back together, building with more power than it had before. Gavin focused on the nihilar within him. He swept his blade at the brambles, drawing the nihilar through him to call on enough energy to shred the bramble. Thankfully, it worked.

Imogen had carved through a couple more. She looked around. "The only thing I can see is that we must keep moving. Gaspar is safe above us."

"I know you don't want me to use this other power, but I might need to."

"Do you even understand it?"

"I don't. Not really."

"That's my concern." She closed her eyes for a moment, and when she opened them, she shook her head. "But I can't see anything more."

254 | D.K. HOLMBERG

"Maybe we can find something for me to see." If there was a bralinath tree here, he might find what they were looking for and get some answers.

They made their way through the trees, and the forest seemed to shift as if there was something here. A different power. A vine started to tangle around his ankles, constricting, sending sharp metallic barbs into him. Gavin pushed out through the nihilar connection and wrapped it around the vine, which crumpled.

Imogen sliced through the vines attacking her and glanced over to him. "We must be careful now. We are close to something. I can't see it clearly, but I know it's there."

They continued deeper into the forest, and Gavin could feel the energy of the bralinath tree, though this one was strangely different than what he had encountered before. Ancient power began to flow into him, but not as easily as it should.

"Have you found anything?" Gaspar asked, his voice coming through the enchantment clearly and with a heavy note of irritation in it.

"Just more metallic vines," Gavin said. Anna had mentioned them before, but she didn't know any sorcerers who used that power. It had to be fragmented power of some sort, but fragmented from where? "Nothing you need to concern yourself with."

"I'm concerned about all of this," Gaspar said. "I can't see anything from up here, other than a steady swaying of the branches, but not much more than that."

"You can see them swaying?" Imogen asked.

Gavin frowned at her. "Why? What does that mean?"

"Probably nothing."

The way she said it suggested that maybe it meant something, though.

They reached a small clearing. In the distance, a small stone building was built into the hillside. As Gavin approached it slowly, the ground began to tremble.

"Are you still out there?" he asked through the enchantment.

"I'm here," Gaspar replied.

"I'm near a clearing. There's a building, but I'm not sure what to make of it."

"Do you need me to come your way?"

The ground trembled again. "It might not be the worst idea."

He looked up as a black shape streaked overhead.

"I'm nearly there," Gaspar said.

Gavin watched the sky, not paying nearly as much attention to what was happening to him on the ground.

Metallic vines slithered toward him, catching him off guard. A mass of them made it feel as if he were standing in a nest of snakes. The vines shifted up out of the grasses, and Gavin had no idea how he had overlooked them before. He stood motionless while struggling with how to react.

The sensible option was to back away.

But the nihilar had worked for him before.

He started to draw on it and began to feel something doing the same to him, almost as if that power had been summoned here. Imogen had warned him, but he had not listened.

A figure appeared near the mouth of the building built into the hill that was more like a cave than anything else. They were dressed in a black cloak, but there was a shimmering quality to it. Metallic.

"Chauvan," Gavin said.

Chauvan pulled the hood of his cloak back, and he chuckled. "And here I thought you would have given up by now."

"I'm stubborn like that," Gavin said.

"Stupid is more like it."

Gavin attempted to take a step forward, but the writhing of the metallic vines pushed him back a step.

Chauvan laughed again. "Did you really think you could come here and stop me?"

Gavin frowned at him. "Considering I don't know where 'here' is or what this means, I guess I did."

Chauvan stared for a few moments. From this distance, it looked like he was moving his hands in a way that controlled the vines, though he had something else on him as well—a ring that had to be a marker of the Sul'toral.

"You claimed their power," Gavin said.

"They didn't need it," Chauvan said. "And I have only been searching for what I was always meant to acquire."

"I thought you wanted to be the Champion."

"What do you think the Champion is?" Chauvan took a step forward, and the metallic vines squirmed out of the way, evading him and giving him space to move.

Gavin wrinkled his nose as he watched the unpleasant sight.

Chauvan grinned. "He didn't tell you, did he?"

"Tristan hasn't been his usual self," Gavin said.

Chauvan took a step toward him, sending the metallic vines in Gavin's direction. Gavin lowered his sword but held the nihilar within it. The vines fidgeted away from it.

"Do you know how long it took me to know what he was after?" Chauvan asked.

"I don't really know, seeing as how you were a failure."

Chauvan had reacted poorly to taunts in the past, and Gavin was determined to do something similar now.

"I succeeded far more than he ever expected," Chauvan said. "But you won't ever see that."

Gavin shrugged. "Why won't I?"

Chauvan took another step toward him. Now they were separated by only five paces. Gavin tensed, calling on the power of his core reserves and holding them at the ready. He wanted to be able to leap at Chauvan if it came down to it, to attack the man. But he also wanted answers. If this was all tied to him and what he intended, Gavin had to understand why.

"You can't see it, can you?" Chauvan said.

Everything inside Gavin went cold. "What was that?"

Chauvan cocked his head to the side. "No. You can't. He thought he made a mistake with me, but I think he succeeded far more than he ever knew."

"What did he do?"

Chauvan stepped closer. The vines began to twist and stand upright as if they were snakes coming to attention.

They seemed to turn their focus onto Gavin. There was something unsettling about it, but they still reacted to the nihilar that he called through his blade.

"I see your failure," Chauvan said. "I understand how it will come to be, as well. You can't understand it. Not yet, but you will."

Gavin rushed toward him, but a wall of vines had circled him. He drew on the nihilar and tried to use that power, but the vines coalesced, blocking access to Chauvan. Distantly, Gavin heard him laughing.

Rage began to bubble within him. What sort of fragmented power did Chauvan use to control these vines? Gavin could carve through them. He'd seen that he could.

When his blade touched the vines, they started to disintegrate. He pushed outward with the nihilar, but he also added the hint of power he had from the El'aras connection. He bound those two together, exploding it with heat and the crumbling power of nihilar.

The vines began to tremble, and then they retreated. They dropped to the ground, but they were not destroyed. They simply withdrew back into the earth. Gavin stared after them, wishing there was something more he could do, some other way he might be able to understand what had just happened.

But worse, Chauvan was gone too.

Gavin strode forward, half expecting the vines to come after him again, but they were not there. He stopped in the middle of the clearing.

There was something quite distinct here.

Power.

Or a memory of it, if not power itself.

Gavin focused on the nihilar, as he'd been holding on to it, but he realized that was a mistake. It wasn't the nihilar that was going to provide him with answers.

The paper dragon circled overhead before diving. Gavin funneled extra power into the creature for the possibility that the vines might attack once more, but they didn't. When the dragon landed, Gaspar looked over at him.

"What is it? You look like you've eaten something terrible."

"I saw Chauvan," Gavin said.

"Here?"

"This has to be another place where he's collecting power."

Gavin had to channel the bralinath trees to try to make sense of it, but he wasn't sure he would be able to. He was starting to think that Chauvan and Timo knew too much, that they would not be able to learn anything in time.

"We will find them," Gaspar said. "Now that Imogen is here, we will find them."

Gavin wished he was as confident as Gaspar.

"I'm not so sure. I think..." He frowned, focusing again, and could almost imagine what had once been here but was now lost. "I think he's targeting these fragments, but I don't know why. Whatever he's after is tying him to power. And I worry that he may become too strong for us to stop."

CHAPTER TWENTY-ONE

IMOGEN

The enchanted energy filled the forest.

Imogen could feel it around her, even though she wasn't quite sure whether there was anything else here. Gavin and Gaspar were behind her, focusing on what Gavin had uncovered, though she was not so convinced that he had the right of what they were dealing with.

Ever since Benji had passed on, it felt like she had been dealing with the residual energy in the world. Fragments of power. Why did everything seem to be so bound up in that? And how was it that she had never known about it before?

Possibly because with the right sort of death, someone would disappear and head to the stars, just as her people believed. Something had happened that had changed that. Now she was pursuing fragments, not for herself or for power but to free them if she could.

She stepped through the dark, shadowy forest, focusing on the power she knew to be around her. She held on to Tree Stands in the Forest as she walked, feeling for that energy and trying to determine if there was anything else here that she might need to find. She struggled as she did.

Timo had been here. She was certain of it.

Though Gavin had only come across Chauvan, Imogen believed that Timo had been here as well, and chased the same sort of power. The challenge for her, however, was that she did not know quite what Timo was after. Power, of course, as that was the same thing Timo had been chasing the entire time she had attempted to deal with the threat he posed, but it seemed like there had to be something else to it.

As she focused, the ground around her began to tremble.

The energies that had been here were not quite gone.

Imogen glanced behind her. She could see Gavin, but he was preoccupied with his search and with what he had come to believe about the power that existed here. It would be better for her to deal with this on her own, she knew. Better primarily because she wasn't quite sure what was here, but also because she didn't know what more she might need to do.

She followed the trembling. Every dozen steps or so, Imogen focused on Tree Stands in the Forest, using that to help guide her. She would take another step, then another, and then slow to a stop.

As she concentrated on her pattern, she could feel something all around her.

The ground trembled again.

The roots of nearby trees began to bend, carving up and toward her.

She still didn't move.

Imogen maintained her focus, using Tree Stands in the Forest to push energy outward. The bizarre bending roots worked their way toward her, but even as they did, she continued to force herself and her connection out against that power. She could feel it, and she could feel what she needed to do.

But within that, it seemed there was something else she might try. Perhaps she could add a bit of the renral's energy.

Zealar was somewhere overhead, circling as he often did. She had not called the renral to her while traveling with Gavin and Gaspar, mostly because others found traveling atop the renral to be an uncomfortable experience, but partly because she was incredibly curious about the enchantment Gavin had. It was powerful in a way she still did not fully understand, but she found herself curious about it.

Imogen added a bit of her own connection and power to the renral energy and let it flow through her. As it did, she began to feel even more power building to the point where it washed outward and swept toward the roots that attempted to bend up toward her.

The air crackled. And there was something else to it.

Imogen focused, feeling everything within her, everything she was summoning, and everything that filled the air, and she knew she could use that. The renral pattern was powerful enough that she could draw on it. And so she did. She called that energy through her, using it to build up with even more power, and then let it wash out from her toward the roots, where they trembled for a moment.

Then they shattered.

She felt something else, different this time.

She was aware of residual power. Fragmented power.

She pushed again with her Tree Stands in the Forest pattern, using that to try to detect anything more to this fragmented power. She had an idea about how she might be able to try a variation of the sacred pattern, as she had done something similar in the past, though she had not attempted anything quite like that in some time. Still, as Imogen thought about what she might need, she began to force different tree patterns up around her, creating a forest of her own. The fragmented power that was there began to push against her with a strength that was almost overwhelming.

It was more powerful than Imogen had anticipated it would be.

Was this what Timo and Chauvan had been after?

She maintained her focus on the pattern and tried to sweep those fragments together, but even as she attempted to do so, there was some aspect of what she was doing that didn't work quite as she intended.

The Tree Stands in the Forest pattern—or in this case, the forest itself—was not enough.

Imogen was not accustomed to that. She tried pushing outward again, but even as she did, she found that it fought her in ways she had not expected. There were dozens of different fragments here. She could not identify each of them, but she could feel the power within them and the way they tried to counter her and what she was doing. As she held on to those fragmented powers, trying to trap them together and swirl them into a single, unified whole, it didn't work.

Imogen continued to squeeze, compressing those various fragments together. Even if they were from different entities, she thought she might be able to use what she was drawing on in order to find a way to force that power together and hold it that way. But even as she did, she found those fragments struggling against her, straining to get free.

There was something else she could try, but she wasn't sure it would do much. Perhaps it would incapacitate those fragments, though, and if that was the case, she had to hope that it might be enough to stun them so she could find a way to contain them.

Imogen was not a sorcerer. She did not know how to make enchantments. But the Chain Breaker had learned how to, though he claimed he couldn't. She'd seen that his modification of enchantments was really just an enchantment. They didn't need a sorcerer. They needed an El'aras. That kind of control and that kind of power would be greater than what Imogen could do.

She reached into her pocket, pulled out the enchantment that allowed her to communicate with Gaspar, and tried to activate it, but some part of that enchantment was not fully functional. Because of the power she was maintaining with Tree Stands in the Forest, she could not activate the enchantment and reach Gaspar.

The only way she would be able to do that would be if she could truly incapacitate these other fragments.

So Imogen focused. She strained. She could feel that energy, could feel it working its way out. The fragments tried to fight her, yet she knew she could find a way to overwhelm them. She had to. She drew on everything she had learned and then focused on the lessons Benji had given her, even calling out to him. Only one possibility opened up before her.

"No," she whispered.

"There is no other way, First," Benji said. His voice came through her mind, a distant whisper. "I'm sorry."

The only way.

But the only way meant destruction.

Imogen wasn't sure if it was possible to destroy magic, but what Benji had attempted to show her would certainly do that, regardless of whether she wanted to or not. Still, she had to think there was another option. She had done something similar before, so couldn't she pull these fragments to herself, like how she had held on to the fragments that were Master Liu?

But a single fragment was one thing. There were dozens, and cumulatively, these dozens of fragments were powerful. Perhaps more powerful than she was.

They were certainly strong enough that Imogen found it difficult to grip them tightly and avoid losing them. The only way she had managed to hold on to Master Liu before had been when she had pulled his fragment into herself, similar to how she had simply been gifted Benji's fragment. In this case, if she were to do that, those two would be at war within her.

"Can't you help?" she asked him.

Even as she did, Imogen could feel the fragments straining. The tree she'd made with her pattern created an invisible barrier, but despite that protection, it still was not enough. Imogen could see that, but more than that, she could feel it. As she maintained that connection, trying to hold it tightly inside of herself, she was aware that she would not be able to any longer.

"I'm sorry, First," Benji said.

And for the first time in quite a while, she had the sense of another presence there. It was Abigail the Lost, the other Porapeth she'd known who had gifted her the tiniest of fragments to better understand the Porapeth. She came to Imogen as if she wanted to alert Imogen of what she saw and how that might differ from what Benji did. Both of the Porapeth fragments inside her shared that same vision, though. Both of them told her that there was only one way.

She was going to lose control over it. The moment she did, those fragments would drift out into the world once more, possibly to infect something else again—that was the only way Imogen could think of it. Other creatures would be twisted and tainted by those fragments.

"Does it destroy the magic?" she asked.

Benji laughed in what was a bitter sound. "What have I told you about magic?"

"Magic does not die," Imogen said.

"It doesn't die. However, you can change form. All you need to do is release this, but it has to lose this form."

That, at least, made her feel somewhat better about what she had to do. If it was merely about trying to shift her form somewhat, to help modify this power, then was it so bad?

Imogen focused on what she was doing, on how she was calling on that power, and then felt for the distant connection to Zealar. He was there somewhere, and she had to let that sense come to her.

As he did, she heard his soft cry.

"Help me," Imogen said.

Zealar shrieked again, and Imogen knew that the renral would offer her the assistance she needed. As she focused on it and felt that power, she remained connected to it as much as she could so that she let the power flow.

She unleashed the renral energy, which crackled out of her. Hundreds of different strands of lightning began to streak away from her, reminding her of how that power flowed out of Zealar through his feathers, shooting along his wings and becoming something else entirely. She focused on that as long as she could, then began to feel something more. That power built, and then she tried one more of her sacred patterns.

Imogen was met with resistance. She couldn't push through it, regardless of how much she tried. She couldn't tell how much of that power was tied to her and how much of it lingered, allowing her the opportunity to draw on more of it. The only thing she knew was that there was a flash, a sizzle of what seemed to be silvery light mixed with a kaleidoscope of colors. Then even that faded. The burst of energy she had felt disappeared with it, leaving her with nothing.

Slowly, she started to release the Tree Stands in the Forest pattern, hating that she did, hating that she had destroyed those fragments—or felt as if she had. They were power, and knowing what she did about Benji and how she had used what she had of Master Liu, the idea that she had destroyed fragments that had once been some other entity left her unsettled, regardless of what Benji might tell her.

She continued to stand and hold on to her sacred pattern, wishing she could feel anything else around her, but there was nothing.

"There was no other way, First," Benji told her.

"I wish I believed that."

"And if there was? Do you think you would have absorbed those fragments?"

Imogen sighed. "I don't know."

"That is not the fight you want, and what you have done may be enough to save others."

Imogen wasn't sure she believed that, but at this point, she also wasn't sure if it mattered.

CHAPTER TWENTY-TWO

G avin crouched down near the remains of the tree. He couldn't see any part of it left, though there was still a flicker of memory, but even that was starting to fade. What he felt of the tree seemed to dissipate slowly, leaving him with little more than a fragment of a memory of what had been. Even that began to disappear.

"There was a bralinath tree here," Gavin said. He still burned with curiosity and worry as he looked up at Gaspar.

"Why would there have been a tree here?"

"I don't know. Perhaps the El'aras came through at one point and settled in this place, or maybe someone else who didn't survive."

"Not a tree," Imogen said, striding forward toward them.

Gavin glanced over to her. "How do you know?"

"It was another fragment. Different than I have felt

before, but it was definitely a fragment. That's what they are after. They're trying to collect power to the point where they will be unbeatable, and we are chasing them when we should be trying to find answers. Unfortunately, there are none." She peered around, a troubled expression on her face. "The trees are a connection to the El'aras power, aren't they?"

"They are a connection to the past," Gavin said. "I assumed it was a connection to their power."

She frowned as she continued staring, her eyes going distant. "What did you know?" she whispered, though it seemed to be mostly to herself. "How is this tied to what I cannot see?"

"Who are you talking to?" Gaspar asked.

Imogen took a deep breath, then let it out and looked over to Gavin. "There are times when I can still speak to the Porapeth. Well, I can speak to his fragment. Magic cannot die, after all. He is what guides me. It's not entirely dissimilar to how your El'aras guide you, at least in what they once had been."

"It is a little different," Gavin said. "They aren't a constant presence, and they don't really speak to me."

"Don't they? What do you experience when they provide you with knowledge?"

"Visions."

"Those visions are another way of speaking," Imogen said. "When I first encountered this Chauvan, he was working with a fragment of power, one of the last remaining Sul'toral. A powerful one at that. I had not fully understood it then, but the Sul'toral had still chased power even in its fragmented form."

"But you stopped him?" Gavin asked.

"It wasn't so much me as it was another fragment. They fought, and Master Liu succeeded. Fragments can be brought back together, and magic can't die. Though it can be corrupted." She closed her eyes for a moment. "Perhaps that is what they are doing, corrupting power. With enough different fragments, they could create an entire dark army, much like the Sul'toral had attempted, though not nearly as efficiently because I suspect they didn't understand the truth of the fragmented power." She sighed. "I wish I could see backward and not just forward."

"Maybe I can," Gavin said.

It was the same thing Tristan had said to him. *Find your past.*

Chauvan had claimed he was able to see something, that he was able to use that to gain power, but what could he have used from the past?

"Let's assume that he has found these other fragments, or places where the fragments could be found," Gavin said as he started pacing and looking down to ensure no metallic vines were slipping out of the ground. "If this is about fragmented power, then he wants the El'aras connection and the bralinath tree power. Could there have been others here?"

"I'm not convinced this is only about the bralinath trees," she said.

"But that's what he's been after," Gavin said, feeling

increasingly certain that was the connection. "Maybe he's trying to keep us—me—from learning about the past."

He glanced up at the sky. They were in a part of the forest that once should have been filled with shade from the bralinath trees. He could still feel the memory of the tree, even if he didn't see any sign of it. Whatever had been here would have been important enough that Chauvan felt the need to attack it.

"We have to find others," he said.

"Other what?" Gaspar asked.

"Other places like this. There have to be other places that have their own fragments that are tied to something I can connect to. Imogen can look forward, but I can look back. If we can find it, maybe I can use the connection I do have to look toward the past and understand what they're after."

"Assuming you do it faster than they can react," Gaspar said. "Also assuming they don't already have Porapeth magic like Imogen so they can look forward and back, unlike you."

"What kind of magic do they have?" Gavin asked her.

Imogen shook her head. "No, it's not that they have magic. It's that they *are* magic. That's why Benji was able to grant me the power that he was. He was able to gift me power from himself because he *is* magic. Or was." She shrugged. "When I traveled with Benji, he always talked about speaking to the wind, the trees, the grasses, and the world around him." She smiled slightly, and a glimmer of sadness flickered across her silver eyes. "There are answers, but they have eluded me."

They continued to walk around. Gavin closed his eyes, wondering if he might be able to find any sort of image, but there was nothing. He connected to the dragon, and they took off. Imogen guided them but then had them stop.

"I wonder if we are going about this wrong," she said. "I have thought that I needed to lead us based on what I can see, but perhaps we need to go based on what has been. Everything I try to see comes up blurry. I can see it fading from places they have been, but that just means we keep chasing them. I'd love to find a way to anticipate instead of reacting."

"Is any place brighter than others?" Gavin asked.

"Perhaps," she said. She spoke softly as she turned and looked all around her. "If I were to follow the brightness, maybe I could track a surge that will help me find where they anticipated going."

None of them said anything for a while as they flew.

After a while, the sun began to set. The dragon descended near a small stream, and they camped for the night. Gaspar was quiet, sitting near the dragon and twisting the enchantments that he wore as Gavin got a small fire started.

"Do you still want to spar?" Imogen said.

Gavin looked up. He'd been crouched near a pile of dried branches, careful not to pick anything living now that he had gained an understanding and appreciation for the bralinath trees, and smiled at her. "You want to test yourself or me?"

"Perhaps a bit of both."

Gavin snorted. "We didn't spar much before you left."

"Because I wasn't ready."

"I don't understand."

"I left my people, and my training, behind. I had forgotten what it was like when I used to push myself. When I wanted to try to test myself against those who were more potent than me."

"How do you think you would fare now?"

She smiled. "I have an advantage now that I didn't have before."

"Your patterns."

"That, though I doubt that advantage is going to offer me what it does against others as you have also seen and mastered many of those patterns." She frowned, and Gavin suspected it bothered her that he could learn her patterns as quickly as he had, but that was the gift that he had been given through the training he'd gone through to become the Chain Breaker.

"Then the Porapeth gift."

She nodded.

He had to admit that he was intrigued. He didn't know what it would be like to test himself against her, and wanted to see what they might uncover, but perhaps now wasn't the best time.

"How about we test ourselves when this is over?"

"Are you afraid, boy?" Gaspar asked.

Gavin took a deep breath. He didn't fear testing himself against Imogen, nor did he fear the possibility of losing to her—which he thought he actually might. "It's not that. It's.... more about a distraction."

Imogen nodded. "I would rather have your full focus anyway."

Gaspar grunted.

They spent the rest of the night in a quiet sort of contemplation, with Gaspar and Imogen talking quietly and Gavin given time to himself to think and rest. He found his thoughts turning to what he might have to do, and his lack of answers, and didn't care for it.

Morning came slowly.

They took flight again, the dragon moving steadily. After a while, the landscape shifted as they all stared off the side of the dragon.

"There's something down there," Gaspar said, pointing to the trees.

Gavin felt something as well. Maybe bralinath power? Or perhaps one of these fragments that Imogen kept talking about.

They were farther east than he had expected them to have gone. In the distance, he started to see the mountains rising, with snow covering some of the higher peaks. Below them was a forested land that appeared impossibly dense.

The dragon circled for a few more moments before it started to descend. Gavin looked over the side, unsure if there was going to be an easy place for it to land. Surprisingly, the dragon started modifying its size so that he could squeeze between the trees. As it did, Gavin stared at the trees all around him. He couldn't see much else, but he could feel something. Power, perhaps.

Once the dragon landed, Gavin felt a strangeness all

around him. He was drawn forward, and at first he thought it was only the energy of the bralinath trees calling him, but something else seemed to guide him as well. Buildings made of white stone and wrapped in vines stood ahead, with tall grasses growing among all of it. There was a sense of power, and there was something familiar to it as well. He wasn't entirely sure what was so familiar to him, but the entire place struck him as strangely recognizable.

He walked through the city.

"It's abandoned," Gaspar said.

Even though it was, Gavin still detected something around him. It was strange that he should be so acutely attuned to it, but it felt as if a memory here lingered within him.

He paused at the towering building made of white stone. The vines wrapped around it so densely that he wouldn't have even known that it was white stone if he had looked out from above. It would've blended into the forest, much like every other place here. All of these gleaming stone buildings would have been overgrown in such a way that they would be obscured.

"There are bralinath trees near here," Gavin said.

"Timo would've known about this place," Imogen said. "It's too close to the homeland. If the intention is to destroy the trees..."

Gavin made his way around the city. There were what looked to be broken bridges that had formed between some of the towers, leaving crumbled stone on the ground. Grasses had grown over much of it, which created a wild appearance. The entire place had a strange energy to it, one that he could feel, but he wasn't entirely sure what it meant. He continued to walk among all of it.

"The El'aras spoke of places they abandoned," Gavin said. "I remember Theren talking about leaving the mountains."

Imogen glanced around. "There are El'aras ruins here."

"Why?"

Imogen shook her head. "I don't know."

"No, that's not really my question. It's more about why this place is here, yet abandoned."

So many of the El'aras places had been deserted over the years. Here, Arashil, Yoran, other cities. At one point or another, there had been many other places, but they had all been abandoned over time, given up to the trees in the forest, leading to an opportunity for overgrowth.

But why? It wasn't as if the El'aras were without abilities.

Gavin stopped. They weren't without abilities. But it was more than just that.

He looked over to Gaspar. "How many El'aras would you say are in Yoran now?"

"I don't know. Maybe five hundred. Probably not much more than that."

"Think about what we've learned about them. There are scattered families, different tribes of El'aras that have been battling with one another."

Gavin didn't even fully understand it. When he had gone off with Anna to Arashil, he had done so with the intention that he would somehow come to terms with what it meant for him to be El'aras and what that power would mean for him as he learned about it. Gavin had not come to know his power as well as he needed, nor had he fully understood what it was like to be one of the El'aras. Anna had wanted him to feel as if he was part of the people, but he found that difficult. He may share a blood-line, and even share some of their power, but he was not truly El'aras, regardless of what she might think of him.

"Maybe this was one of the other families. We don't know where they scattered," Gaspar said.

He was right. There was Anna's faction, but there were others that had moved to various parts of the world. How many different families existed? Where could they all be found? He thought of Theren, who had talked about his family in the mountains, and the place of power he had seen by the volcano near Hester. Brandon and his family had lived in the plains. There were so many different factions, but Gavin hadn't really tried to understand it. Not with any true understanding of the El'aras, or what it meant for himself.

There was one way he might be able to find answers. When he had been in Arashil and the other abandoned El'aras city, he had known there was a possibility of answers, but the bralinath trees hadn't given him anything other than glimpses of his visions.

The only place he had any real vision was in that truly ancient island.

Gavin strode to the edge of the city and paused.

"Where are you going?" Gaspar asked.

Gavin looked around him at the remains of the build-ings before looking back toward Gaspar. "I need to understand. There are answers here. I just don't know what they are. And I intend to find out."

He strode forward, and he found a bralinath tree that seemed unharmed. He stood before it but didn't touch the trunk, mostly because he had at least learned that touching the trunk of a bralinath tree might be dangerous to it. He didn't need to touch it to connect to the tree. He could do so in a different way. As he focused on the power within the tree, he started to feel some greater energy there, and then pushed down.

Using the technique he had learned in the prison realm, he connected to the bralinath trees and linked them with his core reserves. He felt a bit of resistance now, but he pushed through it until he felt the energy of a bralinath tree. Not just any one but this specific tree.

"I need to know," Gavin said.

The tree seemed to respond.

A faint echoing reverberation built within him as if the tree was trying to show him something. Images formed around him. At first he saw the forest, no differently than he did now. He saw the city, which looked similar, with vines wrapping around many of the buildings, but the top of the city itself had been shaded and shielded from view. It took Gavin a long moment to piece together what this tree was trying to show him, but when he did, he realized there was a connection missing.

A tree was no longer here. Another bralinath, one that was ancient and older than many of the others, standing here before the rest.

He continued to call on the power within him,

connecting to the El'aras, feeling the bralinath tree guiding him and showing him what had been around here.

He needed to see more.

Additional flashes came. They were like painted portraits, little more than that, and Gavin thought he understood. To a tree, time was not quick. When he saw streaks of what looked to be people moving, he understood that was the way the tree experienced them. Not snippets or burst of images but delayed, drawn-out events. He saw the city active, filled with the life of El'aras, and though he couldn't see the people themselves in any detail, Gavin had a sense of the power that had been here and a sense of what had once existed in this place.

The vision started to fade. The city shifted, shrinking slowly and retreating until there was nothing. Then he caught a surge of brightness, a blazing light that flashed in his mind, and then it was gone until nothing remained.

Gavin lingered there for a long moment, trying to understand what it meant.

He stepped back, opening his eyes and turning back toward the remains of the city.

"The El'aras were here long ago," he said. "There was another of these trees, but I don't know what happened to it."

He headed toward where he had felt the tree in his image, focusing until he found a section in what had been the middle of the city. Towers stretched out and around, as if he could feel the memory they placed on this land. Something was missing here, though.

"There should be a bralinath tree here," Gavin said, spreading his hands to either side of him. "Much like there should've been one in the last place we visited, and the place before, and before, and…" He shook his head, fully aware of what he was feeling but not aware of why he was feeling it.

"So you're saying there was a tree here in the heart of the El'aras lands?" Imogen asked.

"As far as I can tell, there has been a tree, or trees, in all of the places where the El'aras have lived."

Fragments.

That was what they were, after all.

He was connected to the magic of the bralinath. Fragmented power.

If that was the case, what did that mean for him?

And what did Chauvan want with it?

CHAPTER TWENTY-THREE

The dragon circled, following the image Gavin had pushed through the connection they shared. As they traveled, he began to realize something. There was some part of him that was starting to lose the image that the other tree had given him, as if it was losing the memory of where the other bralinath trees could be found.

He sat up, and he looked over to the others.

The trees.

They were tied to the ancient El'aras power, though Gavin wasn't sure how. The elders had placed themselves into those trees, and what they had done could not be that dissimilar to what Benji had done for Imogen.

"How many Porapeth remain?" Gaspar asked.

"As far as I know, none," Imogen replied. "Abigail was the last one, and she was lost. It's possible there are others, though they remain obscured to me, which is not surprising, as I was obscured to both Benji and Abigail." She fell silent for a moment and then smiled. "My people used to revere the Porapeth. We feared magic, but not theirs."

"Do your people have anything like the bralinath trees?" Gavin said.

Imogen frowned. "Nothing quite like that, but we did have a sacred tree in the Heart of the Leier homeland. Its branches once pointed to each of the sacred temples."

"Once?"

"The tree was damaged. Either before my people left the Heart or shortly after."

"We should see the tree," Gavin said.

"My people are no longer there. All who remain have come with me."

"There may still be memories within it."

"Then I will show you," Imogen said.

The dragon reacted to Imogen's touch, following her commands as they flew to the east. They had to camp again, taking longer away than Gavin cared but increasingly felt like this was important. The night was spent under the stars and mostly in silence.

They soared over the mountains until they reached an enormous valley that seemed to be set inside five peaks. Each peak looked something like a jagged tooth, with the snow capping them lending more to that appearance. A massive plateau of rock rose in the middle of the valley, and the dragon descended toward it.

"This was my homeland. The Heart of the Leier lands," Imogen said. "This is where we fought Aneadaz, stopping him and the other Sul'toral, and saved my people. But then we left because we could not stay here any longer. We came to Yoran, thinking that we could find safety. That is all I want for my people."

Gavin jumped down from the dragon, and he found himself in the middle of what had been a city but now appeared to be abandoned. The buildings were all made out of a stone that looked to have been quarried in the mountains and dragged here. There was a solid practicality to everything. He looked over to Imogen as she made her way through the city, pausing at one particularly large building before moving on to another.

"And your sacred temple?" he asked.

"There," she said, motioning toward one of the peaks.

Gavin couldn't see anything, though snow covered the mountain now. He couldn't imagine anybody surviving up in the mountains like that, or on the land that was gray and barren like what was around them now.

He walked through the village, looking at buildings, studying the stone, and noting shops of all types—bakers, butchers, and blacksmiths, among others. Eventually, he came to an immense clearing that called to him. It seemed to tell him that was where he needed to go. That was the direction of where the answers would be found.

As Gavin approached the clearing, he slowed, feeling some energy here. He didn't know what it was, only that he could sense something. He paused as he looked around.

There was a flutter of energy, little more than that. A flicker of memories, but then nothing.

There had been power here. A tree, ancient and

powerful. Probably not a bralinath tree, as this was not a place of the El'aras, but it was a place of Porapeth power.

A fragment?

If so, it might provide him with information.

Gavin took a seat and closed his eyes, setting his hands down on either side of him. When he did, he started to focus, pushing power out from him. He wanted to try to understand. He had no idea if it would make any difference or if he would be able to detect anything, only that he felt like he could and should feel some power bubbling up within him. It seemed him that an answer was there, but he had to find the key to it.

He pushed the power downward.

As he did, the ground trembled.

It was as if there was something here that wanted to answer him, but as he tried to find it, he couldn't. Though it was perhaps not bralinath, there was a fragment of ancient power regardless. No answers existed in that connection, so he finally gave up. He got to his feet and found Imogen nearby, her eyes blazing silver.

"Do you see anything?" Gavin asked.

She took a deep breath and let it out slowly. "Nothing. I had not expected to, as I had not when I was here last."

"Tell me about the tree that was here."

She frowned at him. "Each branch was meant to point toward one of the sacred temples." She gestured to the mountain peaks. "They were places of power. Of comfort. They were distinctly for my people."

"Then what happened?"

"The tree has been gone for a long time, Gavin. The

Heart has been abandoned for a long time. I'm sorry I don't know more than that."

"I'm sorry you weren't able to stay in your Heart."

He looked around. It was peaceful here, but there was a strange emptiness as well.

"I think we should keep moving," he suggested. "Perhaps we can find some other places or other fragments that might provide more information."

Imogen held his gaze for a moment before nodding.

Gavin headed over to the paper dragon, and he climbed onto it. When the others joined him, they took to the air. They circled, and from above, Gavin saw the remains of the Leier homeland, as well as the mountains around him. He felt a strange stir of power, even though he wasn't sure what it was.

"Not much farther," Imogen said. "I can see a bit of energy starting to glow, and it's to the north."

The wind whipped past them as the dragon streaked toward the north and crossed over mountains, forest, and marshy swamp, taking the better part of another day.

"Are we heading in the right direction?" Gavin asked.

"I've been here before," Imogen said.

"You have?"

"It's called the Shadows of the Dead," she said. "You will find nothing here."

They kept flying. They passed a lake, another desert, and then another mountainside. Each place they stopped, there was no sign of fragments nor of bralinath trees. There was nothing. Just emptiness.

The dragon kept taking them northeast, past mountains that were not nearly as sharp as the ones where Imogen had grown up, and they were situated along the shore. It would be isolated and difficult to reach, though with Chauvan and Timo's abilities, perhaps they could simply fold themselves here. As they neared, the trees became denser, and Gavin felt a sense of power.

"I know this place," Imogen said. "I have seen it. Or Benji has. Maybe even Abigail."

As the dragon started to descend, a tree-sized branch streaked toward them. The dragon banked, and the branch shot over them.

A projectile?

"There are people here!" Gavin cried out.

It was the first time they had encountered others. Maybe that meant they could find information.

The dragon continued to fly lower, and they had to dodge another projectile as they circled toward the ground.

Power exploded and then struck the paper dragon.

CHAPTER TWENTY-FOUR

Gavin's core reserves connected to the paper dragon. The enchantment wasn't alive, but that didn't necessarily mean anything. It could still be damaged, no differently than any other creature. As the energy connected to him, Gavin was forced to push even more power out of himself, and he realized why. The dragon was fading.

"I can feel something," Gaspar called.

Gavin looked over at him and then down. As soon as he did, he realized what was happening. The power that was coming out of him and should have been flowing into the dragon was instead pouring into nothingness. The dragon had been struck with some magical energy, and it was starting to shrink. Anything he tried to do failed.

"I haven't encountered anything quite like that before," Gavin muttered.

"It didn't destroy the enchantment," Gaspar said.

They were still circling, and they managed to hold out long enough that they were able to keep their altitude, but how much longer would they be able to maintain that? He didn't want to lose the dragon, as they may need it if they had to escape. Gavin pushed on his connection to it, and it started to fold in on itself. He started to reach for another paper dragon as they began to fall, but he grabbed for something else instead.

They needed something smaller and more agile. The paper ravens.

The raven fluttered, grabbed Gaspar, and lifted him off the dragon.

"What are you—"

Gavin ignored him. He turned to another paper raven and tapped on it, and the enchantment unfolded. Power flowed out of him into the raven, and then he connected it to Imogen. She did not say anything as the raven grabbed her and carried her away.

There was only one left. If he used it, that meant he would be abandoning the paper dragon. He wasn't willing to do that, but it still continued to fold.

He thought about whether he could layer something onto the enchantment. Would he be able to heal it?

Not from here.

Gavin knew how to create enchantments, but he was better at layering additional power on top of existing ones.

A blast built nearby and streaked toward him. He focused on the paper raven he had remaining, and he pushed power into it. The creature unfolded, quickly grabbing him, yet Gavin held one hand on the paper dragon as it continued to shrink. The raven was straining to stay in the air, fighting against the resistance trying to pull on Gavin and the dragon.

He poured more power into it as it struggled, and finally, it held. The dragon folded down until he could slip it back into his pocket. Only then did he look around, though he had the raven's eyesight to help.

A city stood nestled into the shoreline, but Gavin couldn't make anything else out about it. He focused on that city, on the people he could see within it, when another burst came shooting toward them. He couldn't make anything out about it. It was power of some variety, but he didn't think it was sorcery because his skin didn't tighten the way it did with that presence. As it hurtled at him, the air suddenly thundered.

The raven folded its wings and dove. The suddenness cut Gavin off guard, and his breath was sucked free from his lungs. He clutched the raven until they landed on a rocky ledge overlooking the city. The two other ravens were perched nearby. He hurriedly tapped on each of them to fold them up and put them away. They wouldn't fly nearly as fast as the paper dragon, but they could use them to escape if it came down to it.

First, though, he needed answers.

Gaspar staggered toward him, looking as if he was trying to balance himself. "You could've warned me, boy."

"I didn't expect that," Gavin admitted. "The ravens are a little more mobile than the dragons."

"Mobile? I felt like I was food clutched in some animal's talons."

"Well, they *are* enchantments, so you never would've been food."

Gaspar grunted. "That doesn't make it any better."

Imogen regarded the remaining paper raven with interest. "The raven sees, doesn't it?"

"I can see through its eyes," Gavin said.

"But it also sees."

"Why do you say that?"

"Because it anticipated some of the attacks." She frowned, and her mouth was pinched in a tight line as if she was trying to come up with some answer only she could know. Silver flashed in the back of her eyes, and then it faded again. "I can't tell what it is, only that the raven must be aware of something."

Gavin gave a slight shrug. "Perhaps. The enchanter who made these is uniquely gifted. I never really know what she's capable of, only that she has incredible power."

"'Incredible' would be one way to put it," Imogen said. She tapped the raven on the top of the head. The creature folded as though she was the one controlling its activation. She picked it up off the ground and handed it to Gavin.

He shook his head. "I think you get to keep that one."

"Why?"

"You connected to it."

Imogen stood in her tree pattern and seemed to link herself to the raven. "Perhaps I did." She looked up. "This place seems like it has been hidden from the world for generations. Can you imagine attempting to come by ground?"

"I suspect it would be impossible," Gavin said. The way the land sloped toward the water was incredibly steep. Other than coming by air or ship, there would be no other way to reach this place.

"Why do you think they anticipated an air attack?" Gaspar asked.

"I think the better question is why they would need a bolt of that size," Gavin replied.

"Not just that size of bolt. Why would they need magic? You said you felt something, didn't you?"

"I did, which means that we might get some answers here."

"Or maybe we are simply chasing ghosts," Gaspar said.

"We're talking about trying to understand the past. Everything we have done has been like chasing a ghost. We just need to catch one."

They started down the slope, moving quickly and quietly, and Gavin could tell that Gaspar remained enchanted. Gavin drew on his core reserves to help him, and Imogen... She didn't seem to have any difficulty.

"Would your brother have been able to come here?" Gavin asked.

Imogen frowned. "It's possible. He is more skilled than I give him credit for. They have other ways of traveling. I'm not sure how they learned to transport themselves by vanishing, but they have."

"Folding," Gavin said. "I wish I understood it. It would

be useful." He patted his pocket. "Though I like our enchantments, as well."

After this was over, he would have to try to understand how people like Timo and Chauvan traveled. There had to be a secret he could learn.

They reached the outskirts of the jungle, and he looked down upon a city. The buildings were located away from the growth, providing a slight barrier and giving them a little buffer from the trees. Stone sculptures were set in regular intervals around them, with a wall between them. The sculptures looked like dragons, though they were made out of black stone. Situated in each dragon's mouth were massive branches.

Gavin shook his head. "Think that's the ballista they used on us?" They were far larger than anything he'd ever seen before.

"Look how many they have," Gaspar said. "What do you think they have to deal with that makes these necessary?"

Gavin stared at the figures that were carved into the stone and smiled to himself. "What if it's a dragon?"

Gaspar glowered at him. "Don't be ridiculous."

"I'm not being ridiculous. I'm just saying that they might have seen a dragon."

"Dragons aren't real, Gavin."

"No?"

He pulled out the paper dragon and held it in the palm of his hand. Even in its folded shape, the distinct lines that it would take on when it unfolded were visible. He could feel the damage within it. Whatever magic they used here, whatever power they possessed, would be enough to influence it, and Gavin wondered if he might even be able to overwhelm it. He had no idea if he would have enough power to disrupt what was here or whether he would find that they didn't have enough strength to do so.

But he was curious.

He crept along the wall and studied the ballistae. Each one had to use an entire tree trunk, it seemed. They were sharpened at the end, and he had a sense of power from them, something that he suspected was tied to magic within them.

Dragons.

"You said you saw something about this place," Gavin said, looking over to Imogen. "What is it?"

"I just see the growing brightness and..." She frowned and furrowed her brow. "And I suspect Timo. When I look in a particular direction, I feel like there is a glimpse of him, but nothing that lingers as it should. I've been struggling with that. I feel like I should be able to find him since I am connected to him." She was quiet for a moment. "With this place, I can only see isolation. I don't think they have ever met outsiders."

Despite that, the place looked incredibly civilized. In addition to the wall with ballistae around it, there were buildings made out of a pale wood, some of them stretching several stories high and woven together. Many of them had greenery worked into the roofs, and bridges linked them. There was something about it that reminded him of the fallen El'aras city he had seen.

"Where are the people?" he asked.

"No people here," Gaspar said.

"This place isn't abandoned. They targeted us. We just can't see them."

They crept forward along the wall, and then a wisp of smoke appeared.

Gavin froze. He had seen smoke like that before. Could it be the Ashara? He wouldn't be able to take on any of them if so. Not that he would need to. If Eva or Asaran were here, maybe they wouldn't need to fight them. Maybe they could get help. If these were the Ashara lands...

But did they have lands?

Not for the first time, Gavin wished he had some way of reaching Jayna.

They continued following the wall all the way until it dropped off into a cliff that led down to the sea. Water crashed against the rocks far below.

"We are going to need to get over that wall," Gavin said, "and we have to do it before Timo or Chauvan show up, if they are going to. We'll also have to do it without drawing any attention from the locals."

"Then we wait until dark," Gaspar said.

Imogen nodded. "We wait."

They settled back against the trees to pass the time. As they sat, Gavin watched the sky start to shift. There were a few birds, all larger than any he had seen in his travels, and many of them quite colorful. He caught sight of deep blues and streaks of red and yellow. Others looked as if they were dipped in sunlight. Each of them floated above the jungle for a moment before diving back down. The ballistae didn't move for any of them.

They hadn't reacted to anything since their arrival.

"Do you think it's strange that we haven't seen anybody who was responsible for firing a ballista?" Gavin asked.

"Maybe they're accustomed to seeing attacks like that?"

Gavin leaned against the tree and stared toward the city. He didn't detect any sort of bralinath energy other than what he was distantly connected to. They waited for a while until darkness finally fell.

"What's the play here?" he asked Gaspar.

Gaspar looked at the wall. "Well, seeing as how we don't have any scouts, I think we sneak over, assess what we might find there, and then make a decision."

Gavin let out a laugh. "I thought you might have come up with a better plan. This one is a little… soft."

"Soft or not, it's all we have," Gaspar said.

They headed toward the wall, picking a section near a ballista but also close enough to the forest that they could sneak forward and not be observed. They slipped as quickly as Gavin thought was safe to do without making any noise. When he reached the ballista, he pressed his hand against it and felt heat coming off it. Some magic had flown toward them when the ballista had been fired. Maybe it was connected.

The wall would be easy to jump over. The others could clear it as well, but only with some help.

"How about your enchantments?" he asked, looking over to Gaspar and Imogen. "Are they still intact?"

Gaspar twisted his bracelet and nodded. "Still seems to be," he said.

Imogen reached into her pocket and pulled out a ring, then put it on her middle finger. "I won't need it once we clear the wall."

Gavin jumped.

It was a simple matter of calling on his core reserves, which filled him with power. This allowed him to clear the wall in a single jump. As soon as he reached the top, he flattened himself against it and motioned for the others behind him to wait. He didn't need all of them to risk themselves until he knew what they were going to get into.

People walked in the streets. They looked like they could be from Yoran, other than their clothing, which consisted of long, flowing gowns and robes and odd wide-brimmed hats. Many of them carried lanterns that glowed brightly as they wove through the streets. A crowd milled near the center of the city, but nobody was near enough to the wall that Gavin worried about getting caught. He slipped down the side of the wall and pushed his back against it. As he glanced to either side of him to see if the ballistae were manned, he spotted a man sitting in a chair, looking straight ahead, and scanning the skies.

Gavin focused on his core reserves and pushed power out just as he noticed a serpent figure on the man's black jacket. They did know dragons. Either that, or they just believed in their power. When Gaspar and Imogen landed next to him, he pointed to the men sitting by the ballistae, aiming them up toward the sky.

Gaspar tapped on his enchantment, and he lowered his voice to little more than a whisper. "What's the play?"

"If there's a tree, it's going to be here in the heart of the city," Gavin murmured.

He waited until the street in front of him was clear before he darted forward, Gaspar and Imogen staying with him. They reached another intersection, and Gavin paused again. The buildings were all made of strange circular branches that were woven together and stretched high into the sky. They shaded the street enough that he understood the need for a lantern. He was thankful for his enchantments that allowed him to see more easily.

He focused for a moment, calling on the core reserves deep within him and trying to see if he could tap into that El'aras ability that would allow him to feel for some other power.

Shadows moved toward them, and Gavin hurriedly grabbed Gaspar and shoved him down a side street. He waited to make sure that no one followed them.

"This is going to be a lot harder than it needs to be if everybody is carrying a lantern," Gavin muttered.

"Unless you have some way of concealing us," Gaspar said.

Gavin wished he had better control over his enchantments, but he had not learned how to do that quite yet. When the people moved past, they stepped back into the street.

"There's another possibility," Gaspar said, pointing to a building across from them.

It was a store. At least some part of it looked similar to those in other cities he'd been to, though unique enough that it felt foreign to him. There was a window, though it wasn't made of glass. Rather, woven strands of leaves allowed enough light to pass through them that Gavin could see what they had on the other side.

Clothing.

"Are you kidding me?" Gavin asked.

Gaspar grunted. "Do you have a better idea?"

"Unfortunately, no."

They scurried across the street, and Gavin let Gaspar take the lead. The old thief slipped his blade into the doorframe, and he popped the door open. He hesitated for a moment before stepping inside.

The second he did, light blazed in. Gaspar stepped back out, and the light faded.

"Some sort of enchantment in there," Gaspar grumbled.

"Let me try something," Gavin said.

He pulled one of the paper ravens out of his pocket, and he focused a trickle of power into it, just enough to elongate it. He then focused on what he wanted.

"I don't know if this is going to work, but it's worth a shot."

Gavin pushed the door open and sent the raven inside. As he remained connected to it, looking through the raven's eyes, he could see racks of clothing. Some looked like they might be a reasonable fit for Gaspar. Gavin sent a request to the raven to grab some. It obeyed and carried a jacket to the door. He pulled the door open, grabbed the jacket, and sent the raven back inside for his and Imogen's clothing.

When it returned, he ran his thumb along the jacket the raven had brought him. It had a dragon crest on it, which he thought was amusing, and he slipped it on over his clothing.

"It's not going to be perfect unless we get pants, but I don't have any interest in trying to go through that much hassle to find something that fits us," Gavin said.

Imogen pointed to the street. "Hats."

Gavin followed her finger. She was motioning toward people who not only carried lanterns but also had circular hats perched atop their heads.

"It's too humid to wear those," she said. "Why do you think they need a hat out here?"

"It depends on what they are worried about seeing them from above," Gavin suggested.

The raven grabbed three hats, flying them out one at a time, and then they slipped them on. The hat weighed almost nothing and was far lighter than Gavin would've expected. It looked to be woven out of a dense, fibrous leaf, and he wondered what tree it came from.

"Now we get lanterns," Gaspar said.

"Or we just get moving." Gavin gave a small shrug. "If somebody stops us, we take their lantern and leave them."

Gaspar snorted. "This is why we don't pull jobs together anymore. You would rather just fight your way through everything."

"If that's the case, I wouldn't have stopped to get clothes and hats."

As they strode forward, Gavin tried to mimic the people they passed. The first group who carried lanterns ignored them, but the second did not. One of the men with them held his lantern up, shining the bright light in Gavin's face.

Gavin darted at him, chopping his hand at his neck. He spun and kicked the second person with them, then drove his open fist down on the third. They all collapsed before anyone had a chance to cry out.

He grabbed the lantern and handed it to Gaspar.

"At least you didn't kill them," Gaspar muttered.

"I don't need to kill them." Gavin frowned as he studied the men. "But we do need to tie them up until we're gone. We need to figure out someplace to leave them that won't draw attention."

He glanced around. The city was strange compared to others he had visited. There were no obvious alleys, just intersecting streets. The one building they had broken into had some sort of enchantment inside of it that had illuminated the interior the moment Gaspar stepped inside. They wouldn't be able to use those buildings without drawing attention.

Either way, they needed to tie the men up and leave them somewhere.

Gavin tore strips of fabric off the first man's clothes and used them to bind his wrists and ankles, while Gaspar made quick work of the others. Imogen kept guard.

Gavin looked over to Gaspar when they finished with

the bindings. "Where do you think we should leave them? The last building wasn't going to work."

"Maybe not all of them are like that," Gaspar said. "Let's get going, boy."

He dragged one of the men first, then glanced behind him while waiting for Gavin to follow. They pulled the men through the streets until they reached another doorway. Gaspar picked the lock and pushed the door open. He tentatively stepped inside, and there was no shifting of light.

Gaspar looked back at him with a grin. "See?"

Gavin snorted. "Fine. You were right this time."

He helped lay the people inside, and they stepped back into the street.

"Now it's time to find that tree," Gavin said.

As they walked, he held the lantern, keeping it tilted forward to make them look less suspicious and mask their faces, and no one turned toward them, thankfully.

Gavin felt the draw of power up ahead.

The tree. He was certain of it.

They made their way through the street, and as they neared a large plaza, a shout rang out behind them. Gavin and Gaspar shared a look, but it was Imogen who spoke.

"It seems your captives have awoken."

CHAPTER TWENTY-FIVE

IMOGEN

"What do you think Gavin is doing?" Gaspar asked. He had a pair of his signature long-bladed daggers in hand, and he twirled them the way he often did while also sliding the enchantments he wore farther up his wrist. It reminded Imogen of the first time she had traveled with him and how he had carried plenty of enchantments on him, mostly so he could face whatever they might find outside of Yoran without danger or repercussions.

"I don't know what he's doing, but he's following what he feels, and now I must follow what I feel," she said, sliding toward the edge of the city.

There was something odd here. It had drawn Timo and Chauvan for a reason, but Imogen was not sure what that reason was. She had to find it.

"Now I have to figure out what you're doing," Gaspar

said. "Why are the two of you making this more difficult than it needs to be?"

"I'm not trying to make it difficult," Imogen said. "I'm trying to identify whether there is anything here that we might be able to use."

"Use?"

"Well, perhaps it's not so much what *we* can use as it is what *they* might try to use," she said. She paused and focused on her sacred patterns, while she knew that Zealar circled high overhead, even though she could not see him. He offered his connection to her, as well as the power she might be able to draw from the renral. "Timo and Chauvan are here for a reason. We have to find out what that is and learn if there's anything we can do to stop it."

She could feel that energy around her. All of it continued to build, making it difficult for her to follow. Some of it came from what Gavin was doing, though Imogen wasn't even sure what that was at this point, only that he was getting ready to fight, as he so often was. She needed to find a different purpose, though.

"My brother's after something out here," she said, though she said it mostly to herself. It was nice traveling with Gaspar, but he didn't know the danger that Timo had posed over the last year. Not the way Imogen or those she'd been traveling with did. Very few outside of the Leier could appreciate all that they had encountered.

"I can see it's bothering you," Gaspar said.

"It's not just that it's bothering me," Imogen said. "I need to be the one to stop him."

"There's always going to be somebody after power. It doesn't matter that it's your brother."

Imogen looked over. "It matters to me."

She expected him to argue, but he didn't. Instead, he nodded and then looked back toward the city. "I don't know that we can stay here for much longer. There aren't places like this around Yoran."

"That's just it," she said. She closed her eyes, and she thought about what she had seen while traveling with Gavin. "There are other places like this, only not other places they have been. It's strange. I'm not sure, at least not entirely, what they are after."

"You think it's this fragmented power."

"That's what Timo has been chasing alone. It's the same thing the Sul'toral were after, in their own way. Others as well. That is what I think we need to be able to neutralize, if there is some way to."

And there was a way, Imogen knew. She had done it. It was just that if she did so to Timo... It would destroy him. She had little doubt that if she used what she had been shown, the power that she suspected she might need, it would destroy Timo and all that he was.

That was her hesitation.

Distantly, she once again felt the faint connection that came from Benji.

He was laughing at her.

Imogen knew it was ridiculous for her to think that she had to protect her brother at this point, but she wasn't sure she could consider it in any other way. She had always thought that she could protect her brother, even

306 | D.K. HOLMBERG

when he had proven that he did not want it, and even when she wasn't sure that he cared. She was his big sister, after all.

She turned, and the ground rippled. As soon as it did, she knew she had been targeted. Did Timo know she was over here?

Gaspar turned in place while holding his knives, but those would do nothing against the rippling landscape in front of them. The power she fought against was considerable here. It seemed to flow underneath the ground and stretch outward, as if it was alive.

Magic, Imogen could tell, but the source of it was beyond her—at least she thought it was. But as she turned and focused on what she felt, Imogen increasingly became aware of more of that power, and she became aware of how that was working around her. There had to be some way for her to find access to it.

She pushed down with Tree Stands in the Forest and mixed it with the renral pattern, drawing energy through her so that it crackled in the air. Gaspar jumped and turned to her, but when he saw her, he nodded, almost as though he understood what it was that she was doing.

She poured power out of herself, down into the ground, toward that crackling sense of magic she was detecting, letting more and more of it flow outward. As she did, she could feel that energy taking shape.

But more than that, she felt something else while she pushed.

That power was there. It flowed, and it reminded her of...

Of a tree.

It was similar to the Tree Stands in the Forest pattern, only this seemed to be a magical energy.

As she focused, something rippled close to her, and Imogen was tossed backward. She focused and leapt back onto her feet, but Gaspar cried out.

Imogen hurried toward him and stood over him while holding on to Tree Stands in the Forest, then let that power explode out of her so she could form a barrier that rippled around him.

She felt Timo somewhere nearby.

"He's here," she told Gaspar. "And he's close."

"What do you think he's doing?"

"I thought I knew."

"Is it about this tree Gavin is after?"

Imogen had thought so. It wasn't one of the bralinath trees, though Gavin had seemed to believe it was, but with what she felt beneath the ground and the way those flows roiled beneath them, she couldn't help but question if perhaps there was something more here. All she had to do was try to find some way to grasp it so she could understand the source of power. Yet Imogen wasn't sure if there was going to be any way she could do that. She struggled with it, straining to try to make sense of it, but even as she attempted to, she found that it was more complicated than what she could comprehend.

But that wasn't entirely true. There was something to it that she recognized—fragmented power.

Hundreds upon hundreds, possibly thousands, of pieces of fragmented power.

Everything within Imogen went cold.

She had never experienced anything quite like that before. As she focused on what she felt, and as she recognized that energy, she could not help but wonder if that fragmented power might be accessible—and that might be the very reason this was here, the very reason Timo and Chauvan were too. They might be after it.

"This has to be what they are after," she said, though she was mostly talking to herself. She didn't expect Gaspar to have anything to do with what she felt, nor did she expect him to even understand.

She looked off into the distance, toward where she knew Gavin was. He had learned about that same power, and if he was right, that was what she had to understand, if only so she could prevent her brother and Chauvan from succeeding.

"What power is it?" Gaspar asked.

"Fragments," Imogen said. "That fragmented power is all throughout here."

There was only one way she could stop Timo from accomplishing what he was trying to do. She had to disrupt this fragmented power, but she wasn't sure she would be able to do it.

"I might need you to keep an eye out for me. Alert me if they come," she told Gaspar.

"They?"

Imogen nodded, and she focused on Tree Stands in the Forest, pushing downward as much as she could rather than branching up. There would be no real protections for her, but at this point, the only thing she needed was to grasp the power she knew existed beneath her in the ground and to try to find a way to shield those fragments.

But even as she tried, she felt something shatter.

She had never felt anything close to that before, but she realized that either Timo or Chauvan was impacting these fragments and turning them into something else— even more fragmented energy.

If they succeeded...

Imogen had no idea what would happen, only that she had felt that power in other creatures. She worried that if she wasn't able to intervene, they could take those fragments and turn them into dark creatures that could then be used in their attack.

They were doing all of this to gain power. Timo wanted the power of the Sul'toral. And Chauvan...

Imogen thought that he wanted the power of the El'aras, which he believed was his birthright and what had been promised to him as Champion.

She may not be able to stop that. That would have to be Gavin's responsibility.

Timo was hers.

She focused on Zealar. The connection she shared with him was strong, but as she drew upon the renral energy and sent it through Tree Stands in the Forest, pouring it out through what she felt deep beneath her, she began to recognize that there were limits to how much power she could push out. She did not have an unlimited store of energy coming from the renral, and because of that, he might not be able to do anything. She pushed and strained with her sacred pattern, trying to stretch it as much as she could, but even as she did, she knew there were constraints.

"Don't overextend yourself, First," Benji said.

"I have to do this, or they will—"

"Or you will end up a fragment."

She stopped pushing.

Benji was right. She could see it.

As she withdrew, the power exploded and fragmented around her, sending it outward. Somehow, she felt it become captured. Imogen still didn't know what they did to hold that power, only that they had some means of doing so.

Then it was gone.

She stood in place, the waves of energy around her leaving her uncertain.

That power was gone. The fragments were gone. And, she suspected, Timo and Chauvan were gone.

She looked over to Gaspar. "We have to hurry. Their endgame is near."

CHAPTER TWENTY-SIX

The crowd in front of him surged and started to turn.

There was a sense of pressure on Gavin from someplace up ahead.

Power. He was certain of it.

If he could find some ancient connection, maybe they could get the answers they needed. Once they did, he had to hope that they'd be able to learn what Timo and Chauvan were after. He stayed to the side of the road, keeping the lantern held the way that others did while he tried to blend into the crowd.

When he reached the center of the square, shadows seemed to drift around him, and a part of the ground shimmered in a way Gavin had seen before.

Metallic vines.

That was what had set the people of the city off.

Gavin strode forward. "I know you're there, Chauvan."

He unsheathed his sword, and he started to twist in place, focusing on the power within the blade, within himself, and even within the sense of nihilar. All of that was inside him. When he reached for that power, he could use it.

A laugh echoed from the darkness. "I didn't expect you to find me quite as easily as this. But you are too late." Chauvan stepped forward, and he looked like little more than a shadow cast against the night. "Are you still following the commands of your master? You run off, scurrying after everything he tells you to, chasing down dangers without questioning why or what purpose he had for you."

"It's the same purpose he had for you," Gavin said. "Only, you failed."

The taunt seemed to work. The vines surged and swirled toward him.

Gavin realized that they had taken on a different shape. They didn't look like the same vines that had wrapped around much of the forest. These were thick and cylindrical, and they reminded him of the type of reeds that were used to form the buildings here.

It was as if Chauvan was using some part of this place to command the vines.

Gavin focused on the nihilar. When he did, he spun, swinging his blade around and connecting with the vines. Each one he connected to shattered and, thankfully, didn't come back together. He carved through them, keeping a tight circle as he stepped toward Chauvan.

He was reminded of how Chauvan had sent the vines

away from himself when they had stood in the forest apart from each other, using them to create a barricade around him and defend against Gavin.

Gavin wasn't about to give him the opportunity to do the same thing once more.

He used the power of the nihilar, but something shifted.

Chauvan chuckled. "Such a mistake."

"You're the one who made a mistake in coming here," Gavin said. "My friends and I—"

He didn't get the opportunity to finish as he was struck from behind. He rolled, then jumped to his feet, switching over to his El'aras power and the distant connection he still had to the bralinath trees.

Chauvan wasn't alone. There was another person with him.

Gavin spun his blade and immediately began to use the Leier patterns, focusing on the way Imogen had taught him to twist and turn and find his way through that power.

At first, there was nothing else here other than the shadows, but markings along Timo's arms caught Gavin's attention as they glimmered against the darkness.

Just like the vines.

Gavin frowned at him. "What did you do?"

Timo sneered. "The Chain Breaker. Oh so powerful."

"What did you do?"

Timo started to move his hands, and Gavin recognized the sorcery building within him. Gavin flew forward

314 | D.K. HOLMBERG

using his Leier technique, but Timo shifted and drove a fist toward him, slamming him backward.

Timo gave a low chuckle. "Did you think you could use the sacred patterns against me?"

Gavin bounced back to his feet. "I thought I could. I see now that was a mistake."

Vines immediately began to work around him, entangling his legs. He drew on the nihilar and chopped through them. When he was done, he spun back to Timo. He didn't know where Chauvan had gone, but he had to be around here somewhere.

Timo took a step toward him, and there was a tight smile on his face. "It was the first mistake of many."

"Why are you doing this to your sister?"

"Because she fails to see."

"I think she sees far more than you realize."

"She only sees what *he* wanted her to see. She has been misguided, and now we will change all of that."

The ground erupted around Gavin. Vines stretched up, reaching for him. He attempted to carve through them, but they were too dense. The nihilar power did not work.

He focused on different Leier patterns, using those to slice through the vines while sharpening his blade with his El'aras power. As he cut through them, he cleared a space until he saw Timo off to one side and could practically feel Chauvan near him.

Gavin activated the communication enchantment. "If you can hear me, Gaspar, I need Imogen."

"We are working our way toward you, but Imogen found more of that fragmented power. It seems like the people here stored it. It's strange, like a vast collection. Something oddly overwhelming."

"It's all fragmented power?" Gavin asked.

"Unfortunately."

Which meant that this was how they would gather even more power.

Vines suddenly stretched from the ground, tall and thick.

"Have you been seeing what's happening?" Chauvan asked, striding toward Gavin and Timo as the vines circled Gavin again.

"I haven't seen anything other than you trying to destroy these trees."

"Have I destroyed them?" He chuckled and stepped closer. "Perhaps some, back when I had that ability."

Gavin drew more power through him and tried to focus so he could be ready for whatever Chauvan might do. He eyed Timo, who hadn't moved. He stood with his head tilted to the side as he looked off into the distance.

"Your sister is coming," Gavin said. "She's more powerful than you can manage."

"Do you think I don't know what she has become?" Timo asked.

"And what have *you* become?"

"You will never understand."

Gavin sprinted toward him, sweeping his blade in a series of movements to try to disrupt Timo and whatever power he was calling on, but Timo simply spread his hands again. It was only a simple movement, which created a barricade that prevented Gavin from getting to him.

It was more than sorcery.

"Not much longer," Chauvan said, and Gavin attempted to strike him.

He realized Chauvan hadn't been talking to him. He had been talking to Timo.

Timo stood with his hands on either side of him and pulled at the air. He was more powerful than when Gavin had seen him the last time, filled with the same sort of magic as any of the Sul'toral he had ever encountered. But the kind of power he had was different. Corrupted. Dark.

Gavin had to get to them. The only way he could do so was the nihilar.

Each time he attacked, it seemed as if Chauvan's smirk grew bigger.

The nihilar power carved through vine after vine, cutting through them but getting him no closer to Chauvan. It was almost as if each one Gavin cut down was replaced by another. Every time it did, Gavin wasn't able to get any closer to him. He tried to dart at Timo, but the strange magical barrier he possessed blocked Gavin from doing even that. Everything prevented him from getting close enough.

He was trapped between the two of them. He could slice through the vines around him, but he couldn't get to either man. All while he was forced to continue drawing on the nihilar.

"Soon," Timo said.

This time, Gavin could feel something from him. Why, though? What was Timo trying to do, and how was he trying to do it?

The vines circled Gavin again, but he wasn't about to let them destroy the tree.

He focused on his El'aras abilities and then pushed that power out through his blade. He knew when he did that it would be drawing on more than just his El'aras magic. It would be calling on the energy of nihilar, power that was trapped in a way that would guide him. There would be nothing more that he could do other than to try to hold on to the power, use that against the vines, and stop what they were doing.

Gavin poured that power out of him. When he did, he carved through the vines. They shuddered, and then there came a surge of brightness. It faded until there was nothing.

Timo watched him as he staggered forward, and then he waved his hands again. In that moment, he folded.

As he disappeared, a smile lingered on his face.

Gavin spun back around, facing Chauvan. He hadn't folded away, and it seemed as if he wanted to talk to Gavin—and probably taunt him. What he needed was to understand that folding technique so he could replicate it.

"You still don't understand it, do you?" Chauvan asked.

"What did you do?" Gavin said.

Chauvan chuckled. "It's not what I did. It's what *you* did, Champion," he said, sneering at him. "You who stole my inheritance. You who stole what I was to be. You did this."

318 | D.K. HOLMBERG

"What did you do?" Gavin asked again.

But Chauvan only continued to laugh at him. There was darkness in his voice, pain that left Gavin trembling, and a sense of irritation. Chauvan was mocking him. Finally, he looked over to Gavin and then behind him. "You can tell her that she is too late."

"Tell her yourself. You're not going anywhere."

Chauvan spread his hands and then brought them together. He folded himself in a way that vaguely reminded Gavin of how Alana folded the paper enchantments. Then he disappeared.

"We have to go," Gaspar said, running up to him.

"What happened?"

"We failed," Imogen explained.

Gavin couldn't shake what Chauvan had said. He had stolen his birthright. It was tied to the prophecy of the Champion?

But what was all of this?

"They wanted the fragments of power that were here, and they have succeeded," Imogen said. "With as many fragments as remain here, they will be able to corrupt and turn as many creatures as they want into dark ones."

Could this be similar to the nihilar? A corrupted, strange power.

Gavin had felt bad about the nihilar when he had first connected to it, but he had not known what it was at the time. It had just been an unusual storage of power.

What if what he connected to had been similar to what this city had collected? And worse, what if the nihilar could be replicated?

Maybe that was what Timo and Chauvan were after. Gavin had felt the overwhelming power of the nihilar when he had started to use it, and he knew the danger of it, but he didn't understand the power itself. He hadn't even been trying, which was a mistake.

If they succeeded, where would they go next? Gavin pulled the paper dragon from his pocket and set it on the ground.

Imogen didn't look over. "We have only a few moments before they converge, and I don't see any way of escaping."

Gavin focused on the paper dragon. He had to push power into it.

A flicker.

It came from the bralinath tree that was here, or the remains of it. There was something familiar to him. Gavin wasn't entirely sure why that would be the case, especially as he didn't know the kind of magic that existed in this place, but he could use that.

He concentrated on it, and he pressed downward the same way he did every time he called on the power of the bralinath trees. Then he focused that power into the enchantment, and the dragon began to unfold. The creature filled with power, though there was something distinctly different about it than before.

It seemed to have more blunted edges that were not quite as sharp as it had been, as if it was no longer just made of paper. As the dragon unfolded, it turned toward him. Gavin touched it on the side and felt something different within it, but he wasn't sure what that was, either.

"What did you do it?" Gaspar asked.

"I have no idea," Gavin said.

Imogen jumped onto the dragon and looked down at them. "Come along. We must move before they reach us."

Gavin scrambled onto the creature's back, and even that felt different. The texture was off. Whereas before it felt like rough paper, now it seemed like something else. It reminded him of sandpaper but not quite. Scales? There was heat within it as well. The dragon waited while Gaspar climbed onto it and then took to the air, sweeping massive wings.

Gavin attempted to connect to it as he had before, but resistance pushed against him. The dragon shot out toward the water, not toward the jungle where he was trying to steer it.

"I think the dragon has a mind of its own this time," he said.

What kind of magic allowed that to happen? Was it something these people had connection to, or was it something he had done?

Blazing lights burned beneath them as if the entire city had ignited enchantments.

As much as Gavin wanted to go back to try to see what they were doing and how they were doing it, he didn't dare. Instead, he turned, clutched the dragon, and hoped there was still time to stop Chauvan and Timo from whatever they intended.

CHAPTER TWENTY-SEVEN

They circled out over the water, before banking and circling tighter.

"Can you see anything?" Gavin asked.

"Lines converging," Imogen said. She closed her eyes. "All of them around a bright light."

"For a while, I thought they were coming for me, but maybe that's not it."

"Perhaps not."

"They want power, but they want the right kind," Gavin said, feeling the bizarre, dangerous energy of the nihilar within him and wondering if that was the key to all of this. "I thought they wanted to steal the bralinath power, but maybe that's not it at all. Maybe they want the nihilar because it's easier to fragment and control." He looked over at Imogen. "If that's what they are after, can I destroy it?"

Imogen regarded him, her eyes going silver for a moment. "I can't see it."

"You can't see it in the future, but maybe there is a way of seeing it in the past."

She frowned but then nodded. "I suppose that is possible."

"I have an idea," he said. He leaned forward and tapped the dragon. "You know where to go."

The dragon roared, surprising Gavin.

"What just happened?" Gaspar asked.

Gavin laughed. He touched the dragon's side, and he couldn't help but feel as if perhaps there was something more here that he had not realized before. Maybe he *had* somehow changed the dragon.

"We have to get word to Eva and Jayna and any others who might be able to help with this," Gavin said.

"Do you think they already know?" Gaspar asked.

Gavin looked at Imogen, who continued to frown.

"I don't know. I cannot see. Those two were much like you, and I suppose like me now. They have gained too much power, which makes everything a bit of a blur."

They streaked forward, and Gavin worried that they weren't going to get there in time. He pressed some of his own power, even that of the bralinath trees, into the dragon to help speed them along. They couldn't take the days to return that it had taken them to reach this place. Thankfully, it worked.

But at what cost?

It was dark at this late hour, and he was tired after fighting and sneaking through the city the way he had.

There was a part of him that worried that they weren't going to be there fast enough, and even if they were, he didn't know if they could do much of anything.

They soon crossed over into familiar lands. Forest and trees passed below, and Gavin could feel something he had recognized before. An idea came to him, and he tapped on the dragon. He tried to connect to it, and though the dragon resisted him, it wasn't so much that he couldn't send some of his intention to it.

As the dragon descended toward the ground, he heard Gaspar asking what he was doing.

They were in the middle of the forest, near enough to Arashil that Gavin knew they were getting closer to Yoran, and hopefully close enough that he would be able to help. He still hadn't heard anything from Wrenlow, which suggested that the city wasn't under attack. Yet.

Once they dismounted, they moved forward. Gavin raised his hand, motioning for them to wait. "There's something I need to do here."

"I thought we were on something of a time crunch," Gaspar said.

"We are. At least, something of one."

Gavin started forward carefully. He headed away from Arashil, into the forest. He could feel the bralinath trees and the energy there, and as he did, he recognized a connection to the ancient El'aras. He focused and pushed downward to connect to that power. When he did, he began to sense something echoing, a reverberation of energy that spilled outward as if trying to call to him.

As it did, he concentrated on it, feeling power, feeling

that energy, feeling something building. "I need to know," Gavin said. "Show me."

The tree pushed back against him.

He pressed that power all the way down. He had already connected to the bralinath trees before in the prison realm, so he knew he could reach for that power, but the challenge was in doing so consistently. He knew the magic of the bralinath trees, but he needed awareness and connection. He continued to focus, fighting the tree as it pushed against him. Finally, the tree opened for him.

"Show me," Gavin said again.

Images flickered in his mind.

Lights. Some of them dim, some of them bright, all throughout the El'aras lands. Dozens of bralinath trees, all of them connected. Fragments of power, but those fragments formed something else. A greater entity, and a greater whole.

Along with that, though, was something else. A gray darkness that pushed.

And it seemed to start to spread.

Even more than before, Gavin realized what the danger was. The El'aras had fought against the nihilar, but even that wasn't entirely true. They had *been* the nihilar. At least some of them. Then they had fought, or that was the way it seemed to him. That was the reason he had been so connected to it at first. That dark, gray energy of nihilar power had come from their own people.

They were easily corrupted, and now even more power would corrupt.

"So I will be the reason these fragments—and this power—pass," Gavin said.

Not so much a Champion, was he?

Instead, he would be their downfall. And they would steal that power from him.

He stood in place, rocked by that revelation, unable to comprehend what it meant for him or what it meant for the El'aras. He didn't even know them. They were his people, but at the same time, they were not. All this time, he had been trying to figure out what they were after, but what if this had been Chauvan's plan all along? If it had been, then he had wanted Gavin, and he had wanted to use him.

He had wanted to corrupt him.

But not only Gavin, he had wanted to corrupt other fragments. Dark power. Dark sorcery. It was no different than any of what the Sul'toral had chased before. Only the scale was different.

"Gavin?"

The sudden intrusion of Wrenlow's voice caught him off guard.

"What is it?" Gavin asked.

"I'm supposed to warn you that there is something coming at us. Actually, quite a few different somethings. They're powerful. You need to—"

Wrenlow's voice cut off. Gavin tried to reach him by connecting to the enchantment and channeling power through it, but nothing happened.

"Wrenlow?"

An idea came to Gavin. He turned and focused on the

bralinath power, then pushed downward only through his core reserves. Somehow, he was going to have to separate the power he had gained from the nihilar and use something else. "I need the seeker trees. I will not permit the nihilar to corrupt them."

Gavin touched the bralinath tree. He felt a tremble and then a steady thudding sound as power began to move. He couldn't see what it was from, but he felt a moment of relief.

The seeker trees were coming.

He hurried back to the paper dragon. The others were sitting atop it and talking quietly. Gaspar leaned into Imogen and whispered something to her, then looked over to Gavin when he arrived.

"Yoran is under attack," Gavin told them.

"Then we go," Gaspar said.

Gavin nodded. As they took to the air, he knew it would be a long flight back to the city while worrying about what was to come.

"I think I am tied to the untainted fragments of the El'aras," he said, thinking about what he had seen in his visions.

Imogen frowned, silver flashing in her eyes. "They want to corrupt all the fragments. If they gain control over this nihilar, they will be able to do it for their dark purposes."

"Like the Sul'toral," Gavin said, "and they want to use this nihilar power to corrupt the others. I think the nihilar itself is some corrupted fragment. I had thought that it might be another ancient power, but maybe it never has been. Just corrupted El'aras power. If I am the key to this, I can't let the nihilar do that to the others."

"How do you think you can avoid it?" Imogen asked.

"I may have to destroy it."

Or himself, he didn't say.

Gavin took a deep breath and stared straight ahead. Yoran came into view before he had a chance to answer. As Wrenlow had said, there was a threat heading toward the city.

He felt it as much as he saw it.

Monsters of earth, trees, and stone were moving. Creatures he couldn't even imagine. All of them were drawing on corrupted fragments of ancient magic. All were going toward Yoran—his city.

The dragon circled, and Gavin felt something come from the paper creature.

As they flew, he realized that it was pushing through to him.

Gavin reached into his pocket, and he pulled out the remainder of the paper dragons he had with him. He set them on his lap, and despite the wind whipping around him, the dragons stayed where they were. He touched one after another, activating them, and began to pour power out from himself by focusing on his core reserves, on the connection to the bralinath, and then something else. He felt that strange reverberation that had been in the other land, but he detected it not from that other leg but distantly, almost as if it was an ancient power.

He pushed that through to the paper dragons.

As they began to grow and elongate, they took on

darker and more distinct features. It seemed as if they turned from paper into physical creatures, with scales, wings, golden eyes, and even what felt like the radiation of heat.

"What are you doing with them?" Gaspar said.

"I have no idea," Gavin said. "I think this is tied to the last place we visited. I was trying to reach for that tree, and I felt something I had not detected before. It seems to have changed the connection I now have to the dragon. Or dragons."

Could there have been a different fragment?

If so, and if Chauvan and Timo had gained control over that, what would that have done for their use of the nihilar?

The dragons continued to stretch and grow bigger and bigger. Then they flanked him on either side.

"Do you think they can fight like dragons could fight?" Gaspar asked, his voice hushed.

"There's only one way to find out," Gavin said.

As they circled, he felt something else. There was a darkness down below, a reverberation of energy, and something was calling to him.

Not to him. To the nihilar.

Dark power.

Dark sorcery.

And Gavin had no choice but to answer.

Below him stretched a terrifying battle. Countless creatures marched through the plains outside of Yoran. They were things out of a nightmare, but what was worse was that Gavin had seen many of them before. Tall, towering stone monsters. Creatures made out of tall branches or grasses. Some looked like they were twisting vines. Others were flying and filled with a dark energy.

All were throwing themselves against the defenders of Yoran.

Most of those defenders were the Leier, though the El'aras were helping, thankfully. There were also constables, enchanters, and even some of Mekel's creations.

"These enchantments are different," Imogen said.

"I think it's from this last place. They gained a different kind of power over them. Sort of like the power I now have over the dragon, I think," he said, realization hitting him.

Imogen looked over to Gavin and held his gaze. "Then we need to destroy the ones controlling it."

"Stay with the dragon," Gavin told Gaspar.

"I think you will need me," Gaspar said.

"Then why don't you direct the rest?"

"You want me to lead them."

Gavin focused on his connection to the bralinath and the dragons, and then he pushed that into Gaspar. It was something like linking the enchantment to him, and he had no idea if it would work as fully as he hoped. As he placed it, he began to feel something take hold. It solidified within Gaspar.

Gaspar's eyes widened. "I'm aware of them."

"Good. Because Imogen and I have something we need to do."

He locked eyes with her, and she had her sword unsheathed.

Gavin reached for his own blade. As he did, he could feel the power crackling within it. It started to flow, and not only was the connection they shared to the bralinath there but nihilar was there as well. Always there. As much as Gavin tried to fight that, as much as he knew he needed to resist that energy, he was aware of it. Worse, he was aware that he might have to sacrifice himself in order to defeat it.

But first…

First, he would defeat Chauvan and Timo.

He jumped off the dragon's back.

CHAPTER TWENTY-EIGHT

G avin swirled his blade and copied the pattern he'd seen Imogen using as he descended, not at all surprised that it helped him fall with much more control. He landed with a loud thud, but he had already fortified himself by drawing on the power of the El'aras.

Imogen locked eyes with him for a long moment.

"What now?" he asked.

"They are both Sul'toral, or their equivalent. They will have others there who serve them."

"They would've made preparations," Gavin said.

Imogen nodded. "They would have."

"And your people?"

"They would've also made their own preparations."

Gavin felt the ground ripple around him, and an enormous stone creature erupted from the earth.

He jumped, immediately calling on his connection to his El'aras abilities, and he landed atop the creature before it fully formed. Using his blade, he scratched his own mark to take control over the creature. The golem tried to shake him free, but Gavin held on. Then the resistance trembled and disappeared. He poured his core reserves and his untainted connection to the El'aras through it.

Imogen had spoken of these fragments. Her people believed that their ancestors disappeared into the night sky and became stars. It was possible that they did, just as the El'aras formed the bralinath trees.

The golem turned toward another monster, and stone crashed against stone as they battled. Gavin jumped on one of the golems and traced a pattern that would help him take over the creature. He used some part of himself to flow into the golem and then leapt down.

Imogen was finishing with a cluster of strange creatures that surrounded her, and Gavin recognized that they were real ones, not just enchantments. They all lay maimed or bleeding on the ground.

She clenched her jaw. "I do not care for manalak."

They were enormous creatures that looked like mixtures of several different animals, but she had handled them easily.

"Dark creatures?" Gavin asked.

"They are. They were formed the same way all dark creatures were formed—through pain and violence. It changed something about them." She shook her head. "They should not be here."

"Well, none of them should be here, but I'm starting to think we may have to deal with other dark creatures before this is all over with."

Terrible things were all around him, but each time he found them, he knew that he wasn't getting any closer to what he needed to.

This was all about stopping Chauvan and Timo.

Gavin darted toward several treelike enchantments and carved his blade through them. Imogen stayed close to him.

"How would we draw them to us?" Gavin asked.

"I can't see if we are going to draw them to us or if they are drawing us to them," she said, silver flashing in her eyes.

Another massive creature rose up suddenly, and Gavin caught sight of a glimmer of metal worked into it. It was something like the vines that had tried to grasp at them, but this was different, as well. It shared some of those features, but not all of them.

Gavin pushed power through himself, and it exploded upward. The creature twisted and began to collapse in on itself. Imogen grabbed Gavin, shoving him to the side before spinning her blade around with what looked like lightning shooting from it.

Imogen sneered. "They think to use the renral against me?"

She gave a sharp, shrill whistle, then repeated it two more times.

There came an answering shriek, and dark shapes began to drift toward them and circle overhead.

"How many renral do you have with you?" Gavin asked.

"We have several dozen," she said. "They are skilled hunters. You don't need to worry, Gavin."

"I'm more concerned about things like the darklings and the other dark creatures we have faced."

Imogen laughed. It was strange to hear in this moment, and even stranger still was that it reminded him of the Imogen he had first known, not this mysterious woman who was filled with power.

She glanced up at the sky. "They will hold the other renral off, and hopefully anything else that might come at us. Including the grapaln."

Gavin had forgotten about them, but as soon as she mentioned the name, the air crackled with lightning.

Imogen laughed again. "They are not smart," she said.

"The grapaln, or the sorcerers who are using them?"

"Both."

She left her eyes unfocused. Then she pointed.

Gavin saw what had to be sorcerers, or perhaps Toral. Maybe they were even Sul'toral, as he no longer knew whether there were limitations for others becoming Sul'-toral. Imogen rushed forward, her blade a blur, and she took two of them down with sharp stabs before Gavin had a chance to react.

He wasn't about to let her have all the fun. He lunged, flowing through movements and sending the connection he had with the bralinath trees out from him and into the sorcerers.

Gavin knocked one back, then blocked another, then carved through the next. One after another he went, sweeping his blade and following a series of patterns until they were down.

Imogen turned in place, her eyes still blazing with silver. "Those are meant to be easy," she said.

"How many enchantments do you think they were controlling?"

"Far too many. I wonder what that means."

She glanced up at the sky and strode forward, then she whistled again. It was answered by another shriek of a renral flying above them.

The air crackled, and a grapaln attacked.

Imogen started toward the spot, and when she neared, she guided Gavin toward an unconscious sorcerer. She left him lying motionless.

She frowned to herself. "Where are you?" she muttered.

Gavin suspected she was talking about Timo. But he needed to find Chauvan.

"Go," he said. "Find him."

"Are you sure?" Imogen asked.

"I have Chauvan. You deal with Timo."

With that, she strode away.

CHAPTER TWENTY-NINE

IMOGEN

The battle raged around her, and Imogen held her slender blade, focusing on the sacred patterns as she did. Master Liu would be proud of how she had harnessed the power within the sword and how she intended to use it, though Imogen wondered if he would be concerned about what she intended now.

Timo was up here. Somewhere.

She had to find him.

She'd thought for so long that she could save her brother, that she could somehow bring him back from the precipice of disaster that he had teetered on for so long, but Timo could not be saved. She knew that now. And given what she had seen and what he was after, she also knew that she was going to have to be the one to remove the threat he posed. Not Gavin. Not any others. Her.

If he had trapped fragmented power, Imogen would release it. And from there...

She didn't know what she would do at that point.

Could it be held?

She had placed power like that into enchantments often enough that she understood that it was possible, but doing so meant that some aspect of the power became diminished. Unless she was able to hold that together and find a way of cleansing that danger, perhaps there would be no way of salvaging those fragments.

And unfortunately for her, Benji didn't have those answers either.

As she strode through the battleground, she noticed a towering rock creature lumbering toward her. She shifted her connection to Zealar and used Lightning Strikes, sending a burst of lightning at the creature, which shattered it. There was no sense of dark energy inside of it, as it was little more than a powerful enchantment.

Two more appeared, snaking up from the ground, drawing on vines and earth and even metal, but she did not have the same restrictions Gavin did. She immediately used the connection to the renral to blast at that enchantment, and it flashed with bright energy, heating up before shattering and exploding in a spray of fragmented power.

Timo had to be someplace nearby. He had to be the one controlling this. She needed to be the one to stop him, but she had to find him first. As she swept through the area, cutting down enchantment after enchantment, she could feel the energy building around her.

Imogen whistled, and it didn't take long before Zealar shot toward her. She stood in place, focusing on Tree Stands in the Forest. When Zealar hovered over her

338 | D.K. HOLMBERG

pattern, she released just enough that she could look up at the renral and feel the power he was holding, along with the power that he emanated to her.

"Find him," she said. As she did, she focused on the connection she shared with the creature and on the power that was there.

Zealar streaked into the air, and energy crackled along his black feathers, illuminating him. Someone targeted Zealar, using a burst of power that was meant to bring him down, but Imogen did not worry for him. The renral were naturally immune to magic.

But it gave her a target.

She recognized a sense not far from her.

She hurried forward with Lightning Strikes, which carried her quickly, and she mixed it with a bit of Petals on the Wind. She tended to join those two patterns. By the time she got to where Timo was—or had been—there was nothing left but a ring of enchantments now forming around her. She made quick work of them, her blade carving through each one. It was the blade of the sacred sword master, fueled by their power and augmented by what she could call through Zealar. There were very few magical enchantments that could withstand what Imogen could do to them.

Where was Timo?

She heard shouting, the cries of battle, the explosions of enchantments and sorcery and people using sacred patterns, but Imogen ignored all of that.

She had a single target. A single focus.

For too long, she had been drawn into other aspects of

fighting, but now she had to stay committed to the only one that mattered: find Timo.

A burst of lightning came streaking from Zealar, shooting toward the ground. Imogen darted at it, and she got there in time to see Timo attempting Tree Stands in the Forest, deflecting much of Zealar's blast.

He looked at Imogen with an expression that dripped with scorn. He had a pair of blades in hand, both of them etched with powerful enchantments, she now saw, and they glowed with purple energy. She wondered what kind of power that was.

"Do you think this beast will destroy me?"

Imogen smiled. "This beast?" She flicked her gaze up to the renral circling overhead, now joined by a dozen others, each of them sending the same lightning sparking down their feathers and wings, out from one to the next, creating a ring around where Imogen now stood. "It does not intend to destroy you. I'm not sure the renral could."

He snorted. "It's about time you realized that."

He held up his blades, and then he attempted to fold.

When he couldn't, he glowered at Imogen. "Do you think you can hold me?" he scoffed.

Imogen shook her head. "I've been looking for you for a long time, Timo. The problem is that I've been looking for you from a single direction, and I realize that was a mistake. You have always been a blurry haze to me, perhaps out of familiarity, or perhaps because of everything you've done. But with what Benji provided me, I thought I should be able to see more from you."

She hadn't moved. Timo still hadn't released his full

340 | D.K. HOLMBERG

pattern, though he was attempting to use whatever power he had to fold and likely would soon disappear. If he did, Imogen wasn't sure she would be able to find him again. He, like Chauvan, could simply vanish.

She sighed inwardly. She wanted to be done with this. Once she was, she thought she might finally be able to move on, but she wasn't sure how that would work.

"I've learned that I need to look from different angles," she continued. "Not just the obvious ones. From above and below, not just from the side."

"You're starting to sound like Benji himself."

"That is quite the praise, Timo."

"You could join me," he said.

"I've tried to get you to join me for far too long," Imogen said. "I've only now begun to see that was never going to be possible. You were my blind spot. You were always my blind spot. As much as I wanted to help you, I see now that I cannot. But perhaps I never was meant to."

She breathed out heavily and focused, feeling for the power that was coursing through the renral and streaking from one to the next, holding Timo in place. It would work. She knew it would. There would be no way for him to escape and nowhere for him to escape to.

Somewhere distantly, the same thing was happening with Chauvan. She didn't even know if Gavin was aware of how she had instructed the renral to circle to try to hold him, but she also didn't know if it mattered. Gavin was smart enough to understand that there were certain things he could not control. In this case, he had to trust that those who were with him, fighting with him, were there to help.

"Come on, then," Timo said. "If you think you can save me, then save me."

He spread his hands, his swords clutched in either one, and when he did, there was a part of Imogen that cried out to do whatever she could to protect her brother. It was the part of her that had cried out to help him when he had first come to Yoran what felt like an eternity ago. It was the part of her that had done everything in her power to help him while he was still here, that had continued to try to find a way to save him even while knowing that he had changed. It was the part of her that was his sister.

Now she had to harden herself. It would be the most difficult thing she had ever done. She had to be who she'd trained to be. Not just Imogen Inaratha, First of the Blade, but the General of the Leier, and perhaps something else. A Porapeth, if such a thing were even possible.

"You cannot be saved," she said.

She whistled, and the ring of energy started to constrict.

When it did, it seemed as if Timo understood what she was doing and realized that there was little he could do to counter it. He thrashed, shifting from sacred pattern to sacred pattern, then finally slid into some of the traditional patterns, though he didn't have the fluidity that was necessary to draw real power from them while he battered at the ring of energy that the renral placed around him.

She smiled sadly. "There is something you never

understood," she said to him. "The renral have a resistance to everything you can do."

"You really think they can destroy me?"

"We've already discussed this. No. The renral cannot destroy you in this form. And I did not ask that of them."

She took a step toward him. When she passed through the ring of power, she felt it cascading around her. It wasn't so much that the renral permitted her to pass, though perhaps there was some aspect of that. It was more that she had her own natural immunity to that renral energy, along with a connection to it.

She stood in front of Timo, blade at the ready. "Do you think you are more skilled than me?"

"Such arrogance," Timo snapped. "That has always been your failing, Imogen."

"Arrogance was my failing once, but it is no longer."

Timo lunged at her. She deflected both blades easily, not necessarily able to see what he was doing but able to feel the power he began to build. More than that, the connection she shared with the renral helped her deflect some of it.

He lunged again, and Imogen blocked, forcing him back toward the center. The renral energy continued to constrict.

Timo flailed. He fought with less coordination and less technique than he should have.

But not Imogen.

She studied her brother, watching him for a moment. Timo kept hacking at her, but with his poor technique, he did nothing to her.

"I would have saved you," she said.

"You could never have saved me."

In Imogen's mind, a series of possibilities formed. There were dozens of them, and in all the ones where she tried to protect her brother, to keep from harming him, she eventually failed. Only in ending him, removing him as a threat, was there light in the future.

"There's only one way, First," Benji's voice said, drifting into her mind.

"I know."

"Only you can do it."

"I know," Imogen said again.

He was her brother.

He was the only family by blood she had remaining.

But not the only family.

"Please forgive me, Timo," Imogen whispered, knowing she would get no response.

As he twisted, Imogen brought her blade up. With a burst of Lightning Strikes, followed by Tree Stands in the Forest, she drove her blade into Timo's heart.

His eyes flashed, colors swirling in the back of his eyes —black and purple, even a bit of gray—before he blinked and the color faded.

He sank to the ground.

She cradled him, knowing there was nothing she could do, nothing that she wanted to do. As his fragmented power seeped out of him, the renral power swept over it, shattering it. There would be nothing of Timo left. Then again, she knew nothing had been left for a long time. He had been gone the moment he abandoned everything they were so that he could chase power that was not his.

The renral power crackled, sizzling off the fragments, leaving no trace of Timo.

And Imogen wept.

CHAPTER THIRTY

An overwhelming sense of power began to build, and Gavin turned toward it.

He carved through a series of enchantments, knocking them down. Power exploded to his left, and Gavin moved toward that. Overhead, there was a shriek. Dark shapes circled, and lightning crackled.

Renral.

They were pushed gradually toward the El'aras ruins, which did not surprise Gavin. He fought his way through hundreds of enchantments, staying focused only on his connection to the El'aras side of him, to the bralinath trees, though he feared that even the faint connection was too much, tainting it.

"You wanted me to come here," he said.

Chauvan turned to face him. There was darkness around him, though it didn't seem to engulf him the same way it had before. There was power within him. Gavin could feel it, and he wondered why that would be. It was not just the power of the El'aras, although that was also there.

"You really do take directions quite well," Chauvan said.

"Where's your little friend? I didn't think you could do anything without his help. Or maybe he directed you here. A sacrifice, as it were."

Chauvan chuckled. "A sacrifice? Who do you think granted him the power he has?"

At least that answered one thing. It would also answer something for Imogen, though Gavin wondered if she would be content by that.

"You have me here," Gavin said, spreading his hands. Behind him, he was aware of the distant sound of fighting and the groaning of the earth as enchantments erupted from it, but there was the occasional surge of magic too. He had to hope that it was the enchanters, the El'aras, and maybe even the Leier all fighting together, working to help defend Yoran. He had to hope.

Lightning continued crackling overhead. Imogen claimed that would help but hadn't explained how.

"The Champion," Chauvan said. He still stood near the opening of the El'aras ruins, with darkness swirling around him.

Gavin had a sense that whatever Chauvan was trying to do, however he was calling on the power, it was leading to something Gavin needed to stop—except he had no idea what it was going to be or how he was going to do it. He had no idea about anything when it came to Chauvan, only that he had to figure out some way to stop him. He had already failed once before.

"Have you come to understand the truth?"

Gavin snorted. "The truth of what you've been doing? You never abandoned the nihilar, did you? You wanted to use it to steal what you believe to be your birthright."

"It *is* my birthright. And I will have it." Chauvan took a step closer to him, and the ground surged as metallic vines shot out of it and swirled toward him.

Gavin resisted the urge to draw on the nihilar the way he had in the past. Instead, he focused only on his El'aras ability and then crushed it down, adding as much compressed energy as he could, trying to burn it. It felt like it resisted him in a way that it shouldn't have and fought him in a way that it had not before. He continued to squeeze and constrict, sending as much power as he could down on what he was trying to do to him. Gavin crushed it until it failed.

Chauvan chuckled. "So much rage inside of you."

"You put it there," Gavin said.

Chauvan laughed again. "Did I, or did your mentor?"

"I thought he was your mentor as well."

"Oh, he was, until I found another."

"I heard about him. Aneadaz. Imogen destroyed him."

Chauvan snarled, but then he visibly calmed himself. It was almost as if he tried to push that emotion back down.

Gavin still needed more of a reaction from him.

"I still have this power," he said.

"A corrupted power. One that has proven useful to grant me a connection to something I could not reach otherwise," Chauvan said. "But you have given that to me. The past influences the future. What has been done cannot easily be undone unless you undo the past."

Gavin arched a brow. "It sounds to me like you're talking in riddles."

"It sounds to me as if you can't even fathom the gift you were given. Perhaps you were too young."

"Well, as I said before, I'm younger than you."

Chauvan scowled at him. "You have done everything I wanted. Everything she said you would do. Everything."

Gavin had the sudden realization that he might have been manipulated yet again.

He spun. A trio of people stood behind him. He didn't need his enhanced eyesight to know that they were likely Toral, each of them serving Chauvan. A hint of moonlight reflected off the rings they were wearing, and he was reminded of what Imogen had said about the Toral and the enchantments they used. It was a connection to a fragment. Given all they had been doing with chasing fragmented power, he felt like he had to destroy those enchantments so that he could end this.

Ultimately, he feared he was going to have to sacrifice himself in order to stop Chauvan. But maybe that was what they wanted. Maybe what he really needed was to live and survive—and defeat the other Champion.

He couldn't do it with the nihilar connected to him. Not when he knew what he had come to believe about it.

Lightning crackled around him, almost as if responding.

He spotted two stone golems in the distance, and he

called them to him. He had the sense of the dragon, and even Gaspar, which wasn't too surprising given how he had linked Gaspar to the dragon. He called them to him as well.

Then he darted toward the Toral.

He swept his sword up in a quick arc, using one of the Leier patterns to drive the blade forward at one of the nearby Toral. The tall, slender woman immediately began to move her hand, and vines started creeping along the ground. A Toral who used that power?

He used another one of Imogen's patterns, bringing the blade down with a sharp crack and splitting the vines, before thrusting his sword into the Toral. He instantly shifted toward the two who remained. It seemed that Chauvan gave them time, which suggested that he did so because he wanted something.

Gavin had to do this quickly.

He focused on the protection pattern that Imogen had demonstrated. He looked past the two Toral to watch Chauvan.

"You have to use them against me? You can't do it?" Gavin held his blade in front of him, thinking that once he got past the Toral, he would have to deal with Chauvan.

Chauvan sneered. "Oh, I can handle you quite well, Chain Breaker, but I wanted to let them have an opportunity."

"With stolen power," Gavin said.

"Stolen? The power has been passed on. It is not stolen. It is what it is, and you have seen how useful it can be."

"I've seen what you have attempted to do with that

power, and what you think you might accomplish. You aren't going to succeed."

"I already have."

The creeping vines stretched out from the two Toral and circled around Gavin. Those vines had to be some way of forming an enchantment, or perhaps some sort of containment, that would permit Chauvan to take the nihilar power and the fragments that bridged to an ancient and dangerous power that had been used against the El'aras.

Gavin would not permit it.

He focused on the Leier pattern at first, but he was the Chain Breaker. He was not Leier. Instead, he connected to the bralinath energy and called that through him, through his blade. Gavin brought it down in a sharp strike that cleaved through the vines, exploding the two Toral backward, where they collapsed away from him. They did not get up.

He was done playing with Chauvan.

Gavin was the Chain Breaker. But he was also the Champion.

He released the barrier he held for protection.

Chauvan chuckled. "It was always going to come down to the two of us. And thankfully, I will have this opportunity to claim it."

Renral flew over them. There had to be a dozen or more of the massive, dark, winged creatures, and what surprised Gavin was how it seemed as if lightning flashed from their wings, bouncing from one to another as power continued to build. He had never seen anything like it and had never felt anything quite like that either. Not magic, as he did not think the renral had magic. More than that, though, he had come to learn through Imogen that they had a way of overpowering magic. So them circling could be useful.

He backed away, focusing on the nihilar part of him. He needed for that power to be at the forefront. He had an idea of what could happen, yet he was not sure it would work.

Lightning crackled. Then it began to streak down into Gavin.

Everything burst through him. As it did, he began to feel something strip free.

He couldn't even see Chauvan, but he was aware that he was there. Was this something he was doing?

No, Gavin didn't think that was the case. This was renral power, and it seemed to be attacking the darkness within him. The nihilar was the only thing it touched.

It seemed to last an eternity.

Then there was a burst. Brightness. Light.

And that was all he knew.

Power from the distant bralinath trees—the El'aras elders—surged inside of him.

He was the Champion, not Chauvan.

Gavin flew toward him. Chauvan was quick, and he knew every fighting style that Gavin had learned. It was blade against blade, and when Gavin brought his sword around, Chauvan kicked and sent the weapon skittering across the ground.

Gavin flipped and danced back to reach for the blade,

but he wasn't quick enough. Chauvan was already there, calling on power in a way Gavin had not anticipated.

Maybe Porapeth power. Of course it would be.

He would be gifted with a different ability.

Gavin had known that Chauvan had access to a different kind of magic. He had felt the effects of it before, especially when he had tried to battle with him in the past, but now it was even more different. He darted back until he reached his blade, but Chauvan rested one foot on it.

Gavin punched, driving his elbow toward Chauvan's chin. Chauvan dropped beneath the blow and then blocked, sending a punch into Gavin's side. Gavin twisted, brought his forearm down, and chopped the other man's hand, then swept his knee upward.

He had to use everything within himself—El'aras abilities, what Tristan had taught him, even the nihilar. All of that combined, and still Chauvan matched him blow for blow. Gavin could not stop him like this.

Chauvan leapt back and braced himself. "I was supposed to be the Champion."

"You weren't. You were never going to be."

Gavin felt pressure within him. He was aware of something building from Chauvan, the energy he was trying to channel and push out of him toward Gavin.

Gavin had been gifted with greater power, one that Chauvan did not have. He jumped backward, and he focused on the bralinath trees. There was one connection that lingered within him. One ancient connection.

Chauvan drove his knee toward him. Gavin ducked, rolling out of the way, and he grabbed for his blade. He swung it around, but Chauvan kicked Gavin's arm, sending his sword flying away from him.

Another kick, and Gavin spun, sweeping his boot toward Chauvan.

He got the blade back up, and as he held it, he could feel some sense of energy forming within him. There was power inside, and he recognized that there was something he could do.

He focused, and then he pushed down and up, the same way he had when Timo had attacked.

In this case, though, he wasn't focusing on the bralinath trees that were spread out around him, nor was he focusing on his El'aras ability. Instead, he was concentrating on a different kind of power. One that was unique. One that he had found isolated.

Chauvan laughed at him. "You really think that's going to work against me? I used you. You have given me everything I need. And now I can join them."

"No," Gavin said. "You tried, but you failed. You never understood the past, and you never can."

It was almost as if hundreds of different images coalesced in his mind. Hundreds of different voices. Hundreds of different fragments. All of them called out to him.

Pale light glowed around him.

He formed the tree pattern that Imogen had demonstrated. Within that was the power of the bralinath trees.

Gavin became one, if only for a moment.

Then that power flowed.

He shoved it toward Chauvan. As that power solidified

around Chauvan, forming a massive bralinath tree of white energy, the renral shifted their lightning and poured it down toward Chauvan, holding him in place.

Chauvan cried out. Gavin ignored him and then charged forward, following that power until he reached Chauvan. Once he did, he knew he could not delay. Not any longer.

He thrust his sword into Chauvan's chest, then forced even more magic through the blade and into him until that power exploded.

Chauvan collapsed to the ground.

Gavin sagged, power leaking out of him, no longer able to stand.

CHAPTER THIRTY-ONE

Power bubbled up around Gavin in a continuous presence. The fighting in the distance, mostly Leier, persisted for a while but eventually began to fade.

He slowly got to his feet. Though he was weak and tired, he could feel all the energy around him. Something about it was different than before, almost as if there was some part of that energy reverberating within him. He was aware of different types of power and different energies within him and around him. He was also aware that there was something distinct, even if he couldn't fully grasp it.

He swayed, but Imogen was there sliding an arm around him.

He looked over to her. "Your brother?"

"He will no longer threaten my people."

Gavin waited for her to explain more, and when she didn't, he simply said, "Chauvan is gone."

356 | D.K. HOLMBERG

"He is. And we have dealt with his fragments."

Gavin barely looked up to see the renral flying above, the strange power they possessed shooting out from them and crackling into the ground below. "I think this is over now. Do we need to help with the rest of this?"

Imogen frowned. "Do we?"

Gavin closed his eyes. He could feel the energies around him, and he didn't really understand what they meant, nor did he know why he could feel those powers so distinctly, but they were there.

"I think your people, along with the enchanters and..."

Even the El'aras were there. Gavin was aware of them in a way that he had not been earlier.

Imogen watched him.

"Can you see me?" he asked.

She gave a small smile. "No better than I could before."

"What does it mean?"

"There are many people in the world that I can't see clearly. You are but one, though there are others."

He breathed out. Everything still felt raw and powerful. "What are you going to do now?"

"People lost their homeland," she said, "and we have been diminished during these attacks."

"We could stay together," Gavin said. "I think the El'aras have suffered, as have the people of Yoran and..." There were probably more than that. How many others had been tormented because of this attack? He had no idea what was going to be involved in recovering from it, but he believed it could happen. "Your people could be safe here."

"We would stay if we have permission," she said.

Gavin smiled. "You're not asking me, are you?"

"I thought I would *start* with you."

"I think you might want to ask Gaspar, and then you might need to go to the enchanters, and finally Davel. You know how he can be, especially when it comes to his city."

Imogen returned the smile. "I know quite well."

"I need to check on a few things," he said.

"As do I."

Gavin held out his hand, and Imogen shook it. For a moment, he felt a surge of energy, a sense of power that built between them. Then it was gone.

A dark shape circled overhead, and Gavin looked up in time to see a dragon—not paper anymore—coming down to the ground. Gaspar sat atop it.

"The dragon wasn't going to stay in the air any longer. I don't know what it's doing, but it was no longer interested in my directive to stay airborne."

"It's all done," Gavin said.

"We only got to attack a few enchantments. These things are powerful," Gaspar said, patting the dragon's side. "I don't know how, but I think it's alive."

Gavin chuckled. "You might be right. Or at least something close to alive."

He had no idea if the enchantment could truly be changed in that way, but if it could…

If it could, then he couldn't help but wonder if perhaps there were other enchantments that could be treated like that. How much more power could they bring into the world? How much more did he want to?

"I'm going to visit with my people," Imogen said.

Gaspar glanced over to Gavin before turning to her. "Would you mind if I went with you?"

She smiled. "I would like that."

Gaspar climbed off the dragon, and then it took to the air, quickly joining the other dark shapes in the sky. There was a strange rumble from above, which Gavin suspected came from the dragon, though he wasn't entirely sure.

He laughed to himself. He was exhausted, and he didn't really enjoy the idea of walking back to the city.

As soon as the thought came to him, something grabbed him. He looked up, panic filling him that it might be a renral or grapaln. He was surprised to see that it was one of the paper ravens, only not so paper anymore. It held him in its talons and carried him, sweeping him above the ground, though only several feet in the air.

Below him were the remains of dozens of different enchantments that had been shattered and left broken on the battleground. By the time they reached the city, the raven folded its wings and dove toward the earth. It passed through what should have been a barrier for it, which Gavin detected, but it did nothing to change the raven.

Gavin tested the paper birds by pushing power through himself and searching for anything inside him that he might be able to uncover about it. He felt as if there was some new, strange power within it.

He looked up at it. "Fly freely, friend."

The raven flapped its wings and soared into the air,

hovering above the city for a moment, but it didn't go any farther. It stayed until the other two ravens joined it.

"What did you do to them?" a voice said from the darkness.

Gavin looked over to Alana. "I didn't need to do anything. I'm sorry if I did."

She smiled. "They don't mind. I think they like it. They feel… fuller. I don't know how to describe it any other way."

"It's a different power."

"I can feel that too. You also changed the dragons. They're stronger."

Gavin nodded. "They are."

"They need a little bit more energy, but I suspect you'll know what to do."

"What is that?"

"I don't know. I can only fold them."

"I'm not exactly sure what I did," he said.

"You will figure it out. I'm confident about it." She reached into a pouch, and she handed Gavin a couple of folded shapes. "In case you need more."

"Thank you."

"I might have more that I want your help with," she said. "Butterflies. If you don't mind."

Gavin had seen her room before and knew that she enjoyed the butterflies. He could imagine himself pushing power out into those enchantments, and he wondered what might happen if he did. Would all of the butterflies suddenly be able to fly?

"Are you sure about that?" he asked.

"No," she said, then started to laugh. "Neither are you, so I think that's good."

Gavin laughed too. "I suppose it is."

"I want to thank you. I never got to see them like this before. I can see them in my mind, but they stay folded up." She looked toward the sky, and her eyes lingered on one of the ravens. "This is better."

All of the enchantments had started to take on a different form, though Gavin wasn't even sure why.

"Will you come by later?" Alana asked.

"I will," Gavin said. He had butterflies to activate.

He turned and saw Anna standing in the road, watching him. Her hair was down, and she was dressed in her dark green cloak, with a couple of her El'aras warriors on either side of her. As he approached her, he heard something shouting at him. It took him a moment to realize what it was—a thin and tinny sound that came from his pocket.

Gavin pulled out the marker he had given to Char. "Char?"

"Finally," Char said, his voice coming through the coin. "Your man is awake. He's asking for you."

"Let him know I will be there as soon as I can."

"He's getting irritable. He's going to leave."

"Tell him that if he leaves, I'm not coming for him."

After a moment of silence, Char spoke up again. "He's giving you the rest of the night."

"That's more than enough."

Gavin strode toward Anna.

"You returned," she said.

"You didn't think I would?"

"I couldn't see," she said.

"No? It has been somewhat of a common theme." Gavin looked at the others flanking her before turning his attention back to her. "Your people should be safe in the city. My city, I guess." Strangely, it felt increasingly like Yoran *was* his city and not like it was one he visited. After all of his attempts to leave, he kept coming back.

Now he thought that maybe he would just stay. If he was to learn about his El'aras abilities, he could do that here. If he was going to learn about other magic in the world, he could also do that here. There were other powers that he had to deal with, and this would be the place where he would do it.

Regardless, Gavin was certain that Chauvan was not the last threat he would have to face. He would be here. He would be ready.

And he would understand his power.

Don't miss the next book in The Chain Breaker: An Ancient Return.

SERIES BY D.K. HOLMBERG

The Chain Breaker Series

The Chain Breaker

The Dark Sorcerer

First of the Blade

The Executioner's Song Series

The Executioner's Song

The Dragonwalkers Series

The Dragonwalker

The Dragon Misfits

Elemental Warrior Series:

Elemental Academy

The Elemental Warrior

The Cloud Warrior Saga

The Endless War

The Dark Ability Series

The Shadow Accords

The Collector Chronicles

The Dark Ability

The Sighted Assassin

The Elder Stones Saga

The Lost Prophecy Series

The Teralin Sword

The Lost Prophecy

The Volatar Saga Series

The Volatar Saga

The Book of Maladies Series

The Book of Maladies

The Lost Garden Series

The Lost Garden